THE MULLIGAN

TERRI TIFFANY

THE MULLIGAN

Contact Information: titleadmin@pelicanbookgroup.com

Cover Art by *Nicola Martinez*

Harbourlight Books, a division of Pelican Ventures, LLC
www.pelicanbookgroup.com PO Box 1738 *Aztec, NM * 87410

Harbourlight Books sail and mast logo is a trademark of Pelican Ventures, LLC

Publishing History
First Harbourlight Edition, 2015
Paperback Edition ISBN 978-1-61116-403-9
Electronic Edition ISBN 978-1-61116-402-2
Published in the United States of America

Dedication

To my husband, Curt, who encouraged me to follow my dream and to Peggy Evans and Kelly Sheridan who cared enough to believe.

1

My twenty-two-year-old twin brother knows me better than anyone else. That's why he forces a smile when I enter the hospital room.

"It isn't your fault," he says. His voice cracks.

I want to run from my place near the door but I remain rooted, my feet frozen like two ice pops.

His broken and burned body is covered with a white hospital sheet. I can't see his legs, but the doctor told my parents this morning they'll never be the same. The beam that fell on him crushed too many bones. My lips quiver and my fingers twitch at my sides willing me to touch his arm. I edge closer. "I'm sorry, Robert."

"It isn't your fault." His hand is clammy but he grips mine with his. "I chose what I did."

I squeeze his hand, my time with him running short. Soon my mother will take her turn at his bedside in ICU.

His eyelids waver. I drop his hand and back out of the room where I meet my disheveled mother. She's still wearing her same sweatshirt and jeans from yesterday. The waiting room is empty except for her and Grandpa, who is snoring in a vinyl chair in the corner.

"Where's Dad?"

"Waiting to talk to you." She glances toward the hallway.

"Has he calmed down any?"

She raises her gaze to meet mine. Fresh tears form on her lids. I want to hug her, but I'll need all my remaining strength for my father. "Try to understand, Bobbi. Robert was his future."

"*You* are his future, Mom. He should know that."

She looks away, shoulders slumping. Sometimes I can be too blunt. By now I should know she won't ever go against him.

"Go inside," I say. "Robert's about ready to fall asleep."

My father is waiting for me next to the soda machine, a can gripped in his thickset hand. His wedding band rides between two rolls of flesh. A bandage covers the burn on his other hand. He snaps the can into the trash container. "What were you thinking?" His jaw barely moves as his accusation snarls past his lips.

"It was an accident, Dad. My studio was cold. I didn't mean to knock the heater over."

"Didn't mean to…"

He steps closer. I can smell the soda on his breath. "Then call the police. Call the fire department. Call the whole stinking town. But why did you have to send your brother in there?"

"I wasn't thinking. I was worried about my paintings."

"Your paintings? You almost killed Robert. Do you realize you've destroyed his golf career? He'll be lucky if he can use the bathroom by himself."

My chest tightens. A part of my mind reminds me I'm in the hospital. If I pass out or have a heart attack, I could end up in ICU. Maybe that's where I belong, instead of Robert. "I'm sorry. I really am. I'm going to make it up to him…to you."

His snort makes me jump.

"No one can make up for what happened. What? Do you think you can take a mulligan like in golf? This is real life, Bobbi. There are no free do-overs. Accident or not, you've destroyed your brother with your foolishness."

I know he wants to add "And me," but instead turns around and stalks down the hallway out of my sight.

~*~

My home isn't far from the hospital, but I take my time returning. I swing through a mini-mart to buy Robert a funny gift, hoping to give my folks time to arrive before me. My father is the last person I want to run into again tonight.

I can't stop yawning. No one has slept since the accident, except Grandpa, who falls asleep an hour after he wakes. As I pull into our driveway, lights from my parents' upstairs bedroom greet me. Grandpa's lights are off downstairs, and of course, Robert's bedroom is dark. Leaving him at the hospital was harder than anything I've ever done before. I feel as though I've been split in two.

I take off my shoes by the kitchen door. If I tiptoe, I might be able to get to my room without my mother coming in to talk to me. She's tried already too many times, making sure I'm OK. As I creep up the front stairs, voices hurl down to me.

I haven't heard my father this angry in a long time. Crouching on the third step from the landing, I listen as I did when a child, hoping I might glean an understanding about who my parents really are.

"He'll never golf again. His career is over before it started. I could have been in Florida with him next year if this hadn't happened. Now I'm stuck playing accountant to a bunch of people I couldn't care less about. I don't know how much longer I can take this life."

"Rick, calm down. Maybe he'll get better. We don't know."

"Better? Are you crazy? You heard the doctors. He'll be lucky to make anything of himself—and I know how that feels."

His anger reaches me, choking the wind from my lungs.

"You have made something of yourself. You are important to us. You're my husband and a good father. That should be enough."

I press against the wall—waiting. I will him to say what I need to hear—that we are enough. Instead, their bedroom door opens and he stomps down the hallway to Robert's room. I slide down two steps into the shadows watching. Waiting. Minutes later, I hear my mother's voice. It's filled with this pleading sound that sickens me.

"Leave them alone, please. He'll use them again."

"Not in my lifetime he won't. It's over. The dream is over."

I recognize the metallic sound. I can't help myself. I jump up and run to my brother's room where I find my father hauling Robert's clubs out of the closet. One by one, he takes each club and throws it to the hardwood floor, making both my mother and me jump.

"Stop it, Dad!" I scream. "Put them back. You're ruining them."

At the sound of my voice, he freezes midair, Robert's favorite driver gripped in his hand. His hair is in disarray and his eyes focus beyond us. I've never seen him like this. My mother grabs my arm and moves me back through the doorway. "Go to your room," she whispers. "Now."

I can't. I can't let him destroy my mother's heart because of me.

"Please," she says. She mouths the word again. The blood has left her lips.

"Listen to your mother." My father lowers the club but his face remains a mask of confusion. He stares at the floor, his head drooping on his neck.

It's then, staring down at the golf clubs, that I see the truth, how much of my father's life—our family life—was tied up in knowing that his son would achieve the thing he didn't. A chance at the pro circuit. And I know what I have to do.

"I'll check on Grandpa." I turn around, shutting the door on their grief. There is only one way I can help my father find himself again. Even if it means leaving home and doing something I never thought I would do.

I don't sleep that night. Not only because of Robert lying in a hospital bed but because I fear what lies ahead.

2

Two months later.

I twist the doorknob of my classroom for Golf Psychology. I can't believe I'm this late. Twenty pairs of eyes turn in my direction, making me want to run back to Pennsylvania. Why did I ever think my decision to come to Orlando made sense? I'll certainly be the worst golfer here.

Breathe. I cross the threshold at the same time I hear my name being called. Or should I say the name I've grown accustomed to hearing mispronounced for most of my life?

"Robert Lacy? Are you here?" The instructor stands only a few feet from me.

"It's Roberta, actually. I go by Bobbi. With an *I*." I pray my burning cheeks won't betray my discomfort, but I'm certain they will. All I want is to become invisible. And go home. It's the memory of my brother lying in bed that propels my feet deeper into my nightmare.

I sweep my gaze across the classroom. A few men in their mid-forties cluster toward the front of the room eating ham and egg sandwiches for a late breakfast. To my right, a group of recent high school graduates whisper to each other about some dumb thing they did the night before. And women…I search the classroom again. The admission rep told me women attend this golf college. Maybe they do, but I don't see any in this class, and that knowledge sinks to the bottom of my stomach.

I spot a vacant seat at the end of the third row and rush to it. Once seated, I readjust the collar of my pea-green jacket made for much broader shoulders than mine. Could it possibly look any worse on me than it did this morning? *A requirement,* the brochure said. Requirement or not, the ridiculous coat makes me so hot I want to throw up. I'm in Florida, for goodness sake, not Alaska.

Stuffing my backpack beneath my seat, I shrink into the hard-backed chair. Why hadn't I risen earlier? Tomorrow I won't be the last one. I look up and offer my best smile to the instructor who has finished reading his register. He stands with his hands on his hips, and he's wearing an expression that says he'd prefer be anyplace in the world than teaching at Orlando Golf College. I empathize with him. With only a few hours' sleep behind me, it takes all my effort to listen to his instructions.

"We take attendance at eight. I expect everyone to be on time tomorrow or you can assume the door will be locked." He shoots me a pointed glare and turns toward his desk, giving me adequate time to finish my assessment of him. OK, he is good looking in that slightly-older man genre. Mr. Drew Hastings. Drew. His name rolls over my tongue, and then I catch myself before I whisper it aloud. It sounds like a character from one of my mother's soap operas.

My gaze travels from his sun-bleached hair to his tan oxford shoes, the exact brand my brother bought last year. They still sit on the floor of his closet in the original box, since walking is not in his immediate future. Drew's red polo shirt stretches across his ample chest.

A jock, of course.

I won't ever fit in here. Not even with all the praying I'd done after I'd sent in my application. This situation reminds me of when I'd tried out for cheerleading in the tenth grade. A double flip? Right. I'd walked around hunched over for a week and signed up for the yearbook staff instead. Is earning my degree in Golf Management God's plan for my life? Why would I think it is? My mother wants me to come home. Robert points to Scripture about God's will for my life. Only Grandpa supports my decision to come here. But he isn't in his right mind half the time.

A sudden jolt to the back of my chair causes me to pull up straight. I peer over my shoulder. A guy a few years younger than me is bent over his desk intently listening to a game on his cell phone. His maddening tapping increases.

I take a deep breath. If I'm going to survive here, I can't be a wuss. I slap his desk and point to his foot; his size ten leaves my chair and finds a home on the floor in front of him.

"After class you can sign up in the hallway to play golf. First come, first served." Drew Hastings picks up a whiteboard marker and outlines the homework assignment for the next week. Golf Psychology. More like golf torture by the way the attention span of those nearest me wane. I scribble down the required page numbers and study Drew's face when he turns back toward the room. His eyes remind me of the sky over our back field on a June morning. I blink back tears when I think of home.

When class ends, I sling my backpack over my

shoulder and follow my classmates into the narrow hallway where everyone congregates around the bulletin board. I hadn't planned to play golf today, but I need the practice. Inching my way through the crowd proves useless, and I curse my height. Why aren't I as tall as my brother?

A wayward elbow nudges me in the side.

I rub the area and bite my lower lip. That's it. I drop my backpack to the floor and push forward, digging my fists into the backs of anyone in front of me. My actions cause only one jock to move aside and the others act like I'm a gnat on their necks.

"You need to use a little force or they'll walk all over you."

I turn to my left and look up. Drew (or should I call him Mr. Hastings?) stands next to me wearing a lopsided grin. A hint of cinnamon comes from his direction.

"I thought that's what I was doing." I shrug. "I wasn't planning on golfing today, anyway. I probably should take a lesson first."

"My lesson sign-up sheet is over there." He points toward the water fountain. Two or three blank sheets of copy paper hang in a neat line. "If you're fast, you might get in." Again, that smile. Is he flirting with me? I move as casually as I can and glance at the now almost-filled golf sheet.

"Are you any good?" I give him my best sizing-you-up look.

"PGA."

If he'd said he'd dabbled a little in high school it would have been enough. At least he has offered to teach me, and I haven't met any of the other instructors yet. Besides, I could fall into his eyes.

"You're on." I pull out my pen (one of the twenty my mother packed for me) and walk to the board. I scribble my name into the one o'clock slot. There. It's done. I have officially started my golf career.

The thought makes me want to bawl.

~*~

Drew comes over the slight incline and walks steadily toward me, the afternoon sun sending shots of golden hues through his hair. He twists the cap off a bottle of water and takes a long slug. "Are you ready?" His lips sink into a straight line.

I wipe the sweat dripping from my chin. He'd said we'd practice for a half hour. But his grim look says it will be less.

"Do you want me to hit a few?" I rest my driver at my feet and wait in the unflinching heat.

"Sure. Show me what you've got."

I adjust my wrists on the club and swing the driver the way I'd been taught. When my hips twist and I feel that sweet snap in my body, I watch with satisfaction as the ball races over two hundred yards.

Drew whistles behind me. "Not bad. How long have you been playing?"

"Does it show?"

"What kind of lessons have you taken?"

I study the turf beneath my feet as though it is growing right before my eyes. I look back at him, deciding I should be honest if I'm ever going to make it here. "I haven't taken any. I've only played with my brother. My dad, too."

His eyes widen. "Your brother, is he a pro?"

"He was going to be. My dad was."

"And?"

I can't tell him that my brother almost died saving my stupid paintings. So I don't. I look away.

"I take it you want to be as good as they are. You'll need to sign up for more lessons."

He makes his pronouncement as though he's a dentist telling me I'll need braces because of my crooked teeth.

"I know I will. The question is, can you teach me? I need to be better than good." I stretch my back to lengthen my five-foot-four frame.

Drew meets me with a stance of his own. "I'll see you tomorrow at the same time. Better practice on that downswing this afternoon." He packs his clubs and hoists the bag onto his shoulder still wearing that reserved look.

"You won't be sorry," I call to him as he turns away. I pump my fist in the air.

"I don't expect to be." Drew turns back, catching my gesture of glee. It's then I see what I've been looking for since he arrived at the range—a flash of a smile in his eyes.

3

Finding my way back to my mobile home court in Winter Garden is as confusing as the time my mother tried to teach me to knit. My stomach growls and my eyelids barely stay open as I make a right turn and discover a grocery store in a plaza ahead. My new place is empty of food except for the snacks my mother sent with me.

I park and head to the entrance. After a few minutes of wandering, I stop in the bakery section and taste drool as freshly baked bread scent wafts toward me. We don't have stores like this back home. The selection overwhelms me, but finally I select a loaf of whole wheat marked half off, and then find the cereal aisle where I pick up some shredded wheat. The soup aisle is next, and soon my arms are full of tomato soup, crackers, and a half gallon of milk.

At checkout, I discover I'm short of cash. My credit card is lying back on my dresser with a stash of tissues I took out of my purse that morning. A groan escapes me as I catch the dubious look on the cashier's face. "I'm sorry." I dig deeper into my purse—hoping. An older gentleman behind me offers a few dollars but I shake my head fighting back tired tears. "Please take off the crackers and bread," I tell the clerk, my face heating with embarrassment.

It takes me a while to find my car since the late afternoon sun nearly blinds me. I pull back onto

Highway 50 toward home, Golden Acres, a community for the over-fifty crowd. How I find my way back, I'm not sure, but I park under the awning of the compact silver trailer in relief. I found the mobile home development online.

Actually my mother did. She'd pointed out the pictures of the swimming pool and lighted tennis courts as though I'd have all this free time to enjoy them. What would she think now if she saw their real condition? I will not be lying around any pool in the near future. Especially since this one hasn't been filled since the eighties. Nor will I be playing tennis in the weed-infested courts or walking the non-existent trails in the back.

My home-sweet-home unit sits next to a larger trailer covered with enough purple and red birdfeeders and wind chimes to decorate the entire state. It won't surprise me to find out the owner is a Red Hat Society member. The chimes thankfully lulled me to sleep last night when two acetaminophen pills didn't work.

But my rent is cheap and my student loan won't cover much more. I drop my head on my steering wheel, close my eyes, and let myself dream of the home where I spent my childhood—a two-story colonial with a wraparound porch that rests on a hundred acres. Lush wooded acres surround it. A stocked pond waits out back while the Susquehanna River meanders down the hill across the hard road from the wagon house.

When I turned sixteen my mother papered my upstairs bedroom in a federal blue floral pattern I chose. She updated the frilly curtains (she sewed herself) and bought a new matching throw for my bed. The best part of the room was the closet Dad fitted with cabinets where I'd stored all my art supplies until he built the studio out back for me. In an impromptu party, we hauled all my easels and brushes and paper out there when he completed it. I loved my art studio, as simple as it was for as long as I had it. It served as my oasis, my hideaway, my place to dream.

Until the fire.

I reach for a tissue from the stash I keep in the glove box. Looks like I'd need to refill it already. Did I cry that much on the trip down? I still can't believe I caused my brother to get hurt. If only I hadn't screamed to him to save my work. I could have repainted everything.

I check my face in the mirror. A quick scan of the neighborhood assures me that no one will see my red eyes. Not even the older gentleman who rode his golf cart past my car three times last night. I carry in my purchases while leaving my clubs in the backseat for tomorrow. All I want to do is eat and take a hot shower to wash off this sticky sweat.

An hour later, I dig into my purse for my cell phone, noting at the same time that I need to look for a cheaper plan. This one is taking a huge chunk out of my budget, like everything else in my life. A bowl of sesame pretzels waits next to my elbow. My mother sent three bags and enough chips to bump me up another pants size. But then the soup didn't fill me like I'd hoped it would. I forgot how hungry I get when I golf. I place the call after chewing down another handful.

"Hello?"

Grandpa's greeting sends warmth shooting through me. The gruffness in his voice brings a smile to my face. At the ripe old age of eighty-five, he is our family hero, the man with the golf legacy and the man I have looked up to since I was old enough to understand what a great feat it is to play the Masters. Even though I wasn't as enamored with golf as Robert was growing up, I loved to sit next to Grandpa and page through his photo albums, oohing with him about his trophies.

I raise my voice a notch to be sure he can hear me. "Grandpa? How are you doing?" Snapshots fill my head of him leaning back in his recliner next to the telephone stand with a glass of cold soda nearby. He refused to let that chair go when he moved to our home last year despite my mother's best tantrums. A proud man, proud of his accomplishments and how he lived life the way he chose, he never asked for any help. He seemed to shrink a little the day we came to pack up his belongings to bring him to the farm he'd given my parents when my mother married my father.

But life caught up with Grandpa, and though in his mind he thinks he needs no one, he does. Black and blue shapes tattoo his legs from frequent falls because he refuses to use a walker or a cane. He'd rather die than resort to those "old-man appliances."

"Is this Bobbi-girl? When will you be home, darlin'?"

"Not for a while, Grandpa. Maybe at the end of August in time for some sweet corn. Will you smoke it for me?" His memory is failing by threads each time I talk with him. Though my mother denies what is slowly happening to her father, I can't. I want to tell her that Grandpa is slipping and he'll always be her hero.

But life changes us. If I speak my heart, will it destroy what little strength is left in hers? My mother depends on her father more than a woman her age should, but what choice does she have? I'm not blind to my father's ways. He's not always been here for our family. But when Robert began to golf with him, I saw a glimpse of the man my mother said she fell in love with.

I clear my throat. "You know how much I love your corn."

"Oh yes, my corn. And how about that golf game yesterday?"

"I didn't get to see it, Grandpa. I was driving."

Will he lose all memory before I have the opportunity to make him proud? Will I have enough time to go on tour while he still remembers my name?

"What a shame you missed it. Here's your mother." I picture my mother dressed in her stretch-waist polyester pants, baggy sweatshirt embroidered with red kittens, her tight perm (leftover from the 80s) and her makeup free face. She comes on the line sounding out of breath.

"We miss you, honey. How is it there? Did your first day go all right? Bobbi, I wish you'd change your mind and pack up and come home. You aren't to blame. Don't give up your own dreams."

I grip the phone tighter and lift my bare feet onto the only other piece of furniture in the living room—a stuffed chair that looks like the dogs have taken a liking to it. I trace the muddy stain on the bottom cushion with my big toe. At least I haven't found bugs like I did in the kitchen sink and cupboards. Tomorrow I'll buy insect spray and air freshener for the horrible musty odor that struck me in the face when I came inside.

I ignore my mother's plea—one I've heard over

and over since my decision.

"I took a lesson today. Have another tomorrow and I stopped at a grocery store for food for supper. You'd love the bakery section. All kinds of bread. I miss all of you. How's Robert?" I swallow hard. It's expected I include him in my conversations though talking with him makes me cry every time.

A long sigh trails into my ear. "He misses you."

"Tell him I miss him, too."

"Why don't you tell him? Wait, I'll take the phone to him."

My heart thuds louder.

I'm sure she rushes toward the front of the house—once the good room—now having been transformed via a hospital bed and a three-point commode. He'll be lying with his open laptop next to him and a stack of golf books piled on his nightstand. Of course, his Bible will be there, too, marked up in his color-coded fashion.

How can I end this call in a hurry?

"Hey, sis, how's it going down there?" His voice is deep and familiar. He sounds pleased I've taken the time to include him in my call.

"I'm good. Really good, but a little tired. I had my first classes today."

Silence.

"Are you there, Robert?"

"I was thinking about what you said before you left. How you plan to be the best female golfer ever. Are you sorry yet you're doing this?"

My brother has this way with words. Direct. To the point. Not always what I want to hear and certainly not tonight when I'm bone-tired and trying to survive on rocky emotions. I love him with all my heart, but he has to know that my taking over where he left off is a good thing. For the whole family.

"You know why I'm doing this." The words squeeze between my teeth.

A long sigh. "Come home, please. It won't change anything. Stop being a martyr."

Is that what he thinks I am? I pluck a pretzel from the dish and throw it against the wall.

"That's not why I'm doing this. And don't make me cry."

"I don't want you to cry. I want you home. I want you to be who you really are."

"And then what?"

Watch Dad withdraw every day from a life he doesn't want? Watch Mom hide her tears because her life isn't anything she ever planned it would be? No thank you.

"Listen, put Mom back on."

My mother comes back on the line, breathless again.

"Bobbi, he's right. You should be home with us. You should be painting—opening up your own shop."

I ignore her since there still remains one more person for me to talk to and I will need more than energy for that. "Dad? Is he there?"

"He's in town at a meeting. I'll tell him you called." My mother pauses as though plotting her next words in a minefield. "He misses you, too."

My mother is a good liar. My father hasn't spoken more than three words to me since the accident except to hand me pepper spray for my trip. But of course, it wasn't that much better before the accident. Who am I fooling? Before the fire, he had his hopes set on seeing his son become a major golfer.

I found the faded clippings years ago in the attic. The ones with my father and his trophies. I did the math and figured out why there weren't any more pictures of him on tour. He'd been handed a set of twins and all the trappings that went with us, saddled with a desk job he never wanted.

Robert and his love of golf changed all that. So would I.

I fiddle with a nearby pen, scribbling my name on a napkin. "Tell him I'm doing fine. Tell Grandpa again, too. Remind him about the trophies I plan to win. He likes hearing about it."

"Now, Bobbi, you know he doesn't care about those things. You need to stop thinking that way. The only reason Robert—"

"Mom, I need to do this so let's not discuss it. OK? Listen, I'm going to hang up. I'm beat and we start early again tomorrow. I'll call soon."

I give another fast good-bye and end the call. No need rehashing with them why I have chosen to give up everything I ever wanted in my life to attend this golf school. Besides, it isn't their responsibility. It's mine. It was my studio that burned down. It was my stupid dream that destroyed Robert's. No amount of denial on anyone's part will change that fact.

~*~

The alarm wakes me earlier today. I stumble around in the darkness until I find the wall switch, adding a bedside lamp to my shopping list. I passed a discount store on my way home yesterday. If I can remember how to find it, I will stop today.

After squeezing into what passes as a plausible

shower stall complete with moldy shelving, I throw on another pair of khakis, this time matching them with a yellow polo. Thankfully, we only have to wear those stupid jackets one day a week. When I check the mirror, I see how my hair dances with a life of its own. Oh, the complexities of managing thick hair in Florida's unrelenting humidity. Dropping the brush, I search for my shoes.

A partially opened box lays propped against one wall where I'd let it fall the day before. A different golf hat will keep me cooler so I dig into the assortment of junk to search for a visor, find an off-white one, and set it on my bed. I flip through more items in search of something to pull my hair up with when my fingers meet a familiar object.

My mother has slipped my drawing tablet into the box without my knowledge. My breath catches.

Faint gray sketches of the back mountain on our property greet me. With my finger, I trace the light pencil strokes. Stark images drawn with abandonment on the day of the fire. The only saved remnants. Robert and my father had left earlier that morning for a course in the next town. I'd wanted to get some drawing done for the gallery where I worked so I didn't go with them to caddie. I'd already sold two paintings and was excited about a request for more.

It was chilly that day—the thermometer read only forty degrees when they left, but the cold never stopped Robert. His passion for golf rivaled my own passion for art. His dream was to qualify at Q-School and make it on a major tour like Grandpa had years ago. Robert was good—better than good. He was born to golf.

I hate remembering that awful day, but if I don't,

I'll never be able to get through this school. My mother keeps saying it isn't my fault, that it isn't my guilt to carry. But if it isn't mine, whose is it?

Certainly not Robert's. He didn't ask to have his life turned upside down. Nor my father, whose dreams for his only son now include relentless doctor visits and therapy and the possibility that the two of them might never share those special father-son moments again.

Right. Who left the heater on? Who screamed to Robert to save her precious paintings?

My chest shudders when I replay Robert's last conversation with me on the day I prepared to leave for school.

"You can't do this, Bobbi. It's not God's plan for you. You're an artist. I'll golf again someday. Let it go, please." His normally tanned face had faded to a pasty white, making him one with our living room walls. Tears shone in his eyes as he plucked the cotton sheet that covered his lower body. My mother had tried to supply him with everything he needed during his recuperation, but she couldn't hide what needed to be hid most. Robert's injuries.

I studied his strong nose, the playful way his hair fell across his forehead. "You're my twin. I owe you. Besides, you taught me a lot. I'll be good. You'll see. And when I win a tournament, it'll be for all of us."

"I'm going to pray for you every day. Pray you come to your senses."

I glanced at his well-worn Bible. Yes, he would pray.

Robert's faith is so much stronger than mine. It always has been ever since that day during Vacation Bible School when we were twelve and we accepted what God did for us. He uses the name Jesus as though he is talking about his best friend—in front of his own friends. The first time he did that, I wanted to die from embarrassment, but no one seemed to mind. In fact, it appeared his friends treated him better. Eventually Robert made us pray at meals and Mom dropped him off at church every Sunday until she decided to go with him. I went, too, but worried more about what I was wearing than what I was learning.

I still have trouble accepting that God loves me like he does Robert. I still have trouble with it, especially now living so far from home. But I'm learning that the circumstances in our lives can't always be controlled. I learned after the fire that sometimes we have to step up and do what it takes to make things right again. Like moving here.

The tablet snaps shut. My mother should stay out of my business. I shove the drawings back into the box, grab my keys, and stomp out to my car.

"Good morning. Welcome to the neighborhood." The unfamiliar voice scratches like worn windshield wipers on a dusty day. An elderly woman—who definitely shouldn't be outside in that housecoat—comes toward me carrying an aluminum foil-covered paper plate pressed against her sagging chest. A gold chain with a thin cross circles her neck, and she wears pink flip-flops on her bird-like feet. Her frosted blue eye shadow momentarily distracts me from her sunken cheekbones covered in blush.

She holds out her offering and grins, showing two missing side teeth. She reminds me of the last jack o' lantern Robert and I carved before our father decided he didn't need any more pumpkins cluttering the front porch steps.

"Thank you." I accept the gift with a matching smile of my own. The lady who loves chimes also bakes. I peek beneath the covering. "Chocolate chip cookies. My favorite!"

My neighbor chuckles and holds out one blue-veined hand. "Call me Mattie."

I take the offered hand and shake it politely, hoping she will cut the introductions short. I'll be late again if I don't hurry, and Drew might lock the door. "Bobbi. With an *I*."

"I once had a nephew named Bobby. With a Y." She winks. "Never could get him to do much for me when I asked. Died in a crash."

"I'm so sorry. Listen, Mattie, I hate to be rude, but I'm going to be late for school if I don't get going." I glance toward my car.

"What school do you go to?"

"A local golf college." Balancing the cookies in one hand, I grab my backpack that I'd set by the car.

Mattie steps away and gives a small wave as I call out a quick good-bye.

The cookies will be great for the break between classes. Even though they are the last thing I need to eat. My kinesiology teacher has impressed me with the need to get into shape—so much that I'm considering joining a local gym if I can get a student membership since the one at school is worthless. It's been over year since the last time I jogged. Robert begged me to run every morning with him. I lasted two days.

I pull onto the busy main highway and make it through three green lights before the traffic starts backing up. Two cops speed past me. I look to my right and then my left. Several cars cut through a parking lot but I don't have a clue to an alternate route. I'll be late for sure. I throw my turn signal on and inch my way out of the backlog of traffic to follow behind a pickup truck through a shopping center.

The road curves past several newer housing developments and for a second a wave of fear rolls through me that I might be lost. When I'm about to turn around a sign appears. *Orlando Golf School 1 mile.* A rush of relief leaves my chest.

Nearing the school, I admit that a part of me looks forward to seeing Drew again, though my heart warns against it. I reach for a still-warm cookie and devour it in two bites. It's silly to entertain any romantic thoughts about my teacher. I'm not a schoolgirl anymore. I also don't need complications—especially when I have so much to accomplish. I will stay focused.

The classroom doorknob doesn't budge. *Great.* He's kept his word. My parents did a similar thing to me the time I stayed out with friends the summer after I graduated. I came home well after one in the morning. A curfew at my age made no sense so I'd stormed around to the barn where a pallet of fresh straw kept me comfortable most the night until a mouse squealed near my head nearly sending me into hysterics. Fuming with anger the next day, I swiped my father's house key and went to Big Mike's hardware store in town to make a spare for my purse.

The door opens as I stand entrenched in my memories of Pennsylvania. Drew speaks first. "Miss Bobbi-with-an-*I*. I assume you want in?"

Most people back home think I'm the artsy dreamy type—a girl who would rather paint scenery than attend the Wyoming County Fair and shoot hoops for a stuffed teddy bear. But they are wrong. I won more than Robert last year. I snap back to look up into an expression I would entitle 'the look of impatience.'

"You want to come in or daydream in the hall?"

Drew's height gives him a distinct advantage over me, not to mention he's the teacher and I'm the student.

"There was an accident." My tone always turns deep and scratchy when confronted by anyone. "A bad one." I hate that I don't sound all high-pitched and feminine like other women do when they want to impress someone. "Police and everything." No, my voice finds the basement of my voice box and etches out sentences like blades on ice.

Clearing my throat to try again, I stop as he steps aside to hold the door open for me.

I dip my head and hunker past to the seat in the back, praying it will still be mine to claim on day two. Again, the stares and whispers trail behind me.

"Please don't go to Orlando." My brother's voice comes to me as I slide into my seat. Our conversation happened two weeks before I left home. "You don't understand how tough the competition will be," he said as soon as I entered his room.

"Then you don't know me." I gripped my coffee cup tighter as I settled in the big chair in the front room near him.

"I know that most people who go to a golf college end up working in the industry—not as golf pros." Robert tossed me a magazine. "Read the article."

I picked up *Golf Today*. An article about how to gain employment on a golf course caught my eye. I tossed it back on his nightstand. "So what. That doesn't mean I can't be the one who makes it. I'm going to get the training and maybe learn something more in the process."

I'd found a website the day after the accident and had pored over the details about a golf college. Normally I could convince Robert of anything. Normally.

He and I share this deep sense of closeness. When one of us hurt, both hurt. As kids, we'd watched out for each other, and that didn't change during our growing-up years.

The last time I needed a subject for a portrait, Robert offered to help rather than attend a golf tournament down in the city with some friends. When he needed to snag a date for a last-minute event, I turned down my own date and attended with him. I even bought him a new offset putter for Christmas last year after hearing him talk about it with my father. It had taken a huge chunk out of my savings, but seeing his eyes light on Christmas morning made it worthwhile. But a new club will never make up for this.

A cough sounds beside me. I try my best to pay attention, but can't seem to manage it today. With half a night's sleep, it's a wonder I'm sitting upright.

"We're having a tournament next week for the freshmen. It'll be down at Reunion right after class lets out on Monday. Bring your best attitude and effort." Drew passes out information sheets and drones on about what to expect.

A tournament. I've hardly had an opportunity to improve my shots. One quick glance around the room tells me what I need to know. I'll be living on the course until then.

~*~

When I was twelve, my father built us a tree house in one of the old maples that borders our property. He made certain I could use the narrow steps he'd nailed into the broad trunk before he left me alone to climb up and daydream among the branches.

I'm sure it was there where my dream to paint landscapes was born. No matter what direction I gazed from my towering perch, the lush scenery jolted my imagination like a glass of lemonade on a hot summer night. I would try in vain to press the scenes into my subconscious so I could take them out later at night and study the finer details when I was alone and when sleep eluded me.

My young heart almost stopped beating when I caught my first sight of the distant murky waters of the Susquehanna River. Right then and there, I vowed to paint the river as only I saw it.

Later that day, it took three threats from my mother to get me down from the tree house.

I think of that tree now as I focus my attention and driver on the flag three hundred yards ahead of me.

My lessons with Drew have taken place every day of the week, but today is Sunday and I found a cheap tee time at a nearby club. The pro shop guy tried to get me to start with someone, but I was adamant to play a round alone.

How long has it been? Months? Since last winter before it got too cold to go out anymore. I'd been caddying for spare money on weekends since the gallery didn't pay that much. We hadn't played in a while until Robert made me come out with him one crisp morning.

He drove us to his favorite course. Paradise Hills.

And yes, it looked like Paradise there—huge oaks and rolling landscape. My blood pumped at the sight. I knew it would be a good day.

"I can't believe you made that shot!" Robert high-fived me after my putt from fifteen feet rattled in the cup.

I birdied.

I made par on the next hole and finally an eagle. Robert still won, but I did a pretty impressive job of keeping up. So good that I saved the scorecard in the bottom of my dresser drawer back home. But that was months ago. Today is today, and it's hotter than a bonfire in the middle of a desert. Today I need to improve my playing.

"Loosen up on your grip." A deep voice resonates beside me.

I look up to see Drew ambling in my direction. I tug on my pulled-back hair. "It's Sunday. What are you doing here?"

"Does that mean you can't learn anything?" A whisper of a smile appears. He wears his golf hat low on his forehead so I can't see those eyes. "I play here every Sunday. Now take your shot."

I take my shot.

"Not bad. Want to go another nine holes and I'll show you what to do in a real game? Winner buys soda." He'd parked his cart nearby and cocks his head toward it.

This will be the first game we play together. I'm acting as though it's my first date instead of a golf game. Maybe I should save the tee as a memento.

"Are you going to beat me?"

Drew removes his cap so that his blond hair glistens in the sun. He squints. A nice kind of squint that puts my heart into overdrive. "Going to let me?"

"Not a chance."

"That's my girl."

And forget my heart pounding from his nearness—it leaps right out of my chest into the water hazard to my right. I remind myself that I'm here to learn to be a great golfer, not connect with a jock who might not understand what loyalty means in a family.

He waits as I pack my clubs and stow them into the back of his cart. "What about my cart?" I glance where I'd parked it near the tee.

His even white teeth show. "Already on it." And when he pulls out his cell and speaks into it, I figure he is. More than I am. By the time we take off to the ninth hole, I don't care about a little old cart.

4

I shut down my computer and lean into my sofa. The last time I remember feeling this lonely was on the camping trip to New York State. Our family's one and only camping trip.

My father came home one day and announced his accounting firm could handle the workload so that meant a family vacation. School had been out for a month, and Robert and I were deep into our summer plans.

"Really?" My mother clapped her hands together and rushed around the house throwing an impromptu menu into an ice chest and extra blankets into our sleeping bags for the colder nights in the mountains.

Dad had borrowed a four-man tent from a friend and enough supplies to keep us away from home for weeks.

My brother hoped to play some golf at a nearby resort. I moaned about missing a sleepover at my best friend's house that Friday night. I'd met Amanda the first day of sixth grade and we'd been inseparable ever since.

I was less than thrilled with our rustic accommodations. Outhouses that stank and smoky campfires to cook hotdogs. And it rained. Mud-sopping rain.

I'd finally gotten so bored I slipped away from my father, who had stuffed his nose in a book all day, and my mother, who was crocheting yet another baby blanket for some stranger, and took off on my own hike. Robert had been spending his time hitting golf balls into the lake even though he'd been yelled at twice by the management.

Yeah, I didn't know how lonely my life could get until I'd gotten myself totally turned around on that mountain and my parents couldn't find me for twelve whole hours. By then, I'd huddled tight against a tall pine and took to praying that God would let someone find me and take me home to my own warm bed. God and I got a little closer that day.

This morning, alone in my trailer, I pad over to the screen door to take a look around the neighborhood. Another long Sunday. A metal awning covers my driveway. The only furniture on my patio are the plastic beach chairs I'd bought on a whim for five dollars each at a discount store. I've never yet sat on them. Determined not to pine away my whole day, I slip my toes into my sandals and step outside. Fresh air fills my lungs. Hot fresh air, but I've gotten used to the heat after being here almost two months.

"Morning, neighbor." Mattie must have been watching out her small kitchen window because she comes right out of her trailer and picks her way across the narrow strip of St Augustine grass that connects us. Today she wears her Sunday attire—a combination of a sundress and stretchy pants. "Are you up for some coffee yet?"

I let out a rumpled sigh. At least she isn't bringing more cookies or cakes like she usually does on her frequent visits. Even though I have started to enjoy our short conversations, I don't need anything more to stop me from getting into shape.

"I just drank mine. How are you doing today?" I motion for her to sit. I don't have to ask twice. "Getting ready for church?"

Mattie's chin wriggles reminding me of one of the chickens Robert tried to raise when he was thirteen. When our father chopped the head off one for dinner, that was the end. Robert gave the remainder to a neighbor and swore he'd eat beef the rest of his life. Of course, he didn't, but he held out for a long time.

"We have a luncheon afterward. You should come. No use eating alone all the time. Going to be fresh corn and some good salads."

Somehow, I seem to attract the kind of Christians who feel it's their duty to get me back into church. First, Robert sent an email asking if I'd found something yet, with a few links to local churches, and now Mattie. I stretch my tanned legs out in front of me.

"I'm OK. Still getting used to the area. I might take a run over to the range today and hit a few balls."

"You sure practice all the time. Planning on being the next Arnold Palmer?"

I laugh. At least she knows a golfer. "Hardly, but if I want to be any good, I need to practice. Besides, I hope to qualify for Q-School this fall so I've got to work at it."

Mattie narrows her eyes. "What's a girl like you want to play on tour for? They travel all over the country. You can barely get married and raise your kids."

As though marriage is on my radar. I roll my shoulders and trace the outline of a palm tree with my gaze. A trick I'd learned to help focus while waiting my turn at golf. It actually worked last week. If only it would work now.

"I don't plan on getting married anytime soon, so I don't think I have to worry about that."

Mattie isn't easily put off. She swirls the gold band on her finger. "Just don't wait forever. I married my man late in life. Only wish he was still here with me. It gets lonely, you know, living by yourself and trying to make a life as a single. I never knew how bad it would get until the day after the funeral when everyone went home."

"I'm sorry." An uncomfortable sweat breaks out on my upper lip. I don't like talking about death. Even more since the accident and seeing Robert lying in Intensive Care for days. No, I'd much rather shove those thoughts out of my head and focus on what I need to do to make things right. Like becoming the best female golfer ever and giving the family something to be excited about again.

They'd all had such hopes for Robert. He'd been ready to go to Q-School. Even had his money raised—something I still need to do. People who supported him had helped with spaghetti fundraisers and warm wishes. When he'd almost died, it wasn't only my family who grieved. The entire community rallied around us, bringing in meals and offering to drive him to appointments. Everyone loves my brother.

My lower lip trembles. I will not cry today.

"No need to be sorry for me," Mattie continues with her story. "The Lord has given me some wonderful people to bless. See those pots of geraniums over there?" She points to where two neat rows of tan crocks sit with red geraniums spilling out of each one. I nod.

"I take them around to other lonely folks in this development and to the senior high-rises. They love to see me coming. It brightens their day as much as it does mine." A smile shows her missing teeth, but this time the sight cheers me instead of making me remember the old pumpkins. Maybe Mattie isn't such bad company after all.

"Well." She thrusts her hands on her knees. "I need to get going. Church will be over before I arrive."

"Thanks for coming over. I enjoy talking with you."

A gnarled finger falls on my shoulder. "You know where I live. Don't be a stranger."

She works her way back across the divide to her home, coming back out a few minutes later with a Bible tucked under one arm. After a quick wave, she pulls out of the driveway in her mint green sedan.

Not one for sitting around all day, I change into a polo shirt and shorts. In the past, when bored, I'd pick up a brush and paint for hours, letting my imagination soar. Sometimes I can finish a painting in one day. All I have now is golf. Unless I want to count playing Scrabble online or calling my friends back home.

At least Amanda has been supportive. Spotting my phone on the counter, I place a call to her house. She'd married the star football player two years ago and hinted to me last week that she might be ready to take the plunge into motherhood.

When she'd said that, my heart shrank a bit. I'm not certain I will ever be able to entertain those thoughts. Not if I am going to golf for a living.

But she will make the perfect mother. Her home will be filled with children, all with her same upbeat personality.

"Hey there, long-lost friend." Amanda's voice sounds as breathless as my mother's. I listen to my own steady breathing. Maybe I have nothing to be excited about.

"Hi. What have you got planned for today?" I ask, knowing full well she'll be heading out to church where she teaches five-year-old children about Noah and the ark and the flood and all those stories I once learned.

When I was fifteen, I remember meeting one of Robert's friends—the son of missionaries. At the time, I thought the guy was cute and flirted with him, but he had different ideas. He wanted to know where I was in my walk with God. (That's what he called it.) "Do you really believe the stories in the Bible?" I asked him, wanting him to squirm, or maybe I wanted him to convince me that the flood did happen.

"Of course I do. Don't you? It takes faith."

I remember giving him my best smirk. Somewhere I'd become a skeptic. "I believe in God, but the stories…really?" He had the nicest hair, dark and wavy.

"Let me talk with you more. Will you let me, Bobbi?"

He smelled good, too. But he never got the chance to talk more with me as his folks moved on to their next mission. He sent me a sweet note I've still kept.

"Bobbi? Are you daydreaming again?" Amanda's voice breaks into my memories. "I'm feeling nauseous so I'm laying low today. How's the heat down there? Are you ready to come home yet?"

I roll a piece of cinnamon gum into my mouth and settle back on my couch, feet propped on the arm. I love our talks and hope today will be a good one, especially with the mood I'm in. "Can you talk or should I expect a few holds while you run to the toilet?'

A giggle comes through to my ear. "It isn't like that. I was going to call you myself today to tell you. Are you sitting down?"

"Lying down. Tell me."

"I think I'm pregnant!"

My feet drop to the floor. "Pregnant? Really?"

"Now, I haven't had time to buy the test yet, but I plan to as soon as I can get to town. It's like this feeling hit me last month, and I knew. I've had these wild dreams, too, where I'm rocking this baby girl and she looks up at me with these huge blue eyes and I think, 'Oh my, she's my baby,' and then I wake up. Am I nuts?"

"No, not at all! Hurry and take the dang test and call me back." I don't need to tell her that. I've always been the first person she calls with news. Guilt still gnaws at me that I didn't call her right after I decided to come to school here. Instead, I'd kept my plans a secret and told only my family.

My mother cried the entire day until my father returned for dinner. She tried to get him on her side, to convince me to stay, but it backfired. He had only shrugged and said, "She's over eighteen. She can do what she wants."

"So that's my news, but what about you? Are you happy there?"

She knows me too well. "I'm doing OK."

"I stopped to see Robert the other day. He told me he's making good progress in therapy and hopes to be on his feet soon. But I'm sure you know all that." She pauses, waiting for me to respond.

I don't know what to say. Getting on your feet doesn't mean running laps and having the stamina to play eighteen rounds of golf every day.

"I'll be calling him soon for an update. I'm glad he's feeling good about it."

We make more small talk and I remind her to call me when she knows something about the pregnancy. When I hang up, the closeness we once shared almost paralyzes me with sadness.

~*~

A quick snack fills me after which I drive over to the range behind the school. A golf course borders the school property. As a student, I can use the range anytime I want. Today few students appear to have the same need I do—to practice instead of enjoying life. I drag my golf bag over to the far right and prop it next to me. I've gotten fairly good with my driver and want to try a new stance to make sure the ball fades to the right when I want it to.

But first, I need a bucket of balls. It looks as though the guy who usually gives them out isn't behind the counter yet. I check my watch. No, I'm not too early. After tapping my foot for a firm five minutes (cooling my jets, my father used to say), I spot a good-looking guy coming toward me.

Good-looking in that non-jock sort of way with longish blond hair and wearing an oversized polo shirt. I can't help but think of my mother's favorite old-time actor. I lean against the counter and wait. But the closer he comes, the more certain I am I know this guy. My memory is usually pretty good but nothing comes to me.

"Morning. Need a bucket?"

His voice is familiar, too. I try not to stare at his

rugged good looks but can't stop myself. "Thanks. Are you new here?"

Two dimples peak at my question. "Good observation. I started a few weeks back. I haven't seen you here before. Maybe because they normally keep me stationed at the carts. They must have wanted to give me a break today." He flashes a smile again showing even white teeth. The kind of teeth I would willingly pay for if I could be guaranteed mine would look like his. And still my brain nudges me. Where do I know him from?

"Are you from around here?"

He reaches over and fills the bucket. When he stands back up, a flicker of recognition crosses his surfer-boy features. "You look familiar. Have we met?"

A surge of satisfaction fills me. I have never forgotten a face before. "I'm from Pennsylvania. And you?"

"No kidding. Me, too," he says, openmouthed. Again that knock-her-head-over-her-heels smile. "Whereabouts?"

When I say Wyoming County, he spits into the grass. "Hey, neighbor. Me, too. Out by the lake."

Considering there is only one lake close to where I live, I picture the exact spot. "The one with the pavilion, right?" I'd painted several of my best scenes there, in fact, celebrated many special occasions there, too. The last one when Robert had saved enough money to attend Q-School. We had a huge picnic and invited all of our friends. My mother grilled chicken and Dad acted like he was king for the day, going around to everyone and getting soda and making sure they had enough food.

I push down the desire to grab his hand and dance

around the greens. Someone from back home.

"I'm Mark. So where did we meet?" He seems as intrigued as I am as to the details of our paths crossing and leans against the counter, one hand dangling close to his side. And oh, his eyes.

"Bobbi." I hold out my hand. His grip is strong. "My father owns an accounting business."

"Naw, do my own taxes. Ever roller skate?"

"Not in years." My brain whirls with possibilities. School? A restaurant? Church? And then the moment. Of course, I'd been so mad that morning that I'd not been in the mood to joke about staying out so late. "I remember now. Did you work at a hardware store?"

His eyes twinkle—maybe savoring the same shared memory? "You were one angry woman." A burly chuckle follows. "I couldn't make that key fast enough."

I laugh. "I can't believe this. What are you doing down here?"

His face flushes and I'm sure it is not from the wicked heat. "I moved down to live with my brother."

"And what did you do up north?" Now that I've found a kindred spirit I'm not about to let him go. I think of my mother's comment to me before I left home. 'Watch those strangers down there. They won't be anything like here.' What will my mother say when she finds out I've met someone from home?

"I worked in a hardware store." Again his dimples flash. "But not the one you met me in. I worked there a few years, and then got a job as a manager closer to home. And you? What brings you here?"

I nod toward the U-shaped building that houses the school. "I attend school here." I suppress the urge to tell him the rest. People tend to look at me as though

I'm crazy when I tell them I'm a golfer and not doing what I dream of doing every night. Too many have gone as far as to try to talk me out of it. "Going to make it my career."

He lets loose a low whistle. The kind Robert makes whenever he accuses me of showing off. "You must know my brother, then. He's a teacher here. Drew. I think he teaches golf psychology or something strange like that. The guy's hooked on this game. Went on tour and everything and now does this."

My heart does a flip when he mentions Drew. Of course. The blue eyes. "He's my golf instructor. I didn't know he'd been on tour. He never mentioned that."

"He might not. He blew his shot at fame because of something that happened to him. One thing I know about golf is that most of the game is played between here." He points two fingers above his ears. "Not on the field. Let something bother you and boom…might as well throw in the clubs."

Before I have a chance to respond, two more students come up for balls. Stepping back, I wait a few minutes, but then grab my bucket, not wanting to appear too eager. "I'll see you later," I call and get a return wave. I move over to the driving range but find my thoughts are centered on Drew. Have I met him before, too?

I hit my first ball. No, I would have remembered him.

Another student comes up next to me. "Hey, Bobbi. Want to play later?"

Nate's a nice guy. He's built well and stands taller than Robert. I like the sound of his voice and the way his face lights when he laughs. But he isn't Drew. I turn him down and continue my drives.

5

It's good I enjoy movies, considering free ones are the only benefit to my new job at the mall. My open palm waits for the ticket stubs from an older couple. Action flick. By now I have become pretty good at guessing what movie most people come to see. My game helps pass the time and monotony of this job, but at least I'm working. Some of the guys in my class are still looking. But a few weeks ago, I'd driven around and ended up at the Ocoee mall and this theater. As luck would have it, an employment sign caught my eye and I was hired on the spot.

"Enjoy the show," I say to a couple of teenagers who try to hide a bag of chocolate candy beneath the girl's jacket. Like she needs a coat in this weather. I was told not to say anything unless it is obvious since the theater also sells candy. Three dollars a box. I'd be down at the dollar store, too, bringing in my licorice sticks. So I let it go and act as though I'd not noticed anything. Fifteen minutes more and my shift ends, anyway. I am also fortunate to get shifts on Saturday afternoon and only two evenings a week leaving me time to practice.

"I'll take over. You can take off for the day," my manager says with one of those practiced smiles people use who think they are better than you are.

Smiling back, I shrug out of my little blue vest and go to the employee area where I've locked my purse. I have yet to explore this mall. Today will be as good a time as any. I know it contains the usual anchor department stores and a few clothing stores for younger teens—sizes I couldn't wear when I was twelve. I buy a root beer at the food court and work my way up and down the aisles. Sellers in booths hawk perfume, incense, and hairpieces only Mattie would wear. About halfway down, I come to an abrupt halt.

In front of me is a store that sells art. Not just any art, but landscapes painted in enticing colors. My breath rushes out from the longing that overtakes me. My stomach coils with intensity, and my heart unfurls in pleasure as my lungs fill with the familiar scent. I'm transported back to my studio, surrounded by palettes of paint and creamy canvases stretched across their frames.

"May I help you?" A young salesman sporting facial hair that might, on a good day, pass for a goatee approaches me.

I shake my head. No, he can't help me. No one can. I've created my own world, one in which I've decided to be the hero our family needs to save it from further pain and disappointment. And that means I no longer paint. But can it hurt to look?

"I'm only looking." I say this to him in a casual way so he'll leave me alone and return to his post by the front.

He tilts his head as though pointing me in the direction I should go, but I need no assistance that way, either. I move toward the river scenes as though on autopilot.

"Are you an artist?"

Unwanted tears form in my eyes. I blink. Before, when a stranger asked me that question, I was thrilled to be able to nod and say, "Yes, I'm an artist. It's what I do. It's my passion." But today I can only give the truth. "Not anymore."

My eager salesman shrinks back as though my answer discounts me. I notice it isn't because of my no longer being an artist, but so he can capture the next couple who wanders into the showroom.

Packed rows draw me to a section that showcases the better works. An easel holding one particular painting catches my eye. I study the delicate brushstrokes. A familiar scene. I read the title. *A Susquehanna Day Dream.* I peer closer to read the artist's name. Sarah Adams.

Sarah? Not Sarah. Yet the proof rests before me. When I worked in Art's gallery back home, Sarah had brought in a few of her paintings, but Art refused to take them on consignment. "They aren't good enough for our store," he explained to me after Sarah left in tears.

What made the whole scene awkward for me is I knew Sarah. We attended the same high school and shared the same desk in art class. I'd always been a little jealous (OK, maybe a lot) of her work so when she got turned down, I didn't feel as broken-hearted as I should have for her.

But obviously she'd not let that rejection stop her determination. She'd improved—really improved. Her color choices capture not only my artist's sense of design and depth but make me smile. She followed her dream and didn't give up.

"It's one of our store's best sellers. This artist has become popular for this kind of work. Can I interest you in a purchase?"

I bite back a laugh. If he knew how little money I

had in my wallet, he'd probably kick me out of the store.

"It's beautiful. But I'll have to think about it."

Not one to be put off, he reaches behind him and comes back with a colorful brochure. Perhaps that's why he was voted salesman of the month. I'd noticed his bright ribbon attached to his pocket with the distinction. "Take one of our brochures in case you change your mind. There is an excellent write-up in this about the artist."

With no other choice but to take the offered information, I tuck it into my purse. My phone chooses that moment to vibrate, giving me a good reason to slip away. I dig for it and bring it out to find Amanda's name on the display.

"Hey, I've been waiting for your call. So am I an aunt?" I move toward the center courtyard area where a merry-go-round is entertaining a host of young children in line to experience it. "You never called back. Did you take the test?"

"We decided I should get a professional opinion before I told anyone. Yes! I'm pregnant! Can you believe it? My heart about stopped when they called me. I tried to get you yesterday, but decided I didn't want to leave a message. This means you need to come home for my shower this winter."

I stop by the toy train and move toward an empty bench. My best friend is having a baby. "Oh wow! Does it feel unreal? It's not like we've been out of school all that long."

"Long enough. You're going to be twenty-three in a few weeks, in case you've been so busy and have forgotten. Will you be coming home? Don't they give you a break sometime soon?"

I nod and search for a clean place to sit. A pile of cold french-fries litters one seat and it looks as though someone lost their soda all over the other bench.

I honestly haven't thought about my birthday.

"My semester ends in two weeks. I don't know if I'll have the money to drive back up or not. I started a job at a theater a while ago. I'm not sure if they'll give me the time off."

I dread being alone on my birthday, but the truth is I might have to be. Last year's birthday celebration comes into focus as tired moms herd their children away from the machines that sell cheap toys. Last year my mother baked two cakes, Robert's favorite chocolate peanut butter one and my white one with white icing. She'd invited everyone we knew for smoked corn and barbecued chicken.

The last person left at midnight, and that was only because it was Robert's best friend, Dan. We'd been sitting around the campfire Dad started at sundown, and by then my mother brought out the fixings for S'mores. Even Grandpa stayed up past his bedtime and tucked himself into one of the lawn chairs next to the comfortable blaze.

Later, Dan and I shared a private moment behind the barn. He'd tucked my hand into his and led me there on the pretense of giving me my birthday gift. We had dated only twice but those times had left me hoping for more. "Come here. I've got you something, but I don't want to give it to you in front of Robert. You know how that clown gets." He'd rolled his eyes and I couldn't help but admire his full lips and dark shiny hair.

He was a freak about golfing like Robert was and was already on tour so he didn't get home much. But I didn't care. I'd always thought he was nice and my heart reeled that he asked me out.

He pulled out a tiny box wrapped in blue tissue paper.

I fumbled with it and finally lifted up a silver chain. A miniature heart hung from the end. I remember looking up into his eyes. He leaned forward and kissed me.

"Are you listening to me, Bobbi?" Amanda's stern voice pulls me back to the present.

"I'm here," I say, but I choke on the words. I'm here in Orlando, a zillion miles away from everyone I love. Why is it continually so hard to stay focused? I've almost completed one semester with three left to go.

Anything is possible. Isn't that what Robert always said when he talked about his dream to win the Masters Tournament?

Maybe I have my doubts on days like today, but I refuse to let anything interfere. "I'm here. Tell me more."

~*~

Marketing class teaches me not only how to create a power point that impresses the teacher to give me an A, but also that I need to start marketing myself more. I buy five hundred cheap online business cards and pass them out to every person I meet in the industry, whether or not they run a golf course, give lessons, or know someone on tour. I want my name out there so that when I win tournaments, sponsors flock to pick me up.

In the meantime, I sign up for a lesson every chance I get. Today after class, I hitch my backpack onto my shoulder and hurry into the hallway to sign up for Drew's afternoon lesson. We almost have a standing arrangement for one thirty, and I look forward not only to showing him how well I am putting, but also to our conversations.

"Hey, Bobbi. Want to play a round today at Sunset?"

I turn to my right to see Brad catch up with me, puffing hard. He's a few years old than I am and needs to lose twenty pounds. His receding hairline makes him look even older.

"Can't. I need to sign up for a lesson."

He walks with me to where the sign-up sheets are posted and I look for Drew's list. My usual slot has been filled. My shoulders and spirits fall. I'll have to wait around an extra hour if I want one with him today.

"How's Drew as an instructor? I haven't tried him yet."

No longer in the mood for polite conversation, I scribble my name in and ignore his question.

But Brad isn't easily put off. "Want to go over to the clubhouse and get a bite to eat?"

It would be a way to kill time since I hate to spend two hours at the driving range and then practice again. My peanut butter and jelly sandwich I made in my sleep this morning at five waits for me in my car along with a slice of Matty's homemade pie. I calculate how much it will cost to get a burger in the clubhouse.

"My treat. You can buy next time," Brad says as though reading my mind. His chin hangs on the hope that I will say yes, I know that, but I can't bring myself to give him any reason to believe I'm interested in starting a relationship with him.

"Maybe next time, Brad. I had a cancellation." We turn to find Drew standing nearby, hands on his hips.

Brad gives a quick nod and steps out of Drew's path quicker than a dog looking for a treat.

I push my hair back behind my ears, wishing I'd worn it up. He points toward his office down the hallway. I follow his orange and black golf shirt. I'd almost bought that same color last week and am elated I didn't, as it looks far better with his hair coloring than mine. When we arrive at his office, he holds the door open and motions for me to enter first.

The smell of pizza almost knocks me over.

An open box waits on his desk with two large sodas on either side. He motions for me to sit while he goes around to the other side of the desk.

"I thought you had a lesson?" Once again, my voice lets me down, making me sound like I'm twelve.

"He cancelled, so we're on."

"And it includes lunch?" The inviting smell of roasted garlic and pepperoni makes me salivate.

Drew reaches for a large piece and pushes the box toward me. "Eat up. You're wasting away."

I do as ordered and munch on the crispy crust. Pizza has turned into a delicacy for me here in Florida, whereas back home I'd shared one weekly with friends. I stuff it down as politely as I can and reach for a second piece the same time he does.

I have yet to ask Drew about his past and consider this might be the right moment. After all, he seems more relaxed than I've seen him all semester. He wipes his mouth with his napkin and smiles at me, causing me to choke on my last bite.

I reach for my soda and suck half of it down. So I'm not completely at ease with him. I doubt I ever will be considering the way his eyes sparkle and the adorable way his face crinkles when he smiles. I can't help but compare him to Dan, whom I ended going out with only three more times. His taste in movies and music bored me, and his endless parade of golf fanfare had been the end for me. I kept the necklace though (it was a gift) and tucked it away in a box that I kept in my bottom drawer so my mother wouldn't find it if she decided to snoop.

Drew shoves the pizza box away from us. "So tell me why you're really here, Bobbi. It isn't about the golf, is it?"

My eyes widen. If I could have, I would have gulped, but instead set my soda down and try to come up with a plausible answer. "What do you mean? I told you my plans are to go on tour."

His eyes narrow.

I've been found out. Maybe I'm not as good an actress as I'd hoped to be. Maybe Mrs. Tarpon, my sixth-grade teacher, had been right when she'd put me in the choir instead of giving me a part in the *Pirates of Penzance*. I'd cried all night that I wouldn't get to wear those pretty petticoats like my best friend, but as it was, I came down with the flu opening night, anyway.

My mother kept me home while Dad went with Robert, since he played one of the main pirates. Moustache and all.

"That's not what I mean, and you know it."

A plan forms as I contemplate how much to share about my family's problems. "I'll tell you if you tell me why you quit the tour to work here."

He frowns like a child who has been told they are leaving the playground.

Touché.

Now I'm not normally the kind of person who wants to hurt anyone, but I have my reasons for wanting to keep parts of my life private. I assume Drew does, too.

"Where did you hear that?" he says, eyebrows rising.

"I met your brother on the range. How come you didn't mention we're from the same area?"

I'm not sure which part of my sentence floors him more. That I know his brother or that I know he comes from my hometown.

"So you met Mark? Quite a talker, isn't he?"

The office is getting too warm for me. If someone doesn't keep the weight room doors open, this half of the school overheats. I wipe back hair that sticks on my face. "He's a nice guy. We discovered we've met before at a hardware store."

"Really? What a coincidence. So I guess you've been wondering if we've met before, too."

I shake my head. "At first, but then I knew if we had, I would have remembered you." My hand flies to my mouth. Did I really say that?

"And I'm certain I would have remembered you, too, Miss Bobbi-with-an-*I*."

A shudder runs down my spine, to the dead-center of my stomach. I think of moonlit nights, dancing under the stars, and holding hands on the front porch swing. I think of swapping stories until daylight and plucking strands of long grass from his hair after lying in the dewy morning grass by the river. I let my brain spin all forms of romantic fantasies while I shrink under Drew's steady gaze.

I do the only thing I can do. "Do you like movies?"

6

After my lesson, I drive straight home past the row of century-old oaks and into my development. I slow down to let a golf cart pass driven by a man wearing plaid Bermuda shorts, a collared shirt, and loafers with white socks. He nods his thanks and putts toward a trailer where a matching woman with tightly permed silver hair and a sundress that shows her flapping underarms waits. I'm surrounded by old age, but then much of Florida is filled with the retired.

A block of mailboxes sits near the clubhouse. I use the word clubhouse loosely. When I went to investigate it my first day here, all I found were outdated magazines stacked side-by-side next to a broken treadmill and a set of used barbells. The owner stayed in his office watching TV the entire time I was there. Mattie told me later the building's main usage is as a shelter in the event of a tornado or hurricane. I dread the thought of being trapped for days with people who smell like menthol rub.

After finding my key, I unlock my box and smile when I discover three letters from home. Amanda must have sent a pre-baby announcement already as the pink envelope and her fancy cursive is covered with rattle stickers. I finger the next two letters and decide to wait until I get back to my place to open them. My stomach growls in agreement. Drew's pizza didn't last through nine holes of golf.

My cheeks heat again. *Do you like movies?* Pretty forward. I've never asked a guy out before, and here I ask my own teacher. I put the car in gear and drive around the corner to my place. Good thing a student came into his office before he answered. I'm not sure I would have followed through.

A quick glance at Mattie's place assures me she isn't around and won't be bringing over any leftovers tonight. I look forward to my twenty-nine cent box of macaroni and cheese. I might even have some stale bread I can toast.

My meal takes only minutes to make. With a cold glass of milk, toast with peanut butter, and a plate of the blue box's finest imposter, I sit at my kitchen table with the two other letters waiting before me. My mom writes me almost every day. She sends recipes and notes about the robins coming and going and how high the river is. Robert is more lax so I grin when I pick his up first.

A minute later, I set down his letter.

My mother needs me to come home.

My fingers shake as I slit open her letter and a check falls out. I race through her neat paragraphs written in her favorite purple ink but can't find anything to substantiate Robert's claims. The money is for my birthday if I want to fly up—if I can get time off—but she knows it might be difficult for me and doesn't hold out any expectations.

I drop my head in my hands. "Oh, God," I pray. "Oh, God, please help us."

~*~

Maybe it's because I'm a new employee or maybe

such a fine worker, but my manager gives me the time off when I ask for it the next day. I wait now in my seat at the Orlando International Airport for my plane to take off. I've been fortunate to get a direct flight, but not so fortunate to get a good seatmate. The woman who sits next to me has already pulled out her knitting needles and clicks them while we wait for runway clearance. I'm not sure if I will be able to stand hearing that sound for the next two-plus hours.

I study the other travelers on the crowded plane. A young man and his wife (I can tell by the shiny new wedding bands) sit across from me holding hands as though they've just come off their honeymoon. A set of black plastic mouse ears sticking out of her bag give me a good clue. In front of me, I watch two small children and a tired-looking mother climb in after a tussle about who will sit where.

Normally, airplane rides intrigue me. We took a trip out west to Arizona for a vacation when we were in our teens. Dad thought it was important that we viewed the Grand Canyon, though when I got there I asked to go to a mall instead. Not that it was so boring I wanted to cry; it wasn't. It was just the same everywhere I looked. How many pictures could I take of rocks? Robert had agreed and we took to snapping our new cameras at tourists who were chasing their kids away from the steep edges.

When that got boring, we edged closer ourselves to take in yet another view.

"Watch this," Robert said as he stepped on a rock ledge and dangled one long leg over it. "Ta-da!" I laughed and imitated him from where I stood on my own rock four feet away until I felt the back of my shirt being yanked so hard I stumbled backwards.

"Get back from that ledge!" My father next went for Robert, who had been wise enough to see Dad grab me first and knew better than to wait for him to get there.

We sat in the hot car for over an hour while he and Mom went through the gift shop (now I was bored) and took more pictures. I don't think they ever developed half of what they took, but that wasn't my business.

Later, I tried to paint from my photos but couldn't get them right. It seemed my mountains and river were my muse.

After takeoff, I reach into my backpack and pull out my headphones and a book I'd been meaning to read ever since I arrived in Florida but hadn't had time. Golf. That's what I do in all my free time. Day in and day out. I actually shot a seventy-nine last week, and it seems I'm getting more and more consistent with my swings. I still need to do better, but I'm improving.

"Are you going home?"

I can't help but hear my seatmate's question since I have yet to turn on my music.

"I am. What about you?"

I don't realize being polite means I will be connected to this stranger for another thirty minutes. I actually hate that she intrudes on my time to think about what lies ahead of me, but I decide to be sorry for her instead. She can't help it if her mother just died and she's headed home for a funeral. Can I blame her that she's seated next to me who has my own set of problems to deal with? After losing my grandmother so recently, I understand grief.

So I try not to hate her and instead listen politely until she runs out of words and tears.

In the silence that finally shows itself, I close my eyes and think about my father. I will need to speak to him soon. My heart races as I consider what I will say. I want to tell him how much he hurts the family, that his actions are cowardly, and that Mom deserves better.

I dab my eyes with my napkin. My mother's letter didn't give a hint to her pain. She isn't that way at all, so I'm not surprised. One Christmas, she surprised my father with a new rifle. He'd wanted to hunt small game on our back property for a few years but never took the time to get a license or a gun.

"It's a beauty," he said as he fondled the sleek metal. "It'll come in handy."

"Will you teach me to use it, too, Dad?" Robert moved closer and his eyes practically bugged as he took in my mother's gift.

She smiled from across the room and reached for the discarded wrapping paper.

"Better yet, this gun will be yours. I'll teach you to shoot those old squirrels that keep ruining our roof." He handed Robert the gun.

My mother's smile froze. "But I thought you always wanted one, dear."

Dad tossed his shoulders and scooped up the rest of the Christmas wrap. "Not anymore. That was last year. Robert will make good use of it."

Her expression tipped downward, but she hurried to the kitchen to make us blueberry pancakes. I never saw her cry, but I know he broke her heart that morning. He breaks her heart almost every day but that particular memory has stayed with me the longest. Maybe because it was Christmas, or maybe because of what he did with that gun a few years later.

He didn't always own his own business. He

worked as an accountant for a firm in the next town. But the economy slumped, or so Mom told us, and Dad came home one day jobless. Too old to do much else except accounting, his mood quickly turned ugly.

I twist in my seat and tighten my seatbelt as the plane bumps with my memories.

"Never did like turbulence." My seatmate clutches her drink tighter.

I don't like turbulence in my family, but my father is determined to give it to us. A week after he lost his job, he and Mom got into a huge fight.

I was upstairs at the time but couldn't help but hear their words as my father's voice grew louder.

"It's entirely your fault. If you hadn't pushed me to study accounting, maybe I wouldn't be in this situation now. I'd be doing something I really want to do."

I hid back on the stairs and motioned to Robert to wait next to me when he came up behind me. We were old enough to understand the rage that came from my father. And the accusations.

"You needed to do something. You know that. I was helping." My mother fairly whispered her reasons, and hearing her do that made my skin crawl.

"Stand up to him just once!" I wanted to scream. Robert placed his hand on my arm and pulled me up two steps.

"We shouldn't be listening." His color had reddened. He hated it as much as I did when our parents fought, but I was powerless to leave my place of hiding.

"You don't have to, but I am." I slid back down and trained my ear. Nothing but silence greeted me until I heard mother's broken sobs. It took everything in me to not run down and rush into her arms. A burst of air hit me in the chest as my father flew past the bottom of the steps to the closet where he kept his gun.

"Don't, Rick. Put it away, please."

"I should shoot all of you and then myself. That's what I should do."

"Give it to me. You're upset. We'll work it out."

Robert pulled me up to his room, his hands gripping my shoulders. "He doesn't mean it. He's just mad. In a few minutes we'll go downstairs and everything will be OK."

I didn't believe him then, and I don't now.

I open my eyes to see the attendant leaning over me. "Would you like something to drink?"

"Nothing, thank you."

"Not long now. I can't wait to get my feet on the ground again." Click. Click. My seatmate's needles move faster.

I reach into my backpack and bring out the bag of pretzels I'd thought to bring. I'm sure I can wait.

7

My mother looks the same wearing her T-shirt and Mommy jeans and a pair of white sneakers. Her hair needs highlights badly, but at least it's still shaped around her head, not all wild looking as it tends to get some days like mine. I don't know what I expect; it has only been a few months since I left. Maybe I expect to see more sorrow painted on her familiar features. But no, she smiles widely when she catches sight of me coming from baggage claim.

When I reach her, she grabs hold of me and pulls me into her strong arms, hugging me as though I might disappear from her grip. Only then does she give away any of what she is feeling. I hear the sniff and grab on tighter.

"I missed you, Mom."

"I missed you more."

I grin at the silly game we played whenever I returned home from school. She'd be standing at the kitchen sink with a red and white checked dishtowel wrapped around her waist waiting for us.

Robert and I always tried to outrun each other to the back steps after the bus dropped us off out front. I usually lost, but I think Mom held onto me a fraction of a second longer when I finally arrived and Robert moved away.

Now I step back and look into her eyes, wrinkled around the edges with age, or stress. I am never sure.

"What's happened?"

She hooks her arm through mine and turns me toward the parking garage. "It can wait until we get home. I want to know every little detail about what you've been doing."

I know better than to argue, and maybe this is her way of keeping some sort of control in her life. I understand because I'm so much like her when it comes to certain things. I need to know that my life isn't going to fall down around me if I can stop it somehow. I let my mother have her time for now.

I love Pennsylvania in the summer. We drive past field after field of blazing corn ready to be picked and boiled, roasted, or grilled. I hope we will still smoke some. It isn't summer without our fire pit and racks of corn.

"How's Grandpa doing today?" I ask when we turn down the country road that leads home. So far, my mother has managed to stall my peppering her with questions by asking me questions. What grocery stores do I shop in? How about the Laundromat I use, and is it safe enough? Do I take my pepper spray with me when I go (I say yes, of course) and have I met any female friends (not yet, because my attention is on Drew)? And do I mind the humidity on my hair?

"Grandpa's fine. Just like he usually is. Moving around a little less, but that happens with age. Mom got the same way." It's my mother's turn to lie or refuse to see the truth.

"And Robert?"

A side of her mouth turns up. "Robert's doing well too. He misses you and wanted to ride down to the airport to get you, but I hated to have him wait in the hot car. Tonight we'll play cards like we always do."

"Sure. I haven't played any since leaving. I met a neighborhood woman—I think I wrote you about her. She tried to teach me how to play pinochle with some of her friends. I couldn't get the hang of it."

"I'm glad she took a liking to you. That makes me feel better. It's always nice to know your neighbors."

We turn into our driveway. I almost make her stop the car and let me out so I can stand out front and steady the ache in my chest from seeing home. Has it only been a few months since I left? It could have been years by the dizziness that overtakes me. Honestly, I didn't think leaving home and returning would cause me so much emotional turmoil. I want to bury my head in my lap and cry. I don't because I need to save my tears for what lies ahead of me.

I look for Dad's gray Honda where he always parks it by the barn. Only Robert's old truck sits in its usual spot. My gaze drifts out back to the charred remains of my studio. New grass has grown up where the building once stood. Soon there will be no visible reminder of my dream or my nightmare.

"Let's get your stuff inside. I've got a roast in the slow cooker."

I get out and go around to the trunk and reach for my backpack while my mother takes my small suitcase.

From where I stand, I see Grandpa sitting in his favorite chair on the screened-in porch. We added the porch when I was twelve. Before that, it sat open to the elements and bugs. When a small tornado came across the river, the damage was extensive.

My father hired a local carpenter who suggested screening it in and adding windows and heat for the winter. My mother balked at first, but when Grandpa and Grandma stopped by and agreed with the plans, she relented.

A swirling starts in the pit of my stomach and I swallow bile. I hate what is coming. I hate pretending along with my family.

~*~

The screen door slams behind me as I bend over him. Grandpa hugs me harder than I think he is capable. His tears mirror mine when I raise my head from his chest. "Love you, Grandpa."

"Love you, Bobbi-girl. Glad you're home with us."

I nod and look past him toward the sunny kitchen where Mom has already taken my luggage. "I need to find Robert, OK?" I stroke his shoulder and drift inside.

Already the hearty scent of roast beef fills the space.

"We'll be eating once I get the potatoes going." My mother is grabbing glasses from the cupboard. My favorite red glass is in her hand.

"Where's Robert? I want to see him."

She tilts her head toward the family room. Robert had mentioned in an email he was getting out of bed more often. Evidently, all the therapy is helping. I poke through the doorway and see him slouched in the corner of the couch, his long legs covered in baggy jeans and stretched out before him. A person would never guess how badly his bones were crushed and how his muscles had been damaged only months before. One brow lifts and he raises his arms toward me.

I fly into them. "I missed you, goof."

"Not as much as I missed you. Sit." He pats the cushion next to him.

"You're almost as tan as I am! Do you make them take you outside every day so you can lie out or what?" It's true. His strong features are tanned a coppery color, almost as dark as my legs. When he smiles, his white teeth look even whiter.

"Sort of like that. I wouldn't want you to get ahead of me." Now he tugs my hand and clasps it tightly. "I missed you. You read my letter, right?" He whispers his last question.

I look behind me for signs of Mom and turn back.

"How long has he been gone?"

He meets my stare. "As far as I'm concerned, not long enough."

"You don't mean that."

He drops my hand and looks away.

"Where did he go? Is he in town?" I will see my father and talk to him, even though the idea frightens me more than moving to Florida did. He and I don't see eye-to-eye on much.

His presence over me was more as an added enforcer whenever my mother laid down the law. I've always envied the closeness he enjoyed with Robert and wanted part of that for myself, but it never happened. Talking to him would be akin to talking to a stranger.

"He's staying in the apartment over the office."

I let out my breath and sink closer to my brother.

Happy Birthday.

My mother comes into the room shortly after wearing that same inane smile. I want to tell her to cut it out, that I know what is going on, but decide to let her tell me in her own time.

"Has Robert given you his birthday gift yet?" She looks first at him and then at me. I have totally forgotten to buy Robert anything in my haste to get home. Now I try to think of ways I can make it up to him. Maybe I'll take him for a ride to Dee's Ice Cream Hut. He must get tired of being cooped up here this summer. How many times did he drive around the county with me in the cab of his truck when I complained how bored I was? We'd blasted the radio and sang oldies until our throats hurt. We'd stop at the Dee's for cones and yack about my ridiculous whining.

That was before I found my job at the gallery and before I started selling paintings for real cash instead of giving them away for everyone's birthday, Christmas, or housewarming gift. The entire town owned one of my paintings. After the fire, I refused to eat at Anne's Diner because she'd hung one of my river scenes over the stone fireplace.

"Not yet. She just got here, Mom," he says with a bit of an edge to his voice. He reaches over the side of the couch and that's when I see the shiny rolling walker.

"Did Grandpa finally break down?" I grin at the idea that maybe he wasn't so stubborn after all. "Good for him." Before I left, I'd tried again to get him to use one, but adamant as always, he had refused.

Now Robert turns toward me with a glint of a smile in his eyes. "It isn't for him." My jaw drops as he positions the walker in front of him and slowly pulls himself up to a standing position. The first time I've seen him upright in months. My stomach flips and I cover my mouth with my hand so I won't sob.

"Robert…when? Oh, my…" I'm not usually a speechless person (well, *never* actually) but I can't get a word out past the lump that forms in my throat. I stand next to him and throw my arms around his neck, hugging him as carefully as I can. "This is the best birthday gift anyone ever gave me."

"That's just the wrapping. Watch."

He places his right foot in front of him and then the left one. Robert is walking again.

8

Again, my mother makes two cakes. This time I ask for peanut butter icing instead of my usual white and Robert adds sprinkles to his chocolate. The four of us will be eating cake in our sleep.

"So do we have any ice cream to go with this?" I stick my finger in the gooey frosting and lick the creamy sweetness while my mother hustles around the kitchen preparing our birthday celebration for later that night.

It doesn't take me long to realize that smoked corn won't be on the menu after I watch Grandpa move himself from his sunny place on the back porch to his recliner in the TV room. My bones ache along with his. He hunches over when he walks now, making the trek more difficult. Forgotten are the exercises he performed like a ritual every morning to stay in top shape. After Grandma died, he'd shrunk into himself like a leaf saying good-bye to the hot summer.

I look around the neat kitchen, a familiar meeting spot for my mother and myself. How many times have I shared with her here my disappointing romances or my excitement over a new idea to paint? It has never changed in appearance as far back as my memory can stretch.

Two towels appliquéd with apples rest over the bar on the stove while a matching third one hangs through the kitchen door handle. Mom can't get enough hand towels. She probably has a lifetime supply. Same with mugs. I'm always afraid to open a cabinet in case one might decide it's time to seek freedom.

She stops her chore of cleaning carrots and turns around. Her forehead buckles with worry. "You know, I forgot. I'm so sorry. Do you mind running over to town and getting a half gallon of whatever you want?"

"Sure. Let me ask Robert what flavor he wants." I already know of course. Same every year. Chocolate. But asking will let me tell him my plans.

~*~

Because we didn't get cable TV until I was almost a teenager, I watched reruns like *The Waltons* with my mother. For the most part, everyone in that family got along. Occasionally, one of the kids might get angry with the father or mother, but it always worked out by the time the hour ended. I thought maybe our family was like that until the whispered arguments between my parents became more frequent. I decided TV was fiction and their fights were real life.

I've always wondered why my father took to my brother more than me. It wasn't as though Robert went out of his way to get Dad to do more with him. When I asked my mother once why my father always took Robert golfing and not me, she said it was because Dad loved the sport.

At this point, in her telling, my mother's gaze drifted to the back fields. She pulled on her hair and paused. Then she said something about him being gone too much and she didn't like to be home alone with twins. That's when she skipped to the part of him becoming an accountant and how grateful she was that he took up that career. I didn't find the clippings until later and understood why Mom wouldn't tell me the truth.

I waited two weeks and then told her I knew. She'd blushed hard and fumbled with the dish she'd been washing. "He loves both of you. He just loves golf the same amount."

I always wondered when he ignored us at the dinner table if he wished we had never been born. I wonder now as I park the car in front of the office if he will care that I have come to see him and if he cares that I am trying to fix us.

His office is located in a nicer section of town in an old 1800s two-story brick building with the name of his company painted in gold letters over the door. We'd spent an entire summer cleaning and painting for his grand opening when he decided to start his own business. He'd paid me to paint his office. Money I spent quickly on a set of new paints.

The upstairs apartment is small and dingy and usually rented out for storage. But apparently, the accommodations don't bother him.

Pangs shoot through my stomach—not from hunger, but from fear of speaking to him. I've always suffered with stomachaches when I get nervous and have to work hard at squelching them when I golf. I don't need to double over at the markers.

Chalky florescent lights greet me as I open the door and enter the building. I notice Dad's office in the back room is still lit. The staff has left for the day. Part of me feels sorry I've missed them, especially Kate who treats me like her own daughter whenever I stop in. She keeps a stash of candy kisses in her lower desk drawer. I'd thought for years they were only for me until I saw her popping a few into her own mouth one day after school.

My heart beats faster (in rhythm to my churning stomach) and I take a deep breath before calling out, "Dad? Are you back there?"

He comes around the doorway looking like I expected he would, wearing a dark tie (he never wears the bright ones we buy him for Christmas), white shirt, and crisp ironed pants fresh from the dry cleaner since he doesn't trust my mother to not double crease them. His forehead looks like a fork has plowed through it and his thin lips collapse upon recognition.

I want to turn around.

"What are you doing in town?"

We size each other up. "It's my birthday, in case you've forgotten." Yeah, I'm good at being sarcastic when I have to be, only I hadn't intended to be today. I lower my eyes and take another deep breath.

"Happy Birthday," he says. "I'm sorry I forgot."

I raise my head to study his face. It's crinkled with stress—his crow's feet have grown deeper, and the gray in his hair looks almost white.

"Why are you over here, Dad? Why don't you come home?"

It's his turn to look away. His shoulder falls against the doorjamb and his fist finds his pocket where he jingles loose change. He makes me think about how he always did that when we waited for someone in line or the few times he attended church with us.

"Did your mother send you?"

I shake my head. "She hasn't talked to me about you. I wanted to talk with you myself." My voice takes on a life of its own, shaky and low-pitched, sliding out of my mouth faster and faster. "They need you at home, Dad. What's wrong with you?"

My words pull him straight. "It isn't your business. Go back to Florida. Go back to school and see how it feels to want something so badly and then fail at it."

I swallow hard at his attack. "I won't fail. I won't let this family down. Not like you have."

He shakes his head again and I swear if we weren't inside he would have spit. My tears burn in the back of my eyes. The last thing I want is him to see how much he hurts me. I spin on my heels and rush out the front door more determined than ever to be the hero my family needs.

~*~

We play three more rounds of Spades until my eyes droop from lack of sleep.

"Does anyone want more cake? There's plenty." My mother starts to rise.

Robert shakes his head and pushes back from the edge of the table. He still sleeps downstairs and I can see he hopes to retire soon.

"Robert, why don't I help you to bed?" she says next.

"I'm good, Mom. Go ahead and visit with Bobbi. I want to read my Bible before I crash."

I look away as he struggles to stand and as he takes painfully slow steps toward the front room. Mom told me he hopes to be walking on his own within a month or so, but he still has a long way to go before he's the old Robert.

"How about we get a cup of tea and sit out on the front porch?"

"I'd like that. It should be cooler out there." I nod to the breeze blowing in from outside through the screen in the dining room window. My mother goes to the kitchen while I follow. I set out the rose teacups and pluck two bags from the stash she keeps in the silver canister next to the stove. Within seconds, the teakettle whistles and we carry our warm cups to the rocking chairs to sit side-by-side. The night hushes around us except for a determined chorus of crickets and an occasional bullfrog from the pond behind the house.

I love these moments, and soon I manage to push the scene with my father to the back of my thoughts.

"Have you found a church down there yet?" Of course she would ask me sooner or later (sooner, actually).

"Not yet. I've been busy with school."

"I joined a fellowship class last month. I met four nice women my age." My mother smiles, probably remembering her day.

"Amanda's pregnant."

Her look of surprise tickles my chest. "Wonderful! I'm so happy for her. Her mother will make a terrific grandmother." She lets her eyelids close and rocks back and forth in an easy rhythm. Is she thinking of rocking her own grandchild someday?

I set my cup down near my feet. "I saw Dad today."

Her rocking stops and then starts up again. She opens her eyes and keeps her look glued straight ahead. "And what did he say?"

When my mother speaks in that faraway tight

voice, I never know how to proceed. Usually I tell her to forget it and chase her down another time. But I only have a few days home and I need to figure out what's going on with them.

"Not a whole lot. Something about being a failure. Is he coming home?"

She places her own teacup next to mine and lets her head fall back against the hard wooden chair again. She closes her eyes once more and stays that way for so long I am afraid she's fallen asleep. "I don't know much about anything, Bobbi. My life is off course, and I'm afraid I'm lost."

If she'd told me she wanted to jump in the river and never see the surface again, it couldn't have scared me more. My mother never gives up on anything.

I remember one time when I was in the fourth grade and we were dressing up for the May Day festival. Robert and I were going to be horses so that meant we had to make masks out of paper bags and wear brown spotted vests. She whipped those vests up in seconds but somehow we couldn't make our masks look like horses. We finally ran out of paper sacks.

I started to bawl that I would be the dumbest looking horse in the whole class and Robert rolled his eyes saying he didn't want to dress up like a stupid horse, anyway.

Well, my mother wasn't about to give up. She proceeded to drive to the grocery store, paid the clerk for ten more brown bags and took them over to the art department at our local college.

I won the prize for the most realistic looking horse.

"So what are you going to do?" I ask in a voice I can barely hear myself.

"I've asked God that same thing, but He keeps

telling me to wait. He has plans for me."

I search her profile in the dim light coming off the garage. Tears run down her cheeks and she finally wipes them with the back of her hand. I've never seen her so resigned.

"Do you believe that about the plans?"

"I have to," she says simply.

"Dad should be here, not in some dumb apartment."

"I can't stop him. I found that out a long time ago." Her voice quivers.

"So you're going to wait on God and see what He says?"

She reaches for my hand and squeezes it. "He's had a plan for me since before I was born. I have to trust Him, don't I?"

I lay my head back and gaze into the night sky where the stars spell their names to me. Is it possible?

Does God have a plan for me as well?

9

I rise the next morning before anyone else. The sun is out and the robins announce it's daylight from my open window. Amanda and I have arranged to meet at the state park, take a short hike, and grab lunch at the Silver Diner to catch up on all of our news. Like her baby news and why on earth I'm still down in Florida when she needs me here. At least that's what she told me when I called after my tea on the porch.

I've gotten so use to the warm mornings in Florida, the air chills my bones when I step outside. I run back inside for my light jacket, zipping it to my chin. One point for Florida.

Ten minutes later, I pull into the state park's empty parking lot. A hazy gray mist hiding the earlier sunshine swirls around the swing sets. I can barely make out the rusty slide I use to climb as a young girl. The outhouses probably still show my initials where, one bold day, I'd used Robert's new penknife and carved not only my initials, but my latest crush's initials, too.

I slug a long drink from my water bottle. Amanda is typically late. I spend more time waiting for her than I do in any doctor's office. I dig out my cell to prod her as a car pulls up next to mine. Finally. I shed my coat and open my car door, surprised to see a truck instead of Amanda's red Nissan.

"Hey. Didn't expect to see you here." Dan walks

toward me.

"Hey, Dan." My stomach clenches. He hasn't changed—looks as good as or better than before. My old flame wears black running shorts and a light windbreaker pulled over an orange T-shirt. When he smiles at me, I instinctively reach for the necklace I once wore against my chest. His look flashes to my neck and back again. Maybe I should have returned it.

"How's Florida?" He steps around my car and comes closer. His heady cologne mixes with the morning dew from the trees. "When Robert said you planned to golf professionally, I about fell over." A chuckle follows.

"That's the plan. I heard you're doing pretty well on tour. Good for you." I can afford to be generous. It isn't as though we'd parted after a fight or anything.

Dan was hardly ever in the area, and I wanted a boyfriend who could take me out now and then. And one who didn't talk golf nonstop or watch boring movies.

"I've got a ways to go." His eyes look weary, or is it my imagination? "It's hard being on the road so much with Mom not feeling well. Did you hear her cancer came back?"

Of course. I'd forgotten about his mother. She'd been sick on and off for a long time. "I didn't know. I'm sorry. Mom and I haven't really had much of a chance to catch up yet."

The sympathy in my voice encourages him because he moves closer and leans back against Mom's car. He crosses his arms and gazes past me with a faraway look in his eyes. "They give her about six months."

"Oh, Dan, I'm so sorry." I never know what to say

when someone tells me news like this. Not that I've heard it often, but it makes me uncomfortable. I take my cue from the way others have treated us after the accident. "Is there something I can do while I'm home?"

He shakes his head and studies the ground for a minute. "I like coming out here to run. Remember when we had our senior picnic here? You were so afraid of swimming in the creek because someone saw a snake." A kind-of-cute smile forms at the corner of his mouth.

"And you and Robert ate so much watermelon, you threw up on the bus ride home."

He laughs and I remember now why I'd originally fallen for him. I laugh along with him and our voices echo in the empty dawn around us. As abruptly as he'd brought up our past, he turns to the present.

He steps closer and looks down into my face. "I've missed you, Bobbi."

My phone chooses that moment to announce Amanda's incoming call with a ring tone I'd affectionately chosen for her.

"Sorry," I say and pull my cell from my pocket.

"Bobbi, I'm so sorry I'm not there. I woke up puking and I feel horrid. Is this what pregnancy is going to do to my body? If it is, I'll never live through it." Normally, I would have listened to her tirade, but today with my heart racing wildly in my chest from Dan's presence, I decide to cut in.

"Hey, it's fine. I'm here with Dan. He showed up the same time I did. I'll take a quick hike and drop by later, OK?"

"Dan? As in Dorky Dan? What on earth, Bobbi? Listen…wait, I need to go!" The call ends and I slide my phone back into my pocket, grateful he has stepped away. Had I really called him dorky? I study his strong shoulders and can't help but compare them to Drew's.

"Sounds like Amanda is sick. I'll catch up with her later."

His smile returns and he shrugs toward the path. "Want company?"

The last thing I need to do is open doors I can't walk through. But I do. "I don't run, I walk."

"I can do that." He holds out his hand.

If I take it, will I be able to let go again?

~*~

I climb the back porch steps and open the screen door. "Hi, Grandpa. Where's Mom?"

Grandpa sits in his usual chair, enjoying the warmth from the sun that is already soaking into the floorboards. I drank two bottles of water on the hike, but hadn't eaten any of the snacks I took. "I'm thinking of baking some cookies. How about it?"

"Chocolate chip. Your mother made peanut butter the last time and they didn't sit well with me." He snorts and coughs on his own spit.

"You got it."

I find Robert camped out in front of the TV doing an exercise that is supposed to keep his legs from looking like a newborn colt's.

He raises his eyes toward the ceiling. "In the attic. Said she had some sorting to do."

I hand him another pillow for beneath his legs before turning to the stairs.

My mother's favorite place to hole up has always been the attic, where she keeps everything as neat as though she's going to throw a party there. All my old toys are assigned color-coded bins with my name marked plainly on the sides. Games that have seen better days have their own home on the shelves Dad built for her on the front end of the house. I like to run my fingers down the familiar names and wonder if my children will someday beg to play them as I had.

"It's hot up here." She has the wooden fan going, but my forehead complains with new sweat droplets.

I find her sitting on her knees in 'the corner.' We dubbed the space that because it is where she stores all of our youngest mementos. The ones she said she could never bear to part with until they send her to a nursing home. White baby shoes, soft yellow blankets, and a matching pair of pacifiers slightly molded from our gums.

"How was your hike?" She turns and pats the spot next to her. "Pull up a piece of floor. I'm going through your box now."

Wood splinters come to mind, but I do as requested, sitting with my legs crossed in front of a blue plastic bin. I know from the dates that the treasures in this one will be before I started kindergarten.

"Amanda called off sick."

"That's too bad. Nausea?" She hands me a pile of old clothes. Why on earth does she need to keep my first pair of jeans?

"Yeah. Sounds like she might be in for it."

"Then what did you do?"

I shrug, deciding it won't hurt to tell her. "Dan showed up about the same time I did."

My mother has this sense about her. I never have to tell her everything and she always knows what I'm thinking. She sets aside a pile of baby socks and faces me, cocking her head. "And what did you and Dan talk about?" I'm sure she remembers the night I broke it off with him. I'd run him down deeper than the river.

"He's a friend, Mom."

She turns back to her pile of treasures. "Somehow that wasn't the impression you gave me."

So I see him in a new light. I shrug. Even I'm not clear yet what it all means. He'd held my hand most of the way but hadn't made any other moves other than help me up a particularly sharp incline. We'd stopped and admired the river winding peacefully below. I was sure he felt the sensations I did by the way he glanced at me every so often. When we returned to our cars, I hadn't been sure how to say good-bye.

But Dan did.

"People change. He's playing golf this winter down in Florida and I promised to see him when he gets there."

Now I get my mother's look. Eyes narrowed and a grim set to her lips. Honestly, why do I always blurt my private life to her?

"Do you think that's wise?"

"Don't worry, Mom. It won't interfere with my plans. He's a nice guy. That's it."

Her sigh about rolls off the rafters. She reaches for a blue silky piece of fabric and hands it to me. "Do you remember this?"

I unfurl the slippery cloth and a knot catches in my throat. "My cape."

"I made it when you were four. You wore it to bed every night for almost a year. I should never have let you watch *Superman*." A chuckle escapes through her lips and I warm to it and her memory about my hero worship.

"I wanted to save the world." I hand her the cape, my fingers lingering on the soft fabric.

"You still do," she whispers.

10

Saying good-bye isn't easy. Robert pulls me aside as I pack snacks in the kitchen. Mom figures I must have run low by now, and even if it means checking my bag at the airport, she demands I take the remaining cookies and a bag of pretzels.

"Come home where you belong. You aren't a golfer and you know it." Robert holds my shoulders under his strong hands.

I straighten my back. "I shot a sixty-nine at last week's tournament." I amazed everyone on my team. If I continue to practice like I have been, I might shoot a consistent sixty-six, possibly enough to try out for Q-School—the path I need to go if I'm ever to turn pro.

Robert can't hide his pride or his sorrow. "Wow. Do you know how many average golfers ever shoot that score?" He pauses and looks down at the linoleum floor Dad installed when I was ten. Black and white checks like Mom requested. Sometimes looking at it makes me dizzy. I know Robert is thinking about the time he'd shot a 68 at the Towanda Country Club. He and Dad had stopped for ice cream and came home cheering and yelling that the next Tiger Woods lives in this house. "You're good, Bobbi. You are. You've got this talent I never had, but in the end, it has to make you happy. I know you aren't."

He doesn't know everything even though he is my twin and we never miss a beat on reading each other's thoughts. No, this time he has it all wrong. I *had* experienced a kind of joy when I played that well—not for me, but that I was one step closer to giving Dad and my family what they need. A way to bring us all back together.

"Next time I come home, I want to see that thing"—I nod to the ugly walker—"out of this house. You'd better be ready to hike up back with me." I lean over and kiss his cheek. Robert smells like spicy aftershave. He started wearing it when he dated Sharon, the girl who worked downtown at the five and dime. Their relationship died when he missed a few dates due to a golf tournament.

"Call us when you get in."

I nod and find Grandpa waiting on the back porch to also kiss me good-bye. His normally sharp eyes are glazed. I'm running out of time and need to be a success soon. I have to qualify at the first rounds of Q-School this fall or Grandpa might forget me by then.

Mom grabs my luggage and we hurry to the car. We're already running late. She straps herself in and turns to me. "Do you want to stop at the office?" She keeps her mouth straight but blinks faster than normal.

I shake my head and look across the back yard. "We're going to be late. Not this time."

Part of me can't believe she asked, especially knowing I'd already tried with Dad. What does she think could have changed in a few days? He knows we need him. He knows he's hurt her, yet he remains selfish.

Greg meets me at the Orlando airport and drives me back to my trailer. He and I have been project partners a few times, and so I offered him a few bucks to take me to the airport and pick me up. Actually, I am surprised to see his portly figure waiting for me at the luggage area since he is never good at remembering anything. Greg comes from Minnesota and says his parents farm for a living. He was invited once to play golf and loved it.

"Going to get a job at Celebration and stay here. No more cold winters for me." He sat beside me the third day of school and now seeks me out whenever he needs help.

I'm not sure I like being in that role but using can go both ways. Greg is great at English and writes fantastic papers. We got an A on our last project.

I crank up the air when I enter my living room. Is there a word that means hotter than hot? Someone told me I would love fall in Florida. I can't wait. I find my workout clothes and then reach for my keys. So far, my neighbor hasn't noticed I'm home. If she does, I will be bombarded with another two dozen snickerdoodles.

The gym at the school is empty. I'm probably the only student who works out this much, but I have to. I pick up the free weights, face the mirror, and count as I lift. It's not that I want to get muscles, but everything I've read about golf points to success from a fit body. I check the clock and start to sweat. An hour passes as I climb the treadmill and set the incline at five.

Running doesn't come easy to me. Not like Robert. Thinking of my twin makes my heart skip. The thought of him never running again pushes me on, and I dig my heels into the machine. Sweat pours from every part of my body. I will make it up to him. I will.

My dad's harsh words taunt me.

So I'm not Robert, but I can golf.

~*~

Mark meets me outside the theater the next day. I hadn't wanted to eat dinner with him, but when he called the night before; I didn't have the heart to turn him down. Just friends, he assured me.

He wears khaki shorts and a green polo. His tan has deepened from days spent working at the golf course.

"Did you go home for break?" he asks.

I loop my purse over my shoulder and match his stride through the mall. We'd agreed to eat at a restaurant at the other end of the plaza.

"For a few days. How about you?"

He flips his blond hair back from his forehead with a neat toss of his head. Again those dimples. "Not a chance. Too much to do around here for fun. You can't tell me you enjoyed yourself back there?"

Since I'd yet to become enamored with city life, I laugh. "Hiking. Reading. Admiring the sunsets. What else does a girl need?"

His head tips and he flashes a grin that makes me think of the kind Grandpa gave me when he caught me up to no good. Like the time I found stray kittens in the barn and was sneaking some leftover chicken from the barbecue the night before.

My shoulders rise and drop. "So hate me—I like the country."

Mark turns the corner and I see our restaurant straight ahead. "How are you going to become a big golf pro if you don't like the city?"

I frown. Why does everyone ask me questions like that? I'm getting sick of explaining myself. If only I'd brought a sandwich and eaten in my car. "Maybe I'll change."

He holds up two fingers to the waitress. We are seated in a booth right in the front of the restaurant where I can duck into the restrooms. I excuse myself and run in to check my phone. I'm sure I felt it vibrate.

Drew.

Why is he calling me?

Another woman enters and begins to apply mascara at the sink next to mine. I turn into the corner and listen to his message. He asks if I want a lesson later that day, and if I do, to call him. He wants to talk.

Talk?

I think of his brother waiting for me outside the bathroom door. The two men are nothing alike. I'm not sure whom I like better since both their personalities have an appeal. But Drew can teach me golf, and that makes him more valuable. I shove my phone back into my bag.

Mark has already decided on his meal. I order the veggie platter and sit back with my hands in my lap.

"So tell me why."

His question catches me off guard. An earnest look appears on his face, making his boyish appearance even more charming. In another time, I would have fallen for Mark. But not now. Not with so much at stake. And then there's Dan.

"Why what? Why the veggies?"

I know what he's asking me. I'm not sure I'm ready to answer.

He shifts in his seat. "Ok, I'll go at it another angle. I did some research; nosing around, you might call it. Checked with some friends back home and found out your brother was quite the golfer. Heard he was ready to go pro if he could qualify at Q-School. Something happened and you're here instead of him."

My jaw freezes. I'm not sure if I'm going to be mad or worried or what. "You checked up on me?" I wrap my fingers around my water glass. The cool droplets from the ice don't cool my mounting annoyance. "Why would you do that?"

Now it's Mark's turn to look uncomfortable. He thanks the waitress as she sets our dishes in front of us, and then he pops two fries into his mouth. "'Cause you're an interesting girl. That's why. I know there's a story in you somewhere, and I'm curious."

"Maybe some stories are better left alone. Ever think about that?" I spoon green beans onto my fork and shove them into my mouth, chewing on them instead of him.

"Maybe so." That flip of his hair again. It's beginning to annoy me more than his trip into my past. "But something isn't right. I asked Drew about it, and he said you're a closed case. Not like he doesn't want to know, but he is more polite than I am."

"Obviously." I rip my roll apart.

"It's just you don't look like a jock. You seem more like the kind of girl who likes to write books or something more artsy than golf."

I swallow. Hard.

"I read a lot."

Mark laughs and takes a drink of his root beer. "So I'm pushing too much, huh?" His dimples shoot out and I can't help but power down. I never used to be so defensive, but it seems that's who I am now that I've entered the world of golf.

"If you want to know, I happen to think I golf fairly well. Why not capitalize on that?"

"Why not? Drew tells me you're one of the best golfers in your class." He swirls the remaining soda in his glass. "But something tells me there's more to it. And you."

Am I that transparent? I will work on that. The last thing I need is for the golf community to not take me seriously. I have exactly thirty days before the Sectional Qualifying for the LPGA. I want to be ready. I can't fail or there will be no second chances for our family.

11

The last time I failed horribly (worse than when I tried out for cheerleading and made a fool of myself with the cartwheel) had been when I asked to go hunting the spring before the accident.

My father and Robert loved to turkey hunt, and I'd never been allowed to go with them. This past year, I finally convinced my father I could stand the frigid temperatures and endure using a tree as a potty if needed. I'd wear camouflage and pack their backpacks with better snacks than Mom ever did.

I guess my promises convinced both of them because the following Saturday morning I dressed and rose before the sun so we could get into the woods early. My father carried his rifle over his left shoulder and swaggered ahead of Robert, who occasionally looked back to see if I was following.

Three years earlier I had taken target practice with Kelly, a girl I met at in the cosmetic aisle of the local department store. She suggested it as a way to meet men. I'd been pretty good, if I say so myself, but at the very least I learned how to shoot. So when we finally got into position and I spied my first turkey, I reached for my rifle and took aim.

Too fast.

We heard the squeal seconds before we saw her fall.

I knew Sam since she was a puppy. Ruth, her

owner, let me walk her and work at training her to retrieve. Now the next-door neighbor's dog lay in a pool of blood all because I'd been careless—in a rush. My father took the injured dog to the vet for poor Ms. Ruth while Robert stood with his arm locked around my shoulder so I wouldn't sink to the ground.

I heaved and heaved and crushed my fists to my eyes, not wanting to be further witness to my careless act. Sam lived but I never forgot that day.

I'd failed at hunting. I would not fail at golf.

It seems I am, though.

At my next lesson, Drew throws down his driver and turns to me with a look I have yet to see. "What on earth it wrong with you? What do you call that last shot?"

Sure, I messed up—hit my ball clear into the water hazard—but so does every other pro now and then.

"It was a bad shot," I say and reach for another ball from my bag.

Drew steps closer and I almost flinch, but I don't think he will appreciate me showing fear either. "That's not good enough. And you know something, Bobbi-with-an-*i*? You aren't good enough, either."

I drop the ball, my fingers freezing at my sides. Not good enough? I'd heard that comment from my father so often that usually it rolls off me. But not today. Not from my coach who always encourages me and tells me how I'm the best golfer on campus.

"Let me take another shot."

"I'm done for the day." He packs up his clubs and hauls his bag over his shoulder. "You take the cart in." He tosses me another look and begins the long walk back to the clubhouse, leaving me standing in the middle of the sixth fairway. I want to be any place but

Orlando, Florida. My throat burns and I blink hard. If I don't play well enough, I should pack it in and go home. I sit hard on the cart seat.

This is the first time my chance for success feels impenetrable. Like the mountain I'd climbed with Robert when we were sixteen, and some friends dared us to climb above the gorge in New York State. I was sure I would fall to my death. The mountain would win, and we would perish.

I miss my brother so much.

As if on cue, my cell rings. Robert.

Sometimes it's eerie to be a twin.

"Hello?"

"Bobbi? Just felt like I needed to call. You OK?"

I glance around to be sure no other golfer is coming up behind me. I move the cart to the side. "Peachy. How about you?" My voice squeaks like a five-year-old. Robert will see through me in seconds. Not what I need today. He'll tell me to come home; as well I know I should. I slouch down and stare across the greens.

"You don't sound fine. Besides, I had this urge to pray for you today."

"Pray away. It can't hurt." And now for the Bible hour.

Robert doesn't answer right away. I wonder if he is praying for my lost soul right then while I sit at the scene of my crime wanting to bawl but don't dare. Sometimes he drives me crazy.

"You're good, you know. It's hard for me to say this, but you're better than I ever was."

I slide up.

"I want you to know that I was certain you'd fail down there, and part of me…I hate saying this,"—he clears his throat—"wanted you to fail. How could my sister play better than me? But after you told me your scores and that you are the best golfer in your school, I knew it. I knew you were meant to play maybe more than I was. God has a different plan for me, and I haven't yet found it, but I will. Right now this is His plan for you."

Tears run down my cheeks. Never before has Robert said this. Oh, he's supported me with all my other dreams, but not something that should have been his. I need to tell him the truth. "My coach just told me I stink."

Another long pause. "I hope you don't believe him."

My brother knows me too well.

"He's my coach."

"I'm your brother. I know your determination. You will do this."

"Is that straight from God?" Sometimes I take jabs. Today I need to.

Robert ignores me. "I'm praying for you, sis, and that's all you need to know."

Failure feels like a ton of bricks piled in my wheelbarrow. The more I fail, the heavier my load. I doubt I have much room left in mine. My father has added his own dozen bricks to it, and now Drew.

"Are you there?"

I nod. "Yeah. Just thinking."

"You know what kind of trouble that gets you into." He chuckles into the phone. I'm sure he means the pond fiasco.

The time I tried swimming across before I learned how to swim and he had to drag me out of four feet of water. He'd learned to swim in Ruth's pool the summer before, while I nursed a case of chicken pox. When I felt better I was on to a new adventure. Until the day I thought lessons were only for stupid kids. How hard could swimming be?

"Listen, Robert, I'd better hang up. I need to get this cart back before it rains." Already the late afternoon sky is troubled with dark clouds. I smell a big storm.

An hour later I'm in my car driving down 50 trying to beat the downpour headed my way. Mom sent a weather radio with me this time, so I turn it on as soon as I come through the door.

I also flip on the TV but soon lose reception, so I revert back to the weather radio as the winds increase. As I watch from the front window, Mattie's garbage can lid flips off and blows against my car. I hope she's home, but I can't be certain as it isn't dark enough yet for lights. Again the trailer rattles as the winds creep closer to my part of Winter Garden.

Now the announcer starts talking about possible tornadoes. I don't have a clue where the cities are that are under a warning but figure as bad as it looks outside, it doesn't hurt to take precautions.

I grab a blanket and pillow and toss them into the bathtub. Thinking better of my plan, I grab the radio and my purse and sit on the toilet seat. I tell myself this precaution is only a just in case. What are the chances of Golden Acres being struck by the tail of a tornado today?

My lights flicker and then shut off, throwing me into semi-darkness. The roar from outside increases as the floor beneath my feet vibrates—sway may be a better word—but I don't need any further prodding. I dive into the tub head first and slam the pillow over my head as the roar grows louder and the rain pelts the rattling tin surrounding me.

I squeeze my fists and think of my family. Robert would certainly pray in a situation like this and I find myself crying, "Oh, dear Jesus" a few times when I think of my home being rocked off its foundation.

I've heard a tornado sounds like a freight train coming at you. Those people who've said that don't lie. I hunker down as deep against the basin of the tub as it will allow and shut my eyes, the train roaring close by. Another prayer shoots across my lips. *Save me, O Lord…please save me.*

~*~

When the silence rolls back in, I raise my head, half expecting to see my trailer collapsed around me. The toilet paper remains where I'd put it this morning—on the back of the toilet. My oversized towel lays crumpled on the floor and all four walls surround me. Maybe what I heard wasn't a tornado, but it was the loudest storm I've ever endured.

My feet cramp from my fetal position. I wriggle my toes to stop the stinging, stretch to stand, and step out of my haven. My bathroom doesn't have the luxury of a window so I pad down the hallway and peer across the way to Mattie's.

Her flowers, or what remain of them, are scattered across the patio in piles of upturned dirt and clay pots. Furniture from her porch, and who knows who else's, dangle from sheds and stairs. I open my door and look upwards. Dark clouds greet me but the rain has stopped.

The part of me that doesn't always like to comply

pushes me forward toward Mattie's. Her place lacks lights, and if the power is still off, I expect her to be the first resident outside to survey any damage. That's who she is—always helping someone in time of need. She's shared enough stories that I also know she once worked for the Red Cross and traveled all over the country whenever a disaster occurred.

At the time of the telling, I'd been reluctant to hear all the gory details. Why hadn't I listened better? From the looks of Golden Acres, we have our own little disaster right now.

I step over someone's garbage can and work my way around Mattie's upended pots. Shards of glass broken from several birdfeeders greet my feet.

"Mattie?" I call her name twice more and try her door. It's unlocked. Why does that surprise me? I've only been inside three times since moving across the way, and that had been for an impromptu piece of apple pie and cards. We'd sat at her table built for two and shared a cup of tea like I do with my mother.

"Mattie?" Still no response. I peer behind me. Her car is parked in the driveway, but often her friends will pick her up to drive her to her missions. The screen door slams into my back. I take a few tentative steps into her living room. Everywhere I look she's placed some kind of knick-knack or memento of her life.

I swear I'll never keep that much stuff hanging around when I get old. The strong odor of moth balls tickles my nose. Put that on my list, too. Never buy those darned things.

I creep down the narrow hall, sidestepping a chair that has seen better days and try the light switch. Nothing. Three more doors and the bathroom to search. I start toward the bathroom.

It doesn't take a medic to know something serious has happened to my neighbor. Mattie lays face down next to her tub, and by the way she is positioned I know it isn't because of the storm. I kneel beside her and turn her over—relief flooding me when I hear a soft groan come from her.

"Mattie, what happened? Are you OK?"

She clutches at her chest and moans. I reach for my cell phone and dial 911. She will not die on me. I will not have that on my conscience, as well.

The nice lady on the phone tells me what to do and then asks if I need her to stay on the phone until the EMTs arrive.

"You'd better believe it." I put my phone on speaker, rush to find a pillow, place it under Mattie's head, and cover her cold skin with a blanket off the back of her couch.

Mattie's eyes flutter open. I swear she knows who I am. Even in the midst of her emergency, I see a glimmer of the Mattie who bakes me fresh cookies every week.

"Hey, there. Hold on, OK? The ambulance is on its way." I lean closer and whisper, "You're going to be fine."

She blinks, trying hard to focus on my face. I'm sure it takes all her effort to do so. I stroke her hair back on her damp forehead.

"Check my roses…"

"Don't try to talk, Mattie. Just hang on until we get you help."

I pat her hands that clutch the buttons on her shirt. What else can I do? I try to remember my CPR from when I worked a summer at the hospital as a candy striper. Her breathing sounds labored to me, but what do I know? I strain to hear the sirens and curse them for taking so long.

"She's breathing hard," I report to 911.

"The EMTs are two minutes out."

Two minutes pass like five hours.

"Check my pink roses…for you."

I look back down at Mattie. "Don't worry about your plants. You'll be better in no time to care for them." My words must give her comfort because she closes her eyes and her breathing evens out.

I rise from my knees and wait at the front door as the ambulance works its way into the battered driveway. The EMTs rush pass me and carry Mattie out on a stretcher as I stand out of the way in her living room, trying hard not to cry.

It seems like only seconds, but I'm sure it's longer before I hear the siren leaving the community with Mattie on board. By then, a few other residents have ventured outside to take a survey of the storm damage.

"Is Mattie all right?" one woman asks me.

"She fell hard. I should get to the hospital to be with her." My feet won't move.

The woman touches my arm. "You're shaking, sweetie. Let's get you inside before we have to call an ambulance for you."

"But Mattie…" I can't let Mattie wait out the night alone in a hospital.

The woman takes my arm and leads me toward my trailer. "George will go and check on her." She turns to an older man whom I hadn't even noticed come up beside us. "I'm Alice. You let me get you inside and get you warm."

"George—does he know what hospital?" My question is waved off as George produces a set of keys while this woman guides me into my living room. I can't believe how I'm still shaking.

"Thank the good Lord that Mattie wasn't killed," she says as she covers me with a light blanket she finds on my bed. "That none of us were killed."

I pretend to yawn, and Alice finally leaves me alone after making me promise to come see them if I get scared.

I'm not ready to praise God yet, not like she did. Not when He allowed Mattie to suffer alone over there.

12

The storms didn't damage the golf school by any measure. The next day I sit in computer class wondering how Mattie fared the night at the hospital. The EMTs told me which hospital they were taking her to before they drove away, and I looked it up last night. I intend to visit as soon as I get done practicing today after classes.

Drew passes me in the hallway this morning with a look I can't read, but I am over him. So what if he has the hottest blue eyes and my heart ripples like an accordion whenever I look at him? I have no time for crushes, especially on a jock who thinks he needs to ruin my plans.

If I want abuse, I can call my father.

I try hard to pay attention, but Mr. Barret has the most boring voice of any teacher I've ever sat before. Boring with a capital B. I glance around me and find several students looking at their phones or listening with their earplugs discreetly plugged in. I stretch my feet and count the days left to attend.

A big tournament is scheduled for tomorrow at Orange Lake. We've been told that several companies that make golf equipment will be there, and maybe, just maybe, some lucky golfer might pick up a sponsor.

I need it to be me, and that means I need a few teachers to put in a good word for me. Plus I have to break my own score tomorrow.

When class ends, I rush to my car and grab my clubs. I'll practice at the school range for an hour before finding the hospital where Mattie is recuperating. I smell the thick humidity as I walk up the hill to the range. The heavy air clings to my clothes.

In Pennsylvania, the trees would be turning if it is an early fall. I miss the smell of leaves in a pile and apples being boiled into applesauce on the kitchen stove. Maybe Mark is right. How am I going to travel and be a golf pro if it means staying in cities most of the time?

In all truth, that life isn't the life I'd planned for myself. I'd have been happy buying one of the old cabins along the river and decorating it with my art. I would sit on the porch and watch the fishermen glide down the river. Might even get a dog to lie at my feet and keep me company when I decide to paint. A beagle. A friendly beagle that doesn't bark.

I don't know why I think about painting. This homesickness I carry around with me is making me think about all sorts of things when I should be concentrating on my swing.

I set my ball and pull out my driver.

My fingers find their place and I grip the club the way I've been taught. I try to clear my thoughts. Once, and then twice. My head is too jumbled, and that makes me angrier. The guy next to me swings. His ball flies over 250 yards.

"Nice one," I say, but I don't think he hears me. He's already swinging at the next ball.

Again I try to clear my head, and this time I swing. I slice it to the left. I bite down on a word that aches to leave my mouth. I wriggle my shoulders, loosening stiff muscles. Maybe I am not warmed up.

The player next to me hits another one—farther than before. He holds his hand up and tips his cap when the ball lands. Yeah. Cheer now, I want to say. You might be someone's gift to golf today, but wait until tomorrow when your body refuses to cooperate.

The sun bears down on the back of my neck, stroking it, burning it. I'd forgotten sunscreen and will pay later. Again, I set a ball and take my stance. I swing.

"Nice shot," the guy on my left offers.

Nice shot is right. But will I be able to do it tomorrow?

~*~

The hospital looks like it needs to be torn down. This is Florida, right? New construction happens every day, so why doesn't anyone care about a falling down hospital? I find the front desk and give the lady in the red apron Mattie's full name.

The volunteer looks through a list and consults a computer screen. I hate hospitals. They smell like antiseptic and this one is no exception. My stint as a candy striper convinced me that the people who work in hospitals become immune to the smells and therefore think everyone else should as well. I didn't. Today proves that my theory still holds.

I tap my fingers on the desk. Lightly. Ever so gently. I don't want to push this woman into working—just give me Mattie's room number.

Finally, she looks up. Her lips are turned into a line somewhere between "May I help you" and "What's her name?" "I'm sorry. It seems your friend is no longer a patient here."

"What does that mean? No longer a patient? She didn't go back home. I would have seen her."

Again the thin line. But I catch a flash of something in her eyes. Is that sorrow? I lean across the desk. "She's not here because something happened to her, right?" I'm not sure where my boldness comes from because I don't sound like me. "Please don't tell me she died, because I promised her everything would be OK. Please?"

I'm sorry I put that poor volunteer on the spot. I'm not family. She can't tell me anything, but Mattie has no family. Just the residents of the park who love her and all of those others she helped. The volunteer finally gets her supervisor, and after some hard convincing, they tell me Mattie had passed away last night.

I say "Thank you" and drop my arms to my sides.

She'd passed away alone. Why hadn't I gone to the hospital to be with her?

I make it to my car and sit unmoving for a good fifteen minutes trying to remember Mattie's last words to me. Something about her roses. The pink ones. I hadn't gone over yet and righted her pots. She'd hate seeing them strewn around like that.

I put the car in gear and speed home. When I pull in, I notice the park manager coming up Mattie's walkway.

"Mr. Gordon, have you heard about Mattie?"

"I did—such a sad thing. She had my name down as an emergency contact, you know. Several of our folks do here." Mr. Greer wheezes. His eyes also water, but I'm not sure if that is his normal look or out of sympathy. "Going to get her paperwork and put things in order."

By paperwork, I assume Mattie has written a will and Mr. Gordon will take care of it for her. It seems even sadder that your manager has to also be your executor, but by the time someone is Mattie's age, maybe there aren't many choices left. I wander behind him, eyeing the flower pots.

"Do you mind if I straighten these up? I sort of promised her I would look after her plants."

My host waves his hand. "Sure. Sure. Probably going to put them in the dump. Take any you want or give them away. I don't care." I leave him to his ramblings and turn toward my promise.

I don't know anything about flowers. My mother has the dubious title of gardener in our family. Sure, I've pulled a few weeds under duress, but have never planted my own garden. But a promise is a promise.

I start with the smaller pots, packing the dirt back around the roots. I line them up nicely and consider putting a sign out for people to help themselves. I work on the larger plants that have been upheaved during the storm. When I come to a rose, a pink one, I crouch beside it and study the half-emptied planter. What was it about the pink roses that made Mattie remember to tell me about them?

I pull the plant the rest of the way out of the pot being careful not to prick my fingers. Not only do I not have a green thumb, but I want to keep what I do have intact. That's when I see the pink envelope with my name on the front.

To Bobbi, the girl with an "I"—for living.

I can barely make out the scribble, but it is my name, for sure. In a flower pot. Maybe she was farther gone than I gave her credit for. I slip the envelope under my arm, and hoist the plant back into its container. Later, I will sweep up and water them and maybe put out that sign, but right now, the letter burns to be read. I call good-bye to Mr. Greer and hurry across the way to my place.

I've always loved mysteries. My mother read me all her Nancy Drew books when I was growing up until I found authors I loved on my own. Robert said I could make a mystery out of an anthill if I wanted to badly enough. So what if I didn't read the Bible like he did? My stories were far more interesting.

I grab some cookies and sink down on my couch cross-legged. My imagination goes wild. For an older lady, Mattie sure does surprise me. Maybe we had more in common than I realized. Maybe she had been a mystery buff as well and decided to leave clues all over her house for someone like me to find. Maybe, I should go inside, if old Mr. Watery Eyes ever leaves and see if she has left anything else. Within minutes, I decide that perhaps Mattie was an undercover agent working for the government as a spy.

Or not. Maybe she was just crazy.

I flip the envelope over and over willing the suspense to last.

And of course, my phone rings. Normally I would have ignored the caller, but it is my mother. I have yet to tell her about the storm and Mattie and now this letter. Maybe I will keep the letter out of my story and savor it for myself until I know more.

"Hey, Mom. Did you hear about the tornado that hit Clermont?"

"No, I didn't. Is that near you?" Her voice rises. It doesn't take much to make her worry.

"Close, but we only got some damaging winds. Blew everyone's patio stuff all over creation. I think I have an awning lying across my back yard."

"I hope you used your weather radio."

"First thing I did, Mom. I took cover in the tub. Just in case."

"Well, you never know. I was calling to tell you that I saw in the paper where Dan's mother died. Have you spoken to him?"

I take a sharp breath. She died? Poor Dan. I'd read somewhere that death came in threes. Now I'm worried. "I didn't know. He's probably not down here yet if she was that bad. Are you going to the viewing?"

"Thinking about it. At the very least I'll make a casserole and drop it off." A pause. My mother is good at pausing before a particularly delicate topic.

I brace myself. I'm beginning to doubt I can take any more bad news. I have that tournament tomorrow, and all this stuff isn't going to help my psyche.

"Robert walked today without his walker."

My air comes out in a rush. "Now that's great news! Tell him way to go!"

"I will. He can't go far, as his legs are a bit shaky still, but it's so nice to see him moving on his own. He's trying to get Grandpa to adopt that walker."

"Good luck. You have a stubborn father."

My mother chuckles. I love hearing her do it. Everything is right with the world when she laughs. I start to ask about Dad but decide she'd tell me if anything has changed there.

"I've got an important tournament tomorrow, Mom. I'm hoping maybe I can get a sponsor to help pay for Q-School."

I know how my mother feels about my decision to come to Orlando. She doesn't like it at all, but being my mom, she supports me. She doesn't have the funds I'll need along the way, though. I've managed to scrape together enough from my savings to pay for round one tournaments and maybe, if I make the cut, for round two. A sponsor will make the difference, but it's not like they show up waiting to find the next great golfer. Honestly, I'm not all that sure how it does happen, but I hope if word gets around that I'm good, someone will want to attach their name to me.

"You're good, Bobbi. You know we're praying for you here. Grandpa asked about you today at lunchtime."

I decide not to tell her about Mattie. My mother doesn't need to hear about her dying with Grandpa and all he is going through. She's in denial anyway, thinking her father isn't losing his mind and that she'll be able to continue to take care of him at home. Especially without Dad's help or income.

"Tell him I'll call soon, OK?" The unopened envelope in my lap calls me, so I cut the conversation short.

My mother never seems to notice—there's a lot she doesn't notice these days, and the guilt that I'm not around to help her sometimes swallows me whole. In the long run, though, what I'm doing here in Florida will help more than me being there taking care of Robert and helping Grandpa get dressed in the morning. I'm so sure of it I've given up what I love most to do it.

The last time I opened anything that was a true surprise was a gift for my sixteenth birthday. No one can keep anything secret from me, but that year Robert totally surprised me when he showed me a huge box. Where he'd hidden it, I still don't know. I'd checked the closets and underneath all the beds and found out that Mom and Dad were giving me the outfit I wanted from the mall.

"Try guessing first," he'd said with a smirk across his face.

Yes, I love being surprised. Really surprised, and that's why I was often disappointed when no one ever did manage to do it to me. But this time, Robert outdid himself.

I tore open the box and stood back, my jaw turning to mush. The most beautiful oak chest stood before me. Robert had engraved my name on the lid with the date. I rubbed my hand over the smooth lid. "How? When?"

Let me say this. Robert is not a handy guy. That's what made this gift even more special. It seems he spent all his free periods in school in the shop department learning how to use tools without cutting his hands off just so he could surprise me.

I hugged his neck tightly, trying not to cry.

Why I thought of this particular gift right now as I sit with Mattie's letter in my lap I don't know. Maybe because she'd been a special part of my life the way Robert has been. Is still. Maybe Mattie needed me to remember her, and this is a way that I would.

I flip the envelope over and unglue the flap.

I'm not sure what I expect, but as I reach inside and feel the cool metal between my fingers, delight fills my thoughts. Mattie has given me a jewel. Actually, as I turn it over and over in my palm and take in each delicate detail of the necklace, I know she couldn't have left me a more marvelous gift.

A thin gold chain. A pendant covered in tiny diamonds and could it be? I bring the gift closer to my face. The design is shaped like a golf club. A tiny sparkling golf club. The initials M.M. (for Mattie Montrose, I guess) are engraved on the back.

Where did Mattie get a golf-club-shaped necklace and why?

My shoulders sink against my battered chair as I try to recall any bit of information from our conversations that told me she might have golfed.

Nothing. Or had I not been listening? Sometimes my neighbor went on and on. The most important tidbit I remember her saying is that she had a nephew named Bobby who'd been killed in a car accident. That's it. Nothing more comes to me.

I look down at the piece of jewelry in my hand and slip the chain over my head. The pendant falls to my chest. It's then that I realize I haven't looked inside the envelope to see if she's left me an explanation. I tear the envelope open and find what I need. Mattie has written me a short few words on a sticky note. A sticky note with flowers bordering it.

I've seen that pad on her kitchen table. I'd borrowed a sheet to write down one of her recipes that I'd loved. Now a page holds a few short words to me.

Bobbi,
Superman is a myth.
Mattie

Superman? So she's left me more advice. Advice I don't get. I smile knowing this note is so much like Mattie. But still, I'm not sure how she's connected to the necklace. A golf club, after all, isn't the first choice a woman makes when selecting something to decorate herself.

I go to bed that night with the necklace dangling

from my bedside lamp. First thing in the morning, I dress in my favorite yellow polo shirt. I slip the chain over my head and tuck it inside my collar. I'll wear it for this tournament and think of Mattie.

13

Someone wants to sponsor me. A friend of the man who owns Bud's Sports has been watching the tournament and sees me place second with a whopping score of 66. My shots are some of the best I've ever made. I'm not sure if my good fortune has anything to do with Mattie's necklace nestled against my chest, but I do find that if I hold it between my fingers and concentrate, I hit better.

I might not be a Bible thumper like my twin, but I know enough not to believe in luck. God ordains every step we take: that much I believe, but I still can't help but think maybe Mattie's gift has given me the confidence I lacked.

The next day I get the call from the CEO at Bud's, a large sporting chain here in Florida. Would I be interested in wearing their logo in exchange for money? They'd heard from one of my teachers that my goal was to play professionally. They'd like to market their name via me.

It isn't a big brand name. But at least it's a way to earn money, and their logo doesn't totally rot. I can walk around the course with a brown bear on my hat and on the back of my shirt if it means moving toward my future.

After class the next day, I wait to talk with Drew. He was friendly enough at the tournament, but not like he used to be. He stands at the board writing out assignments for the next class.

"Do you mind if I talk with you a minute?"

He turns around and sets his marker to the side. His face shows no animosity, so I take a deep breath and nod to the chair next to his desk. "Mind if I sit?"

I don't get this man. I was sure when I started last summer there was an attraction between us, but something happened. Maybe for the best, but it has left me unsettled. I take the seat and he sits across from me.

"What's on your mind?" His blue eyes soften.

Oh. dear. I put my hands beneath my armpits and clear my thoughts. "I wondered if you are behind this offer I got from Bud's. If you are, I want to thank you."

His shoulders rise. "You deserve it. Only wish it had come from a bigger company."

"That's not how you felt the last time we played. What was that about?"

He turns away from me for an instant as though what he would say next is written on the backside of the classroom door. Drew isn't an easy man to get to know.

Mark has pretty much implied that. I pressed for more information, but Mark turned the conversation to himself and expertly put Drew off the table. The brothers came from the same area as I did, but Drew never wants to talk about himself or his past. Someone hinted that teaching was not what he wants to do. Play golf on tour had been his plan, but for some reason he didn't make it. I am hoping he will help me make it instead.

He runs his fingers through his thick hair and then sighs. "Listen, Bobbi. When you showed up in my classroom, I couldn't understand why on earth you would want to come here. It's not like we have a million females come through our doors—especially ones who golf as well as you. This school teaches you how to work in the golf industry. You should be playing every day, not hanging out in the classroom. When I first started to teach you, I saw what you have—it's something I never had no matter how much I practiced. And when I watched you throw away good shots, it made me mad."

He pauses, giving me a moment to take in what he's saying. What would he think if he knew why I'm so obsessed with being good? My cheeks burn.

"You're going to make the pros and you're going to be a name to be reckoned with. But you can't let your guard down for a minute. And that means no social life at all."

Is that a frown?

"What social life? I work out and practice. That's my life besides my part time job at the theater."

He nods. "Good. If you can knock off the job, even better, but I know how tight funds can be when you're starting out. Can anyone in your family help?"

"No," I say quickly.

"Sorry to hear that. You'll need all the support you can get."

I look down at my shoes. They need a good polish. "My brother supports me."

"He golfs, doesn't he?"

I lift my eyes. "He used to. He was pretty good until his…accident." I hate that word but that's the term my family uses. It wasn't an accident. It was my fault.

Drew leans closer to his desk. I smell his aftershave. "Sorry to hear that. So you come from a family of golfers. That's good. They'll be behind you."

"Sure. That kind of support goes much farther than money." I chew on my lip. I hate lying.

But Drew has learned to keep quiet about his past and so can I.

"So are you going to take the deal with Bud's?"

"Why not? It might make the difference between affording Q-School or not."

My mention of Q-School snaps his gaze to mine. "Are you ready? The competition will be stiff. There are only so many openings to go on tour."

"I've done my homework. And speaking of homework, I'd better go."

Drew follows me to the door. He bends down close to my face. I hold my stance as he speaks. "I'm sorry, Bobbi. You really can do this."

If I could have danced down the hallway to my car, I would have. It means so much to know that Drew is behind me. Maybe someday…but I can't think like that now. I have a tournament to win. I reach for the pendant dangling down my chest.

Mattie. Who were you?

~*~

The jeweler I stop at on my way home hands me back the diamond-studded golf club. "It's a beauty. I would stick that in a vault somewhere."

The necklace glitters in my palm. "A vault?

"A vault. Unless you want to take a chance of it being swiped from your neck."

My head still can't make sense of the figure he quoted me for the value of Mattie's gift. If she had only cashed it in, she wouldn't have had to live in Golden Acres.

"Thanks again for the advice and appraisal," I say and slip the necklace over my head where it belongs now. Mattie didn't leave it to me to stuff in some safety deposit box. She gave it to me to wear, and that's what I'll do.

On my drive home, I pass several other courses. A part of me wants to stop and see if they are offering any deals, but my stomach protests. Besides, it's hot out today. The heat inside of my trailer hits me with the force of a furnace since I've forgotten to turn down the air. Even though fall has arrived, the temperatures still haven't dropped. I reach for a carton of cottage cheese and smell it. Ugh. Time to hit the grocery store.

My supper will be a TV dinner I bought for two dollars. Not bad when the stuffing tastes as good as my mother's. While it heats up in the oven (I hate to nuke it), I change into my shorts. Another Friday. I look across to Mattie's place. The plants need watering and I have yet to make a sign as promised. I'll do it after I eat. But first I want to check something online.

Mattie Montrose.

Google doesn't let me down. Three full pages of stories about Mattie. I've hit pay dirt.

What I find surprises me, though. Story after story touts accolades about Mattie being a pro golfer eons ago—one of the top LPGA titlists! I whistle and hear it reverberate around the room. A pro? Mattie?

"You golfed and never said a word?" A million questions roll through my brain—starting with how she got so good. What was her secret? If only she'd told me while she was alive.

According to Mr. Google, Mattie won title after title and played until she was injured in a car accident. The article from the *Orlando Sentinel* went on to say that if Mattie hadn't been drinking, her sixteen-year-old nephew would still be alive.

"Bobby with a y. Oh, Mattie. Why didn't you tell me?" I shut down my laptop.

The article also stated that Mattie did community service as retribution. She gave talks to schools and eventually gave away potted plants to remind others *to stay grounded where God plants you.*

I don't chuckle at her slogan.

14

Even though I risk losing Mattie's necklace, I get into the habit of wearing it every place I go. I haven't been able to pin down when she got it and for what tournament, but I figure it was pretty darn special. I mean diamonds? Who gives away diamonds? I doubt I'd ever wear that many diamonds on my finger.

Exactly three days before the qualifying tournaments, Dan calls. He's in town and wants to meet at a restaurant in the Millennium Mall. It isn't my favorite place to go since it means dressing better than I might to go to the Ocoee mall, but I throw on some white khakis and a peach-colored top I'd bought before moving down to Florida.

Again, I add my necklace and a pair of fake stud earrings. I let my hair fall down to my shoulders and brush some blush on my tanned cheeks. My heart starts to beat faster when I pull into the parking lot and find a place near the entrance.

My watch says I have fifteen minutes before we're to meet. I lock my car and hurry across the roadway to enter near the fountains. I've forgotten to bring my phone with me, so I wait at a bench near the restaurant. While I sit, I study the other shoppers.

A woman about my age pushes a stroller past me with a child in it sucking on a pacifier. I smile at the baby, and then stop. What mother wants a stranger ogling her baby? I pass it off to my age and the impending clock-ticking effect or something like that. But will I ever have children of my own? I once tried to paint portraits and started a canvas with a mother and child, using a picture I'd found as my subject. I never finished it.

I glance to the exit. Dan strolls toward me, a definite ten pounds lighter. I rise when he nears and step into his embrace. "I'm so sorry," I say into his ear as he tightens his grip. I'd known his mother a little, and she'd always been sweet to me.

Dan finally releases me and holds me a few inches from him. Tears stand on his lids. "You look great. Golfing is good for you."

I tug on my hair. Compliments I will take. "How long are you here for?"

"I've got a couple of tournaments, and then I move on to North Carolina. I missed a few because of Mom, so I need to make them up if I can."

When we enter the restaurant, he takes my hand. Our booth is comfortable and private. Again, Dan reaches for my hand after we give our orders. His actions confuse me because I can't see any future for us. "Dan," I say and slip my hand free on the pretense of finding my napkin. He takes my cue and spreads his on his lap, too. "How will your father manage your sisters without your mother?"

Dan's sisters are adorable (very precocious for ten- and eleven-year-olds, but then what did I know) and would need a mother's touch.

"My aunt Susie moved in for a while. Did you ever meet her? She was a cheerleader in high school and can still do splits. The kids love her." His smile tries to reassure, but doesn't.

"She can't stay forever."

"I know, but Dad needs the most help now. And I'll try to get home when I can…" His voice trails off and I imagine he is thinking of his sisters and how they will need their big brother.

I lean forward. "Ever think about quitting?"

His mouth falls.

Bingo. Dan has thought of nothing else, I guess.

"All the time. Dad doesn't want me to, but I told him I could work at the local course as an instructor and still be around to help raise the girls." He fists his hand. "I still might after one or two more tournaments—maybe after this season ends."

"I'm so sorry." Is that all I can say? My tongue lies in my mouth in a tangle. I can only say sorry over and over. "I think if it was me, I'd go home, but that's me."

"You always were a fixer, weren't you?" He sits back and narrows his eyes. "Is that what you're doing now, Bobbi? Fixing your family by taking Robert's place?"

I want to deny his question. I really do. In fact, my denial is already on my lips when I look back at his face and see the intent in his eyes. He's looking for an answer to his own dilemma—not mine. "Sometimes we have to do what we have to do for our families."

"My dad says we can't save everyone. Some things just happen."

"Are you talking about fate?"

"No, I'm talking about letting God's plan play out. That's why I'm so torn about what to do. Would I be playing Superman if I went home now?"

I think of Mattie's words. *Superman is just a myth.* Hadn't she tried to play that role, too, when she went around talking to people about drunk driving? I cross my arms. Of course, I'm wrong. She didn't play anyone's hero. Nor am I.

~*~

This isn't the first time my father left us. I was sixteen and learning how to drive. The day before, I'd finally passed my driver's license (after two tries), and Mom let me take the car out by myself.

"Stay on the main roads and no speeding." She kissed the top of my head and gave me one of those worried parent smiles.

"Mooommm. I'm a good driver. Don't worry." I waved her off and slid into the driver's seat of our van. We'd had the monster for about ten years, and I was secretly hoping, since both Robert and I could drive, they would get another vehicle for our use. Maybe something sporty or red or even with a sunroof. I dreamed a lot.

After backing out of the driveway, I drove along the river and turned toward town. My father had not ridden with me. It was Mom who taught me how to drive. After school, we'd gone from one parking lot to another until she'd given the green light for me to inch down a real road.

I switched on the radio and tapped my fingers on the steering wheel to a favorite song. This was the life. The sun shone through the windshield and warmed my face, and when I rolled down the window I smelled the beginnings of spring. My head fell back against the headrest.

Maybe my father would like to take a spin. It wasn't yet lunchtime, but I could drive him to Harry's Hotdog Heaven out on Route 6. Dad liked his dogs piled with sauerkraut and onions. I preferred the plain ones, but today I might splurge.

Downtown never changes. Sleepy. Historical. Old. I could add a bunch more adjectives, but that about sums up the place. My father's office was located at the end of Main. I pulled into the side parking lot. Only one other car besides his was parked there. I smiled. That meant he could leave for lunch.

After locking the car, (I'd remembered my mother's warning about strangers breaking into it) I went around to the back entrance where sometimes my father would come out to the small porch and take a break. His office looked out over Meadow Creek.

"A good place to think and breathe," he'd said when he moved in. My mother thought his office should be situated at the front of the building, but my dad preferred the privacy. That's what he told us, anyway.

Today the back door was shut. I shrugged and started to reach for the knob when I heard giggling. I bent down and peered through the half-open blinds. My father and a woman I didn't recognize were lying on the sofa, locked in a pretty heavy embrace.

I jumped back, fingers splaying against the smooth siding.

It couldn't be true. But my eyes didn't lie. My father was having an affair.

I moved against the wall, heart racing out of my chest, and looked toward the creek. Soon anger replaced my shock and my fingers clenched into fists. What should I do? Should I knock and confront them?

Hardly. I might be bold about some things, but the thought of confronting my father with a lover made me want to throw up. I did gag and hurried off the porch to race down to the creek where my entire breakfast of oatmeal and toast ended up on the bank.

I fell to my knees under a maple tree, pressing my hands to my mouth. Just last week, Dad had attended church with us. For the fifth time in a row.

"Hypocrite," I mouthed.

I'm not sure how long I sat by the creek but long enough until I heard the other car start up and drive away. Eventually, I crawled up the bank, and went around to where I'd parked. I didn't care if my father had seen the van. I wished he had.

I never was good at keeping secrets and when I returned home and handed Mom her set of keys, the tears started.

"What on earth is the matter?" She looked out the window to the driveway. Her first thought must have been I wrecked the car.

Robert came into the kitchen and threw a few cookies into his mouth. "What? You wreck your first time out?" He laughed and put his arm around my shoulder. "Won't be the last time. Promise you that."

"I didn't wreck the van."

"Then what's wrong?" My mother reached for me and put her palm against my forehead. Always checking for a fever. Maybe that was my answer.

"I don't feel so good."

"You do feel a little warm. Why don't you go on up to bed, and I'll bring you some tea later."

Her kindness made me want to bawl harder, but I nodded and slunk up the stairs to my room where I shed my clothes and dove under the covers. How would I ever face my father tonight when he came home? I flipped over and studied the wall where I'd hung some pencil drawings I'd doodled a few weeks ago.

One was of my parents sitting together on the front porch.

I shut my eyes and groaned.

A sixteen-year-old kid shouldn't have to deal with this stuff.

I didn't have to be the one to spill my guts though. That night, my father came home and told my mother everything. He moved out for three months before she took him back.

Where was Superman then?

~*~

I don't know why I'm thinking about my father on the first day of the Q-School tournament. I reach for Mattie's pendant and rub it between my fingers.

Do or die. That's what Jessie, a girl from California, said when we checked in.

My future rests on today's performance and again in December in Daytona at the LPGA headquarters where the final cuts will be made.

The weather isn't helping either. Rain and a light wind will guarantee I'll hit at least a few balls to my right. Maybe even land some in the water, but I can't afford that today. I shiver in my rain gear. Why hadn't I layered better? Maybe because this is Florida, and who expects such cold in October?

One by one, the other golfers tee off. I wait, trying to think of anything but the next few hours. My stomach twists. Not now. I press my hand against my waist, forcing myself to take deep breaths.

It's my turn to tee off. I loosen my shoulders and take a deep breath. I press the gold golf club between my fingers and try to clear my mind. Robert said he'd be praying, and for once I count on that. I want God to see what I'm doing and to help me.

I swing.

My least favorite part of golfing is watching where my ball lands. Today, however, I don't have to worry. It is perfect.

15

Drew meets me at my car, his hair soaked to the scalp. His jacket is rolled up under one arm, drenched too. "How about you let me take you out to celebrate?"

"You were here?"

"I volunteered and drove the carts all over the place today." He gives a show-stopping grin. "So how about it?"

"Can I change first? I can meet you someplace."

"Soup and More in Winter Garden?"

"Give me an hour. I'm starved."

I unlock my car and hoist my bag into the trunk. Drew waits, hanging around like a found puppy. "You can go, you know," I tell him.

He comes closer and I look up at him.

"I'm proud of you. You golfed like a pro today."

"Thanks. I still have a ways to go before I can say that, though."

He rests his hand against the trunk of my wet car. "I plan to be there when you do."

~*~

I consider Drew's comment later when I drive to the restaurant where I'll meet him, my body clothed in dry jeans and a T-shirt. My hair still looks pretty ragged, pulled up in a ponytail, but will have to do. I'm exhausted, considering the stress I've been under all day to stay ahead of the pack. But I did it. Round one. Check.

Later I'll call Robert in the privacy of my trailer. I can't wait to have him celebrate with me.

Drew meets me at the door and we are given a table along the window on the west side. I haven't ever eaten in this establishment, so Drew makes some suggestions and I go with a burger, fries, and coleslaw.

I don't realize how hungry I am until the waitress sets our plates in front of us. I dive in, not waiting for Drew to pick up his fork.

"So when are you quitting school?" He wipes ketchup from his mouth.

"What do you mean?" I set my glass of root beer aside. "I'm not quitting."

Drew tilts his head and gives me a look that pretty much says I should know what he's talking about, but I don't. I plan to finish my degree if I can.

"If you win at Daytona, you go on tour."

"But I'm sure that won't be right away." I hadn't thought about this part of my plan in my eagerness to get down here and connect with the golf community.

"This next season, which would mean you'd be on the road."

I stir my coleslaw (why on earth did I order it? It is nothing like my mother's) and then look across the table. What pulled me to Drew that first day? Couldn't have been his good looks alone. Am I that shallow?

"I haven't thought that far ahead."

He pushes aside his empty plate. "Why don't you tell me what's going on, Bobbi. I'm not stupid, and I also know most serious golfers have their future all marked out. You're going about this like a girl who can't decide what boy she should date."

"Ouch. That hurts. Why don't you tell me I'm a flake and be done with it?" I shove aside my own plate, leaving the pile of unfinished coleslaw for the busboy to clean up. So Drew wants to know why I haven't planned better. I do, too, only I've been struggling to get from point *A* to point *B*. I sigh and roll my eyes.

"So you aren't going to tell me?"

"There isn't that much to tell." Sure there is, but I can't spill my guts to Drew, the only guy who backs me here. At least, not yet.

"Try me. You'll find I'm a good listener. And I might throw in my own story as a bonus."

I straighten. "You never talk about yourself."

"Maybe not to you. I do have family and friends, despite what this loner looks like to you." Again the smile.

I've been wondering what happened to him ever since I stepped into his classroom and he offered to teach me to play. Something is off with him, and it isn't only that he didn't make it on tour. Drew is a great golfer. I've seen his shots. Maybe if I give him something…

"OK. It's a deal."

"Deal You first."

"My father never took me golfing—he preferred my brother. My twin brother. His name is Robert. My father was a pro golfer. So was my grandfather."

"That doesn't explain anything. Only begs the question why you're here and not Robert. Is he already on tour? Playing catch-up?"

Is that what he thinks? I could let him go with this, but I'm not good at lying. Maybe I'll share a bit more. "Robert had an accident and he's relearning how to walk."

"Ohhh. I see." He crosses his arms and leans back against the padded seatback. A pretty waitress stops to ask if he needs his cup refilled. Drew shakes his head.

"Do you? You think I'm here because Robert can't be?"

"Are you trying to impress your father? Because I'd think he'd be pretty impressed right now after today's luck."

"It isn't luck." My fingers find the necklace. "I don't know what it was. But it wasn't luck. Maybe God's plan for me or something. I don't know. But I can't stop and figure all that out now."

"You're right. I should let you go."

"No you don't. You haven't told me your dark secrets yet. Come on. Open up."

"Maybe another time." A grin shows and he grabs the check the waitress has dropped off during my story.

"Now who isn't being fair?"

"Let's just say we might need more time, and I know a sleepyhead when I see one."

I stifle my yawn and reach for my purse. He's right. I'm so tired that driving home might be impossible. I say goodnight and make it back to my trailer going well below the speed limit.

A light is on at Mattie's place. As far as I know, all her belongings are being given away next week, and everything is packed and ready to go. The park manager hasn't been able to find any relatives and all her close friends have no need of anything.

I lock my car. Maybe someone is robbing her place? Hardly possible since this court is the last place anyone would come looking to make a fast dollar. I bite my lower lip and decide. Seconds later, I knock on the front door.

No answer.

When I jiggle the handle, the door opens softly beneath my hand. "Hello? Is anyone here?" I call into the semi-darkness. I make out the piles of boxes, and next I see the shadow. I clap my hand over my mouth to stop myself from screaming.

"Come in. Anyone who would brave an empty house must have cared about Mattie. Don't worry. I don't bite." The florescent lights come on over the kitchen sink at the same time I breathe again. An attractive woman in her thirties or maybe early forties steps forward with her hand out.

"I'm sorry. I wasn't being nosy. I'm…was Mattie's neighbor." I shake the offered hand.

The intruder wears white capris and has pulled her hair onto her head in a kind of fancy twist. Streaks of red add to an otherwise bland color job. "Nice to meet you. How well did you know my mother?"

I choke on my spit. "Your mother? I didn't"—I stutter like a nervous date—"didn't know she had a daughter. I'm so sorry for your loss. She never told me about you."

"Mina." She nods to the sofa, the only piece of furniture not loaded with boxes. "Please sit. It's not a surprise to me that she didn't tell you I existed. We haven't spoken in over twenty years. I was lucky to find out she died through the Internet. Someone picked up on her obituary and ran with it. That's what fame will get you—another article at death."

I want to say "Wow!" about the twenty-year time frame but instead say, "That's a long time." We sit a good foot apart on the couch. My knees shake without my permission.

"It's going to be even longer now that's she's gone. I should have come sooner." She lets her head drop for a fraction of a second and pulls it upright again.

This whole scene isn't for me. I try hard to think what my mother might say but nothing comes to mind except offering tea, and that's out of the question since everything is packed. "I wish she'd told me. She was really special."

"I see she gave you the necklace."

Without realizing it, I have been fondling the golf club between my two fingers—as is now my habit. I drop my hand to my lap.

"It's OK. I never wanted it. She won it on her last tournament—Palm Springs. I was there for her victory, but later that night she wrecked the car and that's history, so they say."

"You weren't in the accident?"

Mina shakes her head. Her eyebrows form a lovely V while she speaks. I feel like I'm sitting in the middle of a TV show where they bring out guests who tell their life story. I cross my fingers, hoping for something good.

"I went home with my friends. She stayed and drank with her friends and gave my cousin and others a ride home. I never forgave her. Never is a long time." A sigh floats from her chest.

"You haven't spoken in all these years? What about her community service and all the good she did? Doesn't that count for something?"

"Does that change anything?"

"I think it did for Mattie. She felt good about it. She felt like she was helping others."

"I'm glad for her. It still didn't change the lives she destroyed."

I don't get her. Why is she here if she's never forgiven Mattie even with all the good she did?

"I'm sorry. It seems to me that Mattie would have done anything to fix things in her life. I bet that included you."

Mina stands and strides over to the sink where she pours herself a glass of water. She turns around. Her eyes are shiny. "Ever wish your life had turned out differently? That you did what you should have done? I was a darned good golfer. Would have been pro, but because of my mother, I put my clubs away and took up knitting. Knitting. Do I look like a person who likes to knit?"

Honestly, I want to say yes, but I keep my mouth shut.

"I got married, raised three kids, and practically won the best mother of the year award, but I couldn't call my mother. You know why? I wanted her to try harder. To make up for what she did and not with community service garbage."

"What more could she have done?" I whisper. I regret now that I looked over here when I got home. I will mind my own business in the future.

She waves her glass in the air. Maybe it isn't water. "I don't know. That's the trouble. I really don't know. She couldn't fix everything, I guess."

Superman is a myth.

"Again, I'm sorry for your loss. Would you like this necklace back to remember her by?"

"No, no, you keep it, honey. I'm sure there was a good reason why she gave it to you."

I don't know what it is, but part of me doesn't want to let go of Mattie's gift yet. But I do want to get out of this conversation. I stand and edge toward the door.

"It was nice to meet you. Let me know if you need any help with any of her things." I let my gaze fall around the room at the boxes filled with what was Mattie's life.

"I'm going to have Goodwill haul this stuff away. I'm not sure why I came. Maybe I thought I'd find some answers here." A loose laugh bubbles from her.

I definitely need to be going. In a minute she'll be sobbing into her glass.

I reach for the doorknob, and then I think of something. Something Mattie told me one day when we were eating hotdogs on her patio. She said she liked to write before she was a golfer, and now all she ever did was write in a journal at night when she could keep her eyes opened.

"Did you look in her nightstand?"

Mina raises her head. "Her nightstand? Whatever for?"

"I could be wrong, but your mother told me how she jotted things down at night. In a journal. I thought..." my words trail off. Mina is already halfway down the hall. In a matter of minutes, she returns with a plastic coated journal in both hands. She looks like she's found the lost city of Atlantis.

I start to sit again but change my mind.

"I'll leave you to it."

Mina looks up at me from where she's curled in Mattie's rocker. Tears trickle down her cheeks. "Thank you for being here with my mother. And thank you for this gift. It might not give me the answers I need, but it's a start. A good one."

I take advantage of my opportunity to leave. I will probably never know what was written in that journal, but I sure hope Mattie wrote about her long lost daughter somewhere in it.

16

Robert answers the phone instead of my mother.

I hold my breath and then speak. "I qualified."

Screams tumble through my earpiece, and I laugh along with my brother. I really need to hear him like this today. His support means everything to me.

"I knew you would do it. You're amazing, Bobbi. So when's the next round of tournaments?"

"Not until December—a week before Christmas." I sink into my chair. "I'm nervous about it. The competition was stiff at this one. I played well, but anything can go wrong."

He's quick to reassure me. "It won't. Not now, because you want this so badly. I still don't agree it's what you should do with your life, but I can't tell you what to do."

"How's Dad? Any word from him?" I cross my fingers, hoping. All this work and effort is for nothing if my father decides he's done with us forever. I want him to be proud of me and regain that pride he had in himself. I want him to be happy we're his family.

"He came for dinner last night. Mom invited him." I hear the resignation in his voice, the concern and the fear for what could go right or wrong.

"And? How did it go?"

"Grandpa acted like nothing was wrong. Like Dad has been sitting in his place every night. But then Grandpa took a fall—hit the bathroom radiator and

Mom and Dad took him to the hospital. They kept him overnight for observation." He lowers his voice. "He's going downhill fast and Mom doesn't get it."

"So he's OK now?" My breath quickens when I think of my grandfather and how I'll keep that promise to win a trophy. Will I ever make it?

"He's been resting. Docs say he probably had a mini-stroke and might have injured his ribs. I don't know though. I don't think he'll be around too much longer."

"Don't say that! He'll be around a long time."

My brother has always been much more realistic than I am in everything. When he injured himself in the fire, it was Robert who told me that his healing would take time and that if he never golfed again—then so be it.

Maybe I should be more like him. But if I was, who would be the one to put our family back together? My mother certainly isn't making my father happy. The only time he was excited about anything was when he discovered how good Robert was at the sport. I know my Dad saw his own dreams come true again.

"Hey. Are you there?"

I'm fading. "I'm here. Just thinking about what you said."

"You'll be home for Thanksgiving. You can see for yourself. You are coming home, aren't you?"

"I plan on it. It won't be for long since they don't give us that many days off and I need to practice."

"I hope you're having a life there, too. You are, aren't you?"

As in life does he mean my ticket-taking job? Or maybe my now-and-then lunches with Drew and his brother?

"Sure. I have a life."

I hang up right after a few more sentences and shuffle into my bedroom where I fall down on my bed, exhausted.

I hate my life. I hate that I have to play golf all day. I hate that I can't date anyone. I hate that Mattie has died and that her daughter never knew her and that she is sitting over there crying over an old journal. I hate that I'm the only one who can put my father back into our family and make him happy.

~*~

Although I seem more and more to be a natural at playing golf, I'm not a natural when talking to my father. Dad didn't grow up in the Northeast like I did. His hometown is near San Diego, a place we once visited to meet his parents, my grandparents, who owned a resort in the mountains. I remember asking my father why he would leave this beautiful place and end up where he did.

"I met your mom and she wanted to live near her parents."

That was his explanation. Not that he loved the Endless Mountains or the countryside and the people. He told me he grew up golfing. When he was on tour on the East Coast, he met my mother who was on vacation with her family to watch the tournament.

My mother said she'd actually enjoyed watching golf, but didn't ever play. They fell in love that week, and my father dated her long distance, coming to Pennsylvania whenever he had a break from the tours.

I could see why she fell in love with him. Even though my description is from a daughter's viewpoint, it is accurate. My father stands over six feet tall and has a head of wavy dark hair that hasn't thinned with age. His face is that kind of face you see on the old black and white movies—dashing, masculine and appealing. I think Robert inherited some of those looks, but I take after my mother's side.

My father also works out—or did up until recently. So all in all, my father looks pretty good for someone in his situation. I'm actually surprised more women haven't thrown themselves at him.

But then again, my mother is still attractive. When I look at their faded pictures together I can see why he fell for her. She is one of those perfume model beauties. Light hair with a slight curl to it. High cheekbones. I can't help it if she dresses awful now and that she forgets to wear makeup. Somewhere along the way, after one of my father's disappearing acts, it seems she gave up on herself.

When Robert took an interest in golf, everything became right again with us. Dad was happy. Mom started smiling more, and Robert loved the attention. That left me trying to fit in with my art until the day my passion ruined everything.

Tonight I want to call my father and tell him about my win. The phone clings to my palm, sweaty and heavy. I punch in his contact information and wait for him to answer. It doesn't take long. He's usually pretty good about answering his phone.

"Hey, what's going on down there in Florida?"

"Hi, Dad. I wanted to tell you I made it through the first round at Q-School. I go to Daytona in December."

"Not bad. I remember going through that myself. Some stiff competition, I bet, huh? I know Robert wishes he could be there playing. Did you hear that he can walk now? Nothing like before, but at least he's up and around. I'll have him out on the course by spring."

"That would be great—for him. I also wanted to tell you I'm coming home for Thanksgiving, and if the weather is decent, maybe we could get in a game?" I close my eyes, waiting for his answer, knowing deep inside what it will be.

"Let me see how work is and I'll let you know, OK baby? Hey, my other line is ringing. Looks like your mom. I'll talk with you soon."

And just like that, he hangs up.

I let out the air I've been holding in, go to my bathroom where I peel off my clothes, and stand beneath the hot shower for fifteen minutes. I don't realize my skin has turned bright red by the time I towel off and notice as I look in the mirror over my dresser.

Will my father only be happy if Robert golfs again? If that's true, what am I doing here?

I crawl between my cool sheets and lay on my back, replaying our conversation. Maybe I've gotten everything wrong? I don't think so. He'll be thrilled when I make the tour. He'll move back home permanently and take me golfing every chance I'm there. I'll be the star he wanted, and he'll finally have back what he lost.

~*~

Greg waits for me after class. I grab my golf clubs and follow him up to the range. I need to work on my putting, but it will be nice to have company to practice my drives.

"So how about your win? Are you psyched?" he asks after his first shot.

I put my gloves on. "I'm nervous about what's to come. Have you ever thought about trying?'

Greg laughs. Must know I'm being polite. "I'll be lucky if I can get my PGA card. I'm planning on getting into Celebration at the clubhouse when I graduate. Maybe I can work my way up to manager."

"That would be great." Most of the guys here have dreams of pro golf, but in reality, will end up working behind a counter or chasing golf balls for rich guys all over the course. One guy wants to be a caddie in England because his wife got transferred there last week. I still can't see the glamour in that job.

I hit ball after ball until my arms ache. So much for endurance. Tomorrow I'll play nine holes after class and work on my short game. I was so close to going into the water hazard last week.

"Want to go for something to eat after?" Greg has that hopeful look again in his eyes. I hate turning him down all the time, but I have a bowl of ramen noodles waiting for me.

"Some other time."

He shrugs and gives a final shot to another ball. I bend down and pick up my balls and turn to put them back in my bag when pain shoots from my foot up to my ankle.

"Ooohhh!" I crumple to the ground, grabbing my ankle and watch it swell before my eyes.

The throbbing tells me all I need to know. I am so clumsy that I've sprained my ankle.

Greg rushes over at my yelp and kneels beside me. "What happened? I saw you twist and go down."

I slam my club into the earth. "I think I sprained

my ankle when I turned around. Now what am I going to do?" I squeeze my eyes shut and see myself unable to play for weeks and weeks, hobbling around on a stupid pair of crutches.

"Let me drive you to the ER. You'll need to have that looked at to be sure it isn't broken."

He's right, but I hate the thought of going to a doctor. I let him help me up, and we hobble back to the parking lot. It takes only ten minutes, and I'm signing in at the ER desk with Greg's help. Another hour later and the x-ray tech takes me back. I wait for the young doctor to tell me what I already know.

"It's sprained. We'll give you some crutches. Stay off it for a while."

I'm sure his awhile is much longer than mine, but I smile and hitch the crutches under my pits and find my way out to where Greg waits for me. He finishes his candy bar and helps me out to his car.

"Good thing it's your left leg. You'll be able to drive."

"Lucky me," I say and shift my butt on his seat so I'll be more comfortable. He drops me off at home, promising to pick me up in a few days, and then he'll help me get my car home after school.

"Be sure to ice it and elevate it for the next couple of days. And don't wrap it too tight. You need to let it breathe."

"You sound like a doctor, Greg."

His face turns red. "I was."

I whip my head around. "What?"

He tells me the story after raiding my refrigerator of the rest of my milk and chocolate syrup.

It seems Greg lived in Minnesota but was able to go to college when he was sixteen. "Some kind of genius," he says as though apologizing. "Maybe gifted is the word today. Anyway"—he helps himself to my last bag of chips—"I excelled in the sciences, so my folks decided I should become a doctor. There weren't any in our family." At this point he chuckles. "Only farmers, actually. I come from a long line of farmers." He passes the last three chips to me. "I got accepted into Baylor in Houston, and I went through faster than most students. Did my residency in orthopedics and discovered I hated it. What I did like was golfing with my buddies."

"You liked golfing more than being a doctor?" Now I know my friend is crazy.

"So it doesn't pay as well, but it feeds this need in here." He pounds his heart. "You know that need? To do what you're meant to do?" He gazes out my side window and looks as if he's seen an angel. I follow his line of sight and see only old Mr. Howard taking his garbage to the curb. "So here I am."

"You don't regret walking away from being a doctor?"

At my question, he shakes his head. "Not for a second. I love golf. Life is too short."

"But what about your parents? What about their desire to see you as a doctor?"

"They saw me as a doctor. Now they can see me golf." With that final pronouncement, he stands and brushes off his shorts. Greg asks me again if I need any help.

I figure I can hop around myself and tell him to go home.

When he leaves, I think about Greg the doctor. He doesn't seem to care what the consequences are about his choices. My hand finds my heart and I pound on it the way Greg did his.

After a few minutes, I reach beside me where I've set the tablet Mom sent, and I start to doodle a picture for him.

17

I hate being stuck in my trailer. The next morning, I haul myself outside and sit down on my plastic chair with my foot propped on a cement block. The humidity clings to my shirt like a piece of slime, and I wonder if October is ever going to cool off like everyone around here told me it should. At this rate, I will melt in approximately two hours.

About fifteen minutes into my sunbathing, Drew's familiar truck pulls in my driveway. He slides out of the driver's side, balancing two cups of coffee and a bag of doughnuts that he tosses into my lap before handing me a cup. I take a sip. The aroma teases the insides of my nose. My taste buds applaud. Perfect. Two sugars and one cream.

"Thought you could use some company. Greg told me what happened. Sorry."

I point to my one other chair, and he pulls it up across from me. I should have washed my hair, but the thought of standing to dry it wasn't appealing.

"What about classes?"

"Guess you forgot—there's a tournament today. No class." He raises his cup to salute me.

I can't get over the strangeness of Drew sitting in my yard. It's not like we have progressed to the point of good friends or anything like that. I lusted over him when I first met him, but ever since he made it clear that he is my instructor only, I have taken my sights off him. But today his blue eyes cause me to shiver even though it is ninety degrees.

"Thanks for the coffee." I peek into the bag and pull out a glazed doughnut—still warm. The glaze oozes onto my fingers. "Oh wow." I bite one in half and pass him the bag.

He does the same and tips his face toward my leg. "What are you going to do about December?"

"It's only the end of October. I have time." I shrug. Sure, he can tell I'm worried. What golfer wouldn't be with this setback?

"Work on your upper body strength. You always need that."

"Anything else you want to tell me?" I had already planned to hit the gym as soon as I can drive and maneuver my way on crutches.

Drew smiles and runs his free hand through his hair, making it stand in peaks. "As a matter of fact there is."

"What? Drink plenty of vegetable juice?"

"I was thinking it's time to tell you my story."

Now, that sentence gets me. I set my coffee aside and slide up in my seat. "What are you waiting for?"

Drew clears his throat, and at first it looks as if he's going to throw up, but then calmness takes over his features. "Unlike you, I started playing golf when I was five years old. My dad bought me a set of clubs for my birthday and made sure we hit the links any day the thermometer read above thirty-two degrees. By the time I was ten, I was playing in all kinds of tournaments for kids and winning. I accumulated a shelf full of trophies. I played with them like other kids played with blocks.

"Anyway, eventually I was good enough that I got

sponsors and tried out for Q-School. I made the tour the first time through. Never ever thought about college back then—just golf. It was my life. I lived and breathed it. That is, until I met Katie.

"I was playing in South Carolina at the time, and she worked at a hotel I was staying in. One thing led to another and I fell in love. Hard. Of course, I proposed to her, and we married within the year against my father's advice. But until then, I'd known nothing but golf, and she was literally a breath of fresh air, if you will excuse my cliché.

"Katie didn't care that I played on tour. She supported me. So much that she never told me she was dying. I don't need to tell you what from, and I never could tell myself except that she seemed to tire easily. But one day I got the call…she passed away."

It is at this point in Drew's story that I wish I can get out of my chair to hug him. Instead, I swallow back the tears that have been building and wait.

He stands with his back to me. His voice softens as he continues. "We had only been married six months, but they were the best six months of my life. I never realized that something other than golf could make me happy. Even though it was my passion and my life, Katie and her love surpassed that. I quit the tour the next day and went home.

"My father was beside himself and begged me to reconsider—telling me to think of my career." Drew turns around and slams his fist into his palm. "My career! It was *my* career, not his. And he wants me to take it back up like nothing has happened. I hung around Pennsylvania about ten months, and then packed my stuff and headed south. A buddy of mine heard about the golf school and suggested I apply." He held both palms up. "The rest is history."

I cradle my cup, not sure at all what to do with my hands or how to respond to this story. "I'm sorry, Drew."

"Don't be. I like my job. The reason I told you all of this is so you can think about what you're doing. I know you haven't told me the rest of your story." He sits back down. "Your turn."

"What does your story have to do with mine?"

"Tell me why you're really here. It isn't about the golf, is it? Everyone has a reason and I know true passion when I see it. You don't have that. You like it well enough, but it isn't what you want to do."

After hearing his love story about Katie, my story about the fire and Robert sounds pretty lame. But I take a breath and speak.

"You're right. I never liked golf. But it so happens I'm good at it. Very good, and I'm grateful. I need to be for my brother and for my family. You see, my brother, Robert, was injured in a fire I caused. He was hurt trying to save my art. My stupid paintings. And because of me, he'll always walk with difficulty and will never play golf again." I'm not going to tell him the whole story, am I? I look up into Drew's waiting expression.

His gaze holds mine. "Go on."

I twist my empty cup and toss it to the steps.

"My father has cheated on my mother. I caught him once when I was sixteen. Anyway, until he figured out Robert might be the next best great golfer, he was miserable being part of our family. But finally he had something—a son who might be a super pro. He started laughing more and taking the family on outings, and my mother turned back into the person I remember her being from years ago. Life was good. Until the fire."

"You didn't cause it."

"Not on purpose, but it was my stupid carelessness that did. My father blames me for everything. It doesn't matter how sorry I am—Robert is done playing golf. My father's dream is over."

"And that's when you stepped in to take over where Robert left off."

"I was always pretty good at the sport." I catch his look. "It's an answer. I have this chance to help my family."

"But it isn't what you want to do." He almost thrusts the words at me. "It isn't your passion."

"But it will save my family, and that's more important." I believe what I say, and saying it aloud gives me that extra determination I need to make it to Daytona. I don't think I've convinced Drew, but that doesn't matter. All that matters is my family will be whole again when my father realizes that he can live his dream through me.

"What about your dream?"

I glance over to the sketch pad where I've drawn Greg's portrait. It looks like him. I plan to give it to him next time we meet.

"This *is* my dream."

"Did you ever stop to think that maybe it isn't your father's?"

"What do you mean? Of course, it's my father's. I've seen how he is when he's involved with golf. He's a different person. He's the man my mother fell in love with."

Drew leans close and touches my chin. I want to pull back but I don't. "Bobbi-with-an-*I*, I care about you and what you'll be. Take some time to rethink what you're doing." His gaze bores into mine. He's so close I want to touch his lips.

Instead, I turn away. I know what I'm doing is right.

18

School is crowded with students today because there's a tournament later (one I won't play in). No one skips. The hallway echoes with shouts and loud comments while I hobble my way to class.

I avoid Drew. Fortunately, I have other classes, and by the time I hop around, I don't have time to chat with anyone. A few guys offer to carry my books (which I politely decline), and a few make wisecracks, but overall I make it through the morning, and then to the gym.

The gym is not my favorite place to hang out. First, the treadmills look like last season leftovers from a defunct sporting goods store. The weight machines are crammed into a corner where it is almost impossible for more than one person at a time to work out. I breathe a sigh when I see I'm the only one here today.

My upper arms are pretty strong already, but working them couldn't hurt. I wriggle into a machine and start doing repetitions. Up and down. Rest. Up and down.

I don't want to think about Drew's question, but my thoughts keep returning to it. What if turning pro won't do it for my father? What if it has to be Robert all along?

I set the weights higher.

No, that's not true. Now that Robert can't golf,

Dad will see that he can be just as proud of me, though he never went on to win titles his daughter can. He and Mom will get back together, and life would be as it once was. We'll be a family. I'll always have a place to come home to on the holidays someday with my own family. Isn't that what we all want?

My mother called last night to check on me. She said Dad has been stopping by and seems more like himself. Maybe what I am doing is already working. When I return at Thanksgiving, I'll invite him for dinner. Grandpa would like that and so would my mother.

As I work out, my fantasies of a happy family balloon. I don't notice Dad standing in front of me until he taps my arm.

"I wanted to surprise you. Looks like I did."

"Dad?" I drop my weights and struggle to my feet. He pulls me into an awkward embrace, and for a moment I forget our past—the last time I saw him. It's just my father and me. I step back and take a good look at him. He's wearing a red polo shirt, khakis, and boat shoes minus the socks. My father looks years younger. Is this what separation does for someone?

"What are you doing here?" My mouth won't close.

"Didn't Mom tell you? I have a conference in Orlando for a few days. I figured I would surprise you." He grins, but it looks forced to me.

Did my mother tell him to visit me?

"Do you want to follow me over to my trailer and see where I live?"

He looks at his watch. "Sure, I've got time. Need help?" He reaches for my crutches and hands them to me. I hitch my way to the parking lot and give him directions in case he gets caught in traffic. On the way to Golden Acres, I worry if I've made my bed or finished my breakfast dishes. My father will think I'm a slob.

I pull into my driveway and his rental car fits tightly behind mine.

"Not bad." He tips his head and looks up at the roof (why I don't know) and glances around the court. I see his gaze stop on Mattie's pile of junk yet to be carted away. I should tell him about her. I reach for my necklace. Maybe he's heard of her.

"Can I get you iced tea? It's what I drink now. The Southerners don't seem to recognize anything but."

My father takes the old chair that is propped in the corner and sits on it all stiff like a robot. He never was too comfortable in social situations. A part of me wishes he would hurry and drink up and leave.

"Not a bad place, Bobbi. Are your neighbors nice?"

I join him and lower myself onto the couch. "Mattie, the lady across the way, just died. She was a pro golfer, Dad. Maybe you heard of her? Mattie Montrose?"

He shifts in his seat. A frown creeps onto his lips. "I might have. Did she have a daughter?"

My fingers tighten on my glass.

"Yes, she does. I met her. Wow, what a coincidence. How did you know her?" Again, I reach for my necklace and wait for the perfect time to show him.

He shrugs.

Is this all I'll get? A shrug?

"Somewhere along the way. She might have been at an event with her mother and we spoke. She's probably married by now."

"She and her mother didn't speak for years. I think that's sad."

He stands and roams into my kitchen area. "So, you cook much?" He lifts a frying pan I'd left on the stove. My father knows I never cook much. That was my mother's job and one she didn't want to give up.

"A little more than before. Easy stuff. So how's Robert doing now?"

He face brightens at my question, and he returns to his seat. His hands, always well-groomed, flatten on his knees. "I think he'll be on the course before you know it. That boy is determined. He's going to pick up where he left off and turn pro someday. I know it."

I curl my lip. "It takes hard work. Do you really think after the accident"—I hesitate on the word none of us are comfortable saying—"he'll be able to?"

My father waves his hand. "No reason not to. It's the plan."

The *plan* is for me to win the trophies in case Robert never can. Last night when I talked to Robert, he told me how much Dad is pushing him. I don't think he likes it, but I don't tell my father. I need him to believe in the dream in front of him. Not one that might never materialize.

"Are you going to be able to fly down when I compete in December at Daytona?"

He looks stunned that I change the subject, let alone ask something like that. "You're going to give it a shot?"

"I already made it through the first phase. Why wouldn't I?"

Again, he shrugs and I try to read his look. Nothing. What will it take to give my father what he needs again? It seems like he's fixated on Robert and I'm not real to him. I rise and reach for my crutches.

"I guess you probably should get to your conference. Thanks for coming by."

He jumps from his seat, relief etching his features. "Sure, baby girl." He leans down and kisses my cheek.

After he leaves, I make my way to my bedroom and pull out my sketch book. On top is a picture of Robert swinging a club. By all rights, he should be camped out in this trailer trying out for the tour—not me.

My father's visit surprised me. He isn't the kind to go out of his way to do something nice. Part of me wonders if he has another motive. Maybe he wanted to see how serious I am about turning pro. Maybe he had to see me here to start believing in me. I like that thought and turn it over and over as I prepare for bed. Tomorrow I plan to leave my crutches behind.

It's time to get serious again.

~*~

For the next several weeks, I do nothing but eat, sleep, go to class, and play golf. Night after night, I dream about my shots and wake up determined to do better. My fellow classmates try to get me to lighten up and attend their parties, but I refuse. I practice my putting, my drives, my short game, and everything in between.

Drew stops me in the hallway one day and puts his hand on my shoulder. I flinch at the sudden touch. "You look tired. How about taking the day off?"

"Can't. I've got to practice." I head toward my car to get my clubs.

"You're killing yourself, you know. Is it worth it?"

I look over my shoulder at the man who could have been my mentor if I'd let him. "Don't ask me that."

It's raining when I get outside, and for a second I want to take Drew up on his advice. But the driving range will still be open. I pull up my hood, grab my clubs, and head up the hill.

Mark sees me coming and races for my bag. "So you aren't giving up, huh? I have to say, I've never seen a woman so determined as you, except for the last chick, who wanted to get her claws in me."

I smile at his joke and reach for a bucket of balls. "You can't win if you don't work hard."

"You also need to pace yourself."

Am I hearing an echo? I wave and head toward the range. I'm the only player out here today, but I like that. I can hit ball after ball without distraction. I work to break my own record at distance and finally succeed.

It's only when I do that I decide it's time to go home and eat. I've lost weight, so I stop at the grocery store and splurge on a sub. The guy behind the counter asks me what I want on it, and I rattle off my favorites.

"I want a bag of chips, too," I say and reach for my purse to pay when he hands me my dinner. The checkout line is long. While I wait, my cell rings. Normally I don't answer when I'm in a store, but with another good ten minutes to wait, I do.

It's Amanda. Sobbing.

"What's wrong? Are you OK?"

"It's the baby. We've lost her."

My breath catches as I clutch the phone tighter.

Amanda tells me between choked tears what

happened. She is beyond calming down. I ask to speak to her husband who gives me the facts like a robot.

"Tell her I'll be home in a few days and I'll come see her."

My promise isn't enough for her, but it's all I can offer. What do I know about such things? It will be years before I can even consider being a mother—if ever. Not if I want to be a pro. I tell Jim again I'm coming home for Thanksgiving. He says he'll tell her and tells me to have a safe trip.

I turn my phone off and look down at my bag with the sub in it. Simple things. I worry about simple things like what my next meal will be while Amanda is dealing with death. It isn't right.

Three days later, I land at the airport where my mother greets me with a huge hug. "I'm so sorry about Amanda's baby. Will you be going over there today?"

I grab my suitcase. The clock over the escalator already reads four. "No, tomorrow maybe. I want to cuddle down with you and Robert and Grandpa tonight. How is Grandpa doing now? Any more falls?"

My family doesn't seem to want to share all their secrets with me anymore. Her secret shows on her face and she tries to cover it. I don't let her. "Mom? Is he OK?"

"He took a bad spill a few days ago. They wanted us to leave him in rehab for a while to work on his balance." Her hair falls across her cheek. "He doesn't like it there."

"Is he at Sunrise?" I know the center at the edge of town. I delivered pizza to the staff there when I worked summers for a local shop. I remember the odor. Even the garlicky sauce couldn't cover it up.

"He wants to come home. They said maybe for

Thanksgiving for a few hours."

"*They* said? He's your father."

"Bobbi. He needs more help than I can give him. I thought I could do it, but without your father around and with Robert still needing so much help…"

"And if I was here."

She sighs and pulls off the highway onto the road toward home.

I admire the passing farms and an occasional windmill. I love living in the country. I miss it.

"Did you ever read that book I packed for you?" She's talking about the Christian book about letting God lead you where you should go.

I'd riffled through it and set it aside. "Not yet."

Again, she sighs. "I'm beginning to wonder if you'll ever get back to trusting God."

Somehow, I'd hoped she and I would avoid this conversation. I pick at a nail. She gets my hint and turns on the radio. We ride in silence the rest of the way home.

Robert is waiting for me on the sun porch even though the temperatures are well into the low forties. "Hey, girl." He smiles and holds out his arms for a hug. He's dressed in the sweater I gave him last year for Christmas and looks good. Very good.

"So show me your new dance moves," I say and chuck him in the arm.

"How about a slow waltz?" I watch him cross the threshold and join my mother in the kitchen. Any second I expect to hear my Grandfather call out "Bobbi girl—my Bobbi girl!" But the house is quiet as though we are at a viewing.

"How about a game of chess after I dump my stuff upstairs?"

My twin agrees and moves slowly into the living room where he will set up for us to play. Robert always wins, but today I don't care. I need to be around the one person who understands me.

Because I'm starting not to understand myself.

19

My mother wakes me at seven the next morning. It's Thanksgiving in Pennsylvania. That means we put the turkey in the oven early. For some uncanny reason, she believes I want to help.

I pull on a pair of jeans and a sweatshirt and pad down the steps. "It already smells good in here." The sweet aroma of golden onions and celery simmering in a pot of butter on the stove pulls me close. I check out the counter that is laden with goodies. My mouth waters.

"You can crack the walnuts for the salad." She nods toward the unopened bag and the bowl stationed on the counter. My mother always makes my favorite fruit salad for the holidays.

"You know they make shelled walnuts now." I grab the bag and nutcracker.

"What? Take away all your pleasure?" She's dressed in her holiday sweatshirt—a plump bejeweled turkey wearing an apron. She purchased it on sale last year after Christmas. I remember. I tried to talk her out of it. So did my father.

"What time are we going for Grandpa?" I slip a nut into my mouth.

"I told them around eleven. They said they'll have him ready by then." She doesn't turn as she tells me this. Instead, she stirs the celery mixture into the bread crumbs.

"He doesn't have to stay there, you know. You can sign him out."

Now she turns around. Tears streak down her cheeks. "I don't think I can care for him anymore, sweetie. I feel awful about it." Her chin drops to her chest. She covers her eyes with her hands, and silent heaves come from deep inside of her.

"Mom," I say as I pull her into my arms. "Grandpa will get stronger. He's going to, I know it." It's my turn to avoid the reality of Grandpa's health.

She pulls away, wiping at her face with her apron. "It's more than I can do. Robert can't help, and with your Dad living in town now—I'm not sure if I can keep anything together anymore. You were right. Grandpa's getting bad."

When she mentions my father, I stiffen. He should be here helping. Doing his duty like everyone else. Isn't that why I'm golfing now instead of painting? So I can win tournaments and show him that our family is worth it? I can't help my mother like she needs me to, and that knowledge drives a wedge into my heart.

"If you quit that school and come home…" she says, more tears welling up in her eyes.

"You know I can't. Next month I try out for Q-School again, and when I make it, I'll be touring."

"*When* you make it…What if you don't, Bobbi? What if this is a wild dream that God never intended for you? You aren't Robert. Golfing was his dream—not yours. When we chase something we shouldn't, it never works out. I know that."

"What do you mean? What dream did you ever chase?" I don't want to sound mean, but my mother has always been a homemaker. Period.

She turns back to the turkey and begins stuffing

the breaded mixture deep inside of it. Handful after handful. I expect the bird to explode by the time she finishes.

"I chased your father." Her words come as a whisper. I step over to her and lean against the counter.

"You chased Dad?"

She slathers butter onto the wings and breast. "He didn't want to leave the tour. So I got pregnant knowing that was the only way he would. See?" She lifts her shoulders. "I'm the reason your father is the man he is today."

"You aren't the reason. He was fine until this spring." I want to say he was fine until the fire.

My mother stops her ministering to the turkey, wipes her hands on her apron. She grips her hips. "I'm not blind. Robert and his love of golfing might have kept your father here, but it didn't change who he is."

"But he stayed with us. That's what counts."

She raises her hands into the air. "Where is he when I need him?" Her question shuts me up.

I don't understand my father. I don't understand why he acts the way he does. But I do know he's needed in this family, and he needs a reason to be part of it. My becoming a pro will ensure that.

We finish the preparations in silence.

Robert has made his way into the kitchen and by ten forty-five, the table is set with our special china. He helps by pointing out whether I've placed the silverware correctly or not.

"Let's go or we'll be late." My mother shrugs into her winter jacket—the one with the fur around the hood. I reach for mine and give Robert last minute orders to not nibble on the pie crusts while we get

Grandpa.

The rehab center isn't far. Cars and families fill the parking lot of the dilapidated brick buildings.

Already, as I go through the front door, the odor of deterioration greets me. Grandpa shouldn't be here. I plan to convince my mother of that today.

"Is my father ready?" My mother speaks to a nurse at the desk in his wing.

"Yes, he's sitting right there." She points to a man hunched over in a wheelchair.

My heart rises to my throat. Can that be Grandpa?

I follow my mother who has made a beeline to her father. He raises his face when she calls to him. I swallow upon seeing his forlorn expression. Again, I choke back my sadness and reach out to his other side.

"Grandpa. It's me, Bobbi. Are you ready to come home?"

His eyes are glazed over. What kind of medication do they have him on? I want to stalk back and demand to see his chart, but instead I help my mother get him into his walker.

Yes, he walks—although slightly off-balanced. We find his coat and shuffle him out to the car where I put him in the front seat. Grandpa hasn't figured out yet who I am. It makes me want to cry, but I keep up the banter until he finally smiles as we near the river.

"We're almost home, aren't we?" he says to my mother. She pats his arm and swallows hard.

"Turkey is in the oven, Dad. I also made your favorite corn casserole."

"Corn casserole. Oh, yes. We have it every Thanksgiving." He smiles again.

Maybe it's just me, but I think his voice is growing stronger the closer we get to home. We pass over the bridge and drive beneath tree wings lightly coated with snow. Soon our driveway comes into view.

Grandpa leans forward. "Time to paint the place again, isn't it, girlie?"

"This spring, Dad. Maybe you can help us do it."

My father painted the house four years ago. He complained the entire time that Robert and I needed to speed it up. It seems we weren't the best of helpers. But then, why did I want to paint houses when I could paint landscapes?

It takes some doing, but we get Grandpa into the house and into his favorite chair. My mother and I exchange glances when he sighs and shuts his eyes for a moment before reaching for his glasses and the local paper.

"Let's check on the turkey." She pulls me into the kitchen where Robert is propped in a chair nibbling on pickles and olives.

I push the dish aside. "He seems better, doesn't he? Now that he's here?"

My mother doesn't answer me. Instead she opens the oven door and draws out the turkey. The kitchen fills with the delicious scent.

"Let me help." I hold the bowl while she spoons out the hot stuffing. How would Rockwell draw this scene? Mother and daughter doing kitchen duty in silence.

"He did seem to brighten as we came around the bend." She gives me that.

I take the steaming bowl into the dining room and add it to the mix of other amazing dishes my mother made. I stick my finger into the jellied cranberry, licking the sweetness before Robert catches me.

"Hey, who told *me* to keep out?" Robert stands by

my side and drapes his arm over my shoulder. "Grandpa is doing better."

"Tell her that," I say and then pull out the chair so Robert can sit. Standing isn't yet easy for him, and he walks carefully when he does. He slides down and looks up at me.

"She knows. She's just afraid."

"But he still needs to be home. As soon as I go on tour, I can pay for help."

My phone rings and I grab for it where I'd stashed it in my pocket. I glance at the number and shrug at Robert. It's Drew. The front room comes into focus as I hurry to answer.

"Hey, Happy Thanksgiving," he says.

My voice squeaks as I force out, "Thank you." I add, "Where are you?"

"About ten miles from you."

I glance out the picture window and see only trees that protect the river. "You came home?"

"Mark and I flew in last night on my mother's orders. Seems she wants the whole family for dinner. Anyway, I thought I'd call and see if you wanted to get together on Saturday. That is, if you're free…"

I pick at a piece of lint on my mother's good couch. I've been avoiding Drew all semester so I can concentrate on my golf game. I can't use that excuse here. Just hearing his voice sends chills to my stomach. But I don't need a relationship to mess me up. Not now.

"Lunch at the River Bend?" I say, knowing I will regret my decision.

"Noon? You've got it."

"Have a happy Thanksgiving with your family, Drew."

"You, too." I hear a smile in his voice, the same one that is in his eyes whenever I see him.

I slide my phone back into my pocket. Time to think about my own family. That's when I hear the back door open. I return to the dining room to find my father standing next to Robert.

"Dad. I didn't know you were coming."

Again my father is dressed immaculately. He wears a blue knit sweater, and his hair falls across his forehead. Not a good contrast to my mother who stands behind him looking like she flew in from the fifties. He stands and gives me a kiss on the cheek. I smell his cologne—the one he wore when he and my mother went out for their date night when I was a teenager.

Who's he wearing it for now?

My trust in my father isn't what it was, but I'm trying hard to change my opinion of him. I must or my entire plan is for nothing. It's evident to me that my mother still loves him. Even now, she guides him into the kitchen where they whisper together and she giggles. My dad has that effect on her.

"Good to see we're all here." Grandpa hobbles into the dining room. He finds his usual chair and works himself into it. "My stomach tells me it's about that time."

"I think you're right. I smell the turkey." My words sound falsely happy.

I leave Robert to entertain Grandpa so I can help in the kitchen with the final preparations.

My father is carving the turkey as I enter. "Good to see you, sweetheart. Wish I could have spent more time with you when I was in Florida, but business is business. I see you are walking better. Ankles can take time to heal, so be careful."

"It's much better now. I've only got three weeks until Daytona so I'm glad."

He turns back to my mother. "Do you think this is enough white meat?"

My shoulders and spirits fall at being ignored. I gather up the pitcher of water and bowl of applesauce before returning to the dining room. Minutes later, with the turkey placed in the center, the table is completely set. My mother has outdone herself.

Dad sits at the head of the table like he usually does, his hands folded together in front of him.

It's then that Robert speaks up. He sits beside me in his usual seat, as well. "I'd like to say grace, but first I'd like it if we went around and said what we're thankful for."

My groan stops at my lips. Not this ritual again.

"I'll start." My mother smiles at my father.

I want to choke on my spit.

"I'm thankful we are all here today. I'm also thankful that we're a family again."

A family again? I glance at my father who's smiling as though he knows a secret I don't know. My hope shoots up like a fast-growing weed. Maybe something has happened that I'm not aware of.

He takes my mother's hand and squeezes it.

"I'm thankful for all of you, too." He gazes around the table. "I'm thankful that Robert is on the way to good health."

Next to me, Robert shifts in his chair. He clears his throat. "I'm thankful to the Lord that He has healed me and that I can go on with my life. I'm thankful for great parents and that my sister and Grandpa can be here today."

Go on with his life? What does that mean? Yes, he's walking, but not too well yet. If he means golfing like he once did, then my brother is delusional. I know firsthand how hard it is to be good. I know the hours of practice that have to be endured. I know the frustration of hitting a ball and watching it go crazy. I know the wrenched feeling of losing and the harshness of competition.

Robert is not ready for that even if he can walk a course.

"Your turn, Bobbi." He pokes me in the arm.

"I'm thankful for Grandpa doing better and being with us today. I'm thankful that my ankle has healed and that I might qualify at Q-School next month." I shoot a look to my father who studies his empty plate.

Doesn't he get it? I'm doing this for him—for all of them!

Grandpa interrupts my anger and speaks next. "I'm grateful for a loving daughter who puts her sick Dad before herself."

A choking sound comes from my mother's throat. Guilt does that to you—cuts off your windpipe.

"We're so glad you're here, Dad," she finally manages to say.

Robert eventually says grace—a little long-winded, but that's my brother—and we eat.

My father hangs around to help dry dishes and plays a game of backgammon with Robert while I entertain Grandpa with stories of my school. More and more, he comes back to me.

I can't bear to return him to the nursing home.

After my father leaves, I corner my mother in the kitchen. "It sounds like Dad is intending to stay. Is he coming home?"

A grin creeps onto her face. "He's bringing his clothes back after the weekend."

"Why wait that long?" I play devil's advocate. Someone has to. My mother is too easily swayed. She must be sure this time. Even though my father's return is what I've hoped and prayed for, I want this time to be the one that sticks. Part of me hopes he's coming around because he sees me giving him back that part of golf he once had.

"He has work to do and it would be better if he stays there to do it. Besides, that gives me time to get Grandpa settled back in here." She turns to face me. Her eyes are filled with tears. "I can't send him back, Bobbi."

The fear I'd held inside me leaks out. "I wish I could help more. But with Dad here, you can do it."

My plan is coming together. Now I need to go on tour and win those trophies.

20

Amanda looks awful. Her butter blonde hair falls across her face, and her makeup is nonexistent. Her house looks worse. Never before would she leave tissues and dirty mugs all over the coffee table. Her housecoat hangs over the back of a chair and her socks are littered across the carpet.

We sit in her front room where her husband has left us to talk. She has decorated it in a traditional style—all fluffy and flowery. The painting I gave her for her twenty-first birthday hangs above the fireplace. She cried that day, too.

"I'm so sorry," I say for the third time since she greeted me at her door. Tears continue to spill down her cheeks. How many tears can a person cry in grief? Her pain fills the room like black smoke in a fire.

"What are your plans?" I stroke her arm that's covered in a wool sweater.

A shrug followed by another sob.

I'm not good at comfort. I should have sent Robert in my place. He would have prayed with her and said words that meant something. Instead, I sit and finger the growing hole in my jeans.

"Do you want to go for a drive or a walk? It isn't that cold out."

My best friend shakes her head no. I'm running out of options.

"She was our child, you know? A part of us, and

now she's gone." Amanda speaks in a whisper.

I lean closer, nodding.

If only she will continue to talk. "We had already named her. Jada. Pretty, isn't it?"

Again I nod, hoping she will go on. "You can have more, right?"

"The doctor says this was an accident." She buries her face in her hands. "But I'm afraid to try, you know? Afraid it will happen again to us. Am I crazy or what?"

"I think it's good to keep trying. Things happen. Maybe God needed her in heaven."

Lame, I groan to myself. God needed her? I bite my lip hoping she didn't hear me.

She did. "I've thought of that. Maybe it wasn't her time. Maybe she was supposed to live only that long. Everything has a time limit—like an expiration date. It's like God gives you a certain amount of time to do what you should and that's it."

I don't like where our conversation is going. "I think it's a little more complicated than that. We don't always know what God wants from us. We have to hope we do and then do it and see."

"Like you playing golf?"

I pull back. Where did that come from?

She turns to me—her eyes more focused than before. "Like you taking Robert's place. Doing what he should. Is that why you're doing it? To see if it's God's plan for you, and not for your brother?"

"What do you mean?"

"It's Robert who should be doing everything you are, but God stopped it. His time was over. So you stepped in and are trying to fill that role."

I shake my head. My best friend has known me a long time. "Don't worry about me. I'm worried about you and how you're coping." She's crazy with grief. I need to turn this conversation around. I search the room for her husband who hasn't returned since I arrived. Probably he needed a break, too.

"I'm not talking crazy here, Bobbi. What you're doing is crazy. You are a painter." She points to my painting. "You should be painting—not hitting a stupid white ball around the grass. Just like I'm meant to be a mother…" Another sob.

"What can I do for you?" I stroke her arm again as she bursts into tears. Maybe I can try one prayer. I search my brain for words that might comfort.

"Hey, let me pray," I say and take her hand. In her current state of mind, she doesn't remember that I, Bobbi, have never prayed out loud with anyone. All those years in church, I always let someone else take the lead. Through Sunday school, VBS, and in adult groups, I will sit quietly and let the more verbal speak up. Besides, I am not sure God will hear me—knowing how far away I am from Him these days. But today I decide to try for Amanda.

"Dear Lord, please take care of my friend here. She needs You and needs to know that her precious baby is in Your arms right now. Please fill her with Your love…" I stumble. The picture of her baby wrapped in Jesus's arms gets me. I remember the picture from my youth that hung on the wall of one of the church rooms—a picture of Jesus with children crowded at his feet.

Is Jada there now?

Amanda squeezes my hand and picks up where I leave off. She's like that—a caretaker. "Thank You, Lord, for my good friend, Bobbi. Please show her Your plans for her life, too."

~*~

My eyes still burn with tears as I drive away from Amanda's home. I still can't believe she thought of me during her own time of trouble. I guess that's why she's my best friend. My thoughts take me to town where I drive up and down the empty streets. I turn left onto Madison and drive past business after business. Max's on Madison, Pete's Office Supply, Downtown Hoagie Shop…until I come upon the place where I've spent so much time.

Arthur's Art Hut.

I park in front of the one-story building that houses more art than I could ever dream of producing. The sign in the window takes my breath away.

ART STORE FOR SALE

OWNER RETIRING

Arthur is retiring? The idea is disconcerting to me since Arthur is only in his fifties. He has a wife named Joyce who has been sickly. Maybe she's worse? I park my car in the lot next door and get out. Chances of finding him here are slim, but Arthur is the kind of shop owner who comes in almost every day—rain or shine—holiday or not. He's that dedicated to his business. He's also one persuasive salesman. When someone comes in looking for a painting, he makes sure they leave with something. Arthur can talk a dog off a meat wagon.

I rattle the door knob. The back lights shine in the office. Soon, Arthur opens the door.

"Bobbi! So good to see you again! How is Florida treating you?"

Arthur is a big man. When he hugs you, you know

you've been hugged.

"Good, I'm good."

He steers me inside and points to a stool at the counter. The smell of paint makes me dizzy. Dizzy with love.

"I saw the sign. What's going on? Why are you selling?"

He sits across from me, mopping his bald head with a brown paper towel. "It's Joyce. You know she has her allergies. Well, she tells me enough is enough. We're moving to Colorado as soon as I can unload this place."

"Colorado?" I echo. "But you love it here."

"I love my wife more." His grin shows his white teeth. Arthur is of Mediterranean descent and his bronze skin gives him a healthy appearance.

"Do you have any prospective buyers?" I gaze at the paintings propped on easels throughout the space. I know this shop well. I've spent hours inside here chatting with other artists and watching people fall in love with art.

His rounded shoulders arch. "Maybe that's why you're here?"

"Me? I don't think so. Even if I could, I don't have the funds."

"I plan to owner finance to the right person. And I think I'm looking at the right person."

My heart slips out of my chest and jumps up and down in front of me. The right person?

"I can't, Arthur. I'm a golfer now."

He waves his hand in front of his face. "Golfer, golfer. And when did golfing become your passion? Since your fancy brother Robert got hurt?" He leans closer. "I know what you're up to, and it won't work. I know where your love and your passion lives." Again he waves his hands around the store. "It is here, in this place, surrounded by what you're inspired to do."

I grasp the counter. "No, you're wrong. I can't."

"You're a fool, little girl. I say that with love because one day you will see the path that has been chosen all along for you. When you get over this silly notion that you are the blame for a stupid accident and come home. I can't wait too long, but I will wait awhile for you to come to your senses."

My senses? Is this what my choice looks like to others? I spin off the stool. "I need to go, Arthur. Please tell Joyce I wish her well." I lean forward and kiss him on his plump cheek.

His sigh reaches me. "It was meant for you to stop here today. You know that, don't you? God planned this meeting, not me."

God and His plans. What about free choice? I inch toward the door before the idea of owning this shop swallows me whole. "Happy Thanksgiving."

"You know I'm right."

I close the door on his last sigh, reaching my car as fast as I can walk. My heart is spinning upside down. Within minutes, I drive out of town and head toward the county park where I can walk and think clearly.

As I leave my car, snowflakes begin to fall. Light, airy reminders of past winters. I pull up my hood, shivering. The park is empty. No other fool would come here on this kind of day—dreary and overcast. But I'm here because I need to clear my head. I steer toward the overgrown path that leads up the hillside. My shoulders bend into the increasing wind.

Am I dumb to think I can pull my family together by taking Robert's place on the golf course? Has all my trying been for nothing? I dig my hands deeper into my felt-lined pockets. Maybe Arthur is right. Golf isn't my passion.

Or is it?

I think about the last game I played a few days ago with some of the guys at school. They still joke with me about my abilities, but I beat all of them. I play well—that much I know for sure. But does playing well mean it's something I should chase after the rest of my life? I paint well, too. How can I tell what my passion is?

I kick a stone, overturning it into the grass. I know my truth. I still can't get the smell of the art shop out of my senses. I love to paint. Besides, my father doesn't care that I'm golfing. My mother tells me to come home, and Grandpa doesn't know what I'm doing.

Maybe it's time to give up my quest to save my family and do what I love. Maybe it's time to think about me.

21

Our home is well lit—the bay window in the front room glimmers from the golden glow of my mother's Tiffany lamp. I often wonder why she turns that one on at the first hint of dusk. I would much rather the weightier standing lamp behind Dad's chair. Its cast is so much farther and deeper.

"I wondered where you went for so long. How's Amanda doing?" My mother greets me at the back kitchen door while I peel off my wet coat. I'm freezing and go to stand near the register where rivulets of heat rise up between my feet.

"I wasn't much help. She's pretty depressed."

The delicious odor of chocolate wafts to my nostrils. I inhale. My mother has been baking again. I don't know why, since we still have all those leftovers from yesterday. The glass cake dish sits on the counter. "What are you baking?"

She wipes her hands on her flowered apron. "It's a celebration cake. Your father is coming home today." She grins so wide her teeth could fall out of her mouth.

"Today?" I slide onto a stool.

She moves beside me. Putting her arm around my shoulder, she pulls me close and kisses my cheek. "It's all because of you and what you're doing."

My chest tightens. "Me? What do you mean?"

"Your golfing, silly. He told me how much it means to him, and he can't wait to go to your first tournament. He's thinking of flying us down to be there when you compete at Q-School."

I swallow the lump that has formed in my throat. "Really?"

"I've already asked the neighbor if she would stay with Grandpa and Robert for a few days. It will be like a second honeymoon for us." She leaves my side and spins around. I haven't seen my mother so animated in a long time.

"So you really aren't taking Grandpa back to the nursing home?"

"I told you I wouldn't. Not with your Dad coming home to help. And to think I tried to talk you out of going to Florida. You're my hero, Bobbi-girl." She swoops down on me again and gives me a tight hug.

I hug her back.

Her hero.

Funny—that's what I wanted to be once upon a time.

~*~

Later that evening, after my mother climbs the stairs to bed with my father, I slink down on the couch next to Robert, who's watching some mystery thriller. After a few of my sighs, he clicks off the set.

"What's the matter?"

My twin knows me. It doesn't matter if I try to fake my emotions, Robert always sees through them. Tonight is no exception.

"What do you think about Dad coming home?" I study his eyes. For what I'm not sure.

"I think Mom is happy."

"Just Mom?"

His bowl of chips finds its way to my lap. I munch and reach for his glass of cola.

Robert turns toward me. "Not just Mom. Me, too. I think Grandpa even perked up when he saw Dad's stuff come into the house."

"Hmm," I say, taking another bite of the chips.

"What's that mean? Isn't Dad's coming home what you've been trying to accomplish all along? He told me about wanting to see you play next month. Wish I could make the trip, but it might be too much walking."

"Of course, I was hoping he'd come home. And Grandpa, too. We're one big, happy family." I say this without smiling.

"Tell me what's going on. Now."

I drop the bowl and stand, wandering over to peer out the window. The snow has continued to fall. Our lawn looks ghostly now. White lumps rise here and there, and the tree branches swing low to the ground.

"I stopped to see Arthur today. He's selling the store."

"Good for him. Hasn't he talked about doing that for a few years now?" Robert pulls himself to a standing position. He joins me at the window. "Tell me what that means."

"It means what I said. Arthur is moving to Colorado."

"And what...you're going to miss him?"

I spin around. "Don't you get it? Owning the store was my dream! Now I don't get to do it—ever."

Robert steps back, his jaw opening and closing like a marionette. "Bobbi, you need to stop golfing." His statement is whispered, as soft as the falling snow.

Of course, he's right, but how can I quit now? I've

saved the whole dang family. "It isn't a choice I can make anymore. You saw how happy Mom is."

We both glance toward the stairway. Voices filter down. My parents are making up and putting aside their differences because my father has hope in my career. I have offered him a way out of a job he hates. Why, he's probably already planning on being my caddie.

"She'll understand. She wants you to be happy, too."

I shake my head. "No, it's too late."

Robert puts his arms around me and pulls me into a warm hug. I try to force my tears to disappear but they don't. Robert understands. We've talked about our broken family for years. Now that we're a real family again—neither of us wants to risk breaking it.

I sleep little that night. When morning shakes me out of bed, I remember my lunch date with Drew. I can't think of a way to get out of it. He's my teacher, too, not just a friend. The water from my hot shower pours over my head. My fingers ache along with my lower back. What if I get arthritis and have to quit golfing early in my career? I flex my toes, checking my body from top to bottom. Of course, I'm fit. Why would God let it be otherwise now that I have taken His course for my life?

"For I know the plans..." an old verse pops unbidden into my mind. *Do you really, God?* If He did, why do I feel like I do now?

My hair hangs wet around my shoulders. Drooping like my spirits. I remind myself that this whole plan was my own idea—no one else's. Not God's either, but evidently He likes it enough to make it work. When I go downstairs, my parents are sitting at the dining room table drinking coffee.

"There you are. I wondered when I'd see you today." My father rises from his seat and greets me with an unexpected hug. No, he isn't a hugger, so when I get one, the motion takes me by surprise.

"I have a lunch date with a friend."

I look at my mother. Is that lipstick she's wearing? Also gone is the baggy sweatshirt. Instead, she wears a silky blue sweater, the one I bought her for Christmas last year. What happened when I went to bed? She's transformed herself into a younger, prettier version of my mother.

"Will you be home for dinner? We're having roast beef." A twinkle actually forms in her eyes. Roast beef is my father's favorite meal. It has been ever since I can remember. Whenever he takes us out to dinner, he orders the roast beef, peas, and mashed potatoes and gravy. I can guess what dessert will be.

"And we're having apple pie for dessert," she adds.

Of course.

"I'm not sure. I'll call you with an update."

Disappointment rings her eyes, but she smiles, anyway. That's my mother, the everlasting peacekeeper. My father could rob a bank, and she would explain away his motives with the ease of a psychiatrist.

The skies make me blink from brightness when I go outside to my mother's car. She has been generous to let me use her sedan on my break. I dig through her CDs until I find the one I want and insert it into the dash. I have a short ride to River Bend, but I want to clear my mind. The scene in my dining room tells me my plan is working. My parents appear happy again.

So why am I not happy?

A squirrel runs across the road. I brake instinctively, not wanting to hit it. The car skids to the left. I tighten my grip on the steering wheel and take my foot off the brake. After a quick glance in my rearview mirror, I press the gas pedal, my heart throbbing in my chest along with the beat of the music. Accidents take only seconds. I know that from experience.

By the time I reach the restaurant, my shoulders have stopped aching and my breathing has slowed.

Drew is waiting by the door, wearing a forest green jacket. Funny, I expected to see him in khakis and a golf shirt. Instead, the collar of a sweater peaks out near his chin.

"Good to see you." He draws close as I get out of the car. We haven't talked much since I began in earnest to practice for Q-School. I've been aware of his glances when I walk down the hall at school, though.

"You, too. Here, I mean. How's it feel being home?"

"Strange. I haven't been back in a while. Cold, too." His grin lightens his eyes. Maybe it's just the sun that has decided to shine through the clouds. Either way, he looks adorable. Drew takes my hand in his. There are no other customers in the parking lot right now. It's only the two of us.

"How are you doing with your family?"

I shrug, my thoughts still focused on the way his fingers entwine mine. Deep warmth travels from my gut upward. This is not a feeling I want to have now, not with so much riding on my golf. I untangle our hands. Immediately, I see the effect my gesture brings to him. He raises his brows.

"My father moved back home."

"That's a good sign, right?"

"If he means it, yes." I turn toward the entrance. I would rather talk inside. I've found that our town is small enough that everyone knows your business if you are dumb enough to share it in public. Our booth will give us more privacy.

He follows me to where our waitress seats us. I order my usual. Burger and fries. Drew orders the same. As we wait, he crosses his arms on the table. I know what he wants. He wants me to pick up where we left off and spill my guts about my decision.

"Do you think you'll qualify?"

"I have to. Besides, I want to." I sip from the water the waitress brings us. "What about you, Drew? What are your future plans? How long are you going to teach instead of doing what you really want to do?"

My question makes him sit back. Folds ripple in his forehead. I've hit a nerve. Should I even be asking him about his private life? But he started with me.

"I enjoy teaching."

"Right."

"Where else can I get free golf?" A smirk appears on his lips. He knows I won't stop until I get answers.

"Life is about free golf," I say. "Nothing but."

"What would you have me doing instead?"

"Oh, sure, put it on me. You know what you should be doing. You're the one who should be qualifying at Q-School, getting ready to go back on tour and playing like we both know you can." How did I get this bold? I want to take back my statement, but it's too late.

He's already reacting. His cheeks color. "That's not an option."

"Like me quitting golf isn't an option."

We sit in our own silences, sipping our water until our meal arrives.

Drew takes a bite of his burger, swallows, and pushes it aside. "I'll make you a deal." His face is tense, his mouth taunt. I put my fry down. Whatever he's going to say, I'm sure it will be totally out of character for him. Drew has never looked so determined in the months I've known him.

"I'm listening."

He exhales a long breath. "You stop qualifying for Q-School, and I'll go back on tour."

22

Good-byes tear me up. Today is no exception. Mom has decided to drive me to the airport with Robert while Dad stays with Grandpa. First, I say good-bye to my grandfather who is resting in his chair by the window. He's wearing his comfortable plaid shirt today tucked into a pair of tan pants. I imagine how he must have looked on the golf course years ago. The word *debonair* pops into my brain. My grandfather still slicks his head of white hair back each morning with tedious care.

I bend down in front of him. His skin sags around his chin. His attention is focused on me. I believe he is with me 100 percent this morning. "I'm headed back to Florida now, Grandpa. I'll see you at Christmas."

His smile warms me. "Florida? I remember a few good tournaments down that way. Seems like I won a few of them, too." He winks and catches my hand in his larger fist. "You take care, Bobbi-girl. I want you to come home to us."

I want to come home, too. But not yet.

"I'll be back before you can blink," I say, repeating the phrase he always said to me when I was young and not liking the idea of him crisscrossing the country.

Next, I go up to my father. He's waiting by the back door holding my suitcase. "So, I'll see you and Mom in Daytona?"

"Planning on it. Wouldn't miss seeing you make

the tour." His smile makes my stomach lurch.

I take my bag and get into the waiting car.

Robert is sitting up front so he can stretch his legs.

I don't mind. I prefer being alone right now. The bare trees pass by as we roll down the road toward the highway. Winter has never been my favorite season. When I painted, I loved to paint the vivid spring and summer scenes. Maybe I don't like winter because it was winter the first time my father left us. The day before Christmas. I didn't know or understand what he was doing then—I only remember opening presents with my mother and brother at Grandpa's house without him.

Within an hour, we reach the airport. My good-byes to Robert and my mother take place quickly. I don't like seeing their tears. I wipe my eyes and hurry to board. Thank goodness no one sits next to me. They wouldn't have found me to be good company.

I have three weeks to prepare to compete in the most strenuous contest of my life. Drew's challenge comes back to me as does Arthur's about the bookstore. If it wasn't for the look on my mother's face yesterday morning, I would jump on either. Now I no longer have a choice. I need to say good-bye to my painting career forever.

~*~

"Are you kidding me?" My jaw hangs at least five inches.

"Sorry, kid. But business demands it."

The man I'm staring at is my boss—or my former boss—where I work at the theater. He's dressed in his white shirt and black pants as usual. I spot an oil stain probably dripped there from the popcorn I've seen him steal.

"But I need this job."

"Not enough business. Try some of the other stores in the mall. They might be hiring for the season. You can turn in your uniform over there." He points to the familiar employee lounge and edges away from me. He's never been that good of a boss, but at least he gave me hours that worked with my schedule.

What will I do now? I need practice time but also a way to make money to pay my rent and eat. I toss the jacket on the pile of dirty uniforms. Grabbing my purse, I stalk out of the theater vowing to never return.

Garland and red paper bells decorate the mall. Santa and his female photographer are busy enticing parents and their screaming kids. I shuffle past the food court, unaware of my direction. Why would they fire me over lazy Eddie who eats all the leftover tacos? I stomp the tiles a little harder. The recession has hit Florida hard. Getting another job might be near impossible. I had applied at all the retailers before getting the movie job, so I know my odds at success are low. Or zero.

I hear the voice before I see where it's coming from. "It's gorgeous. We have to buy it for the living room." Shrill mixed with excitement. A woman wearing designer clothes clutches her husband's sleeve while pointing to the painting propped on the easel. I'm standing in front of the art store.

"It is pretty amazing, isn't it?" Her husband doesn't sound as convinced.

The amazing picture they drool over is not amazing. A river scene with trees that looks like a four-year-old child has painted them. I edge closer.

"Look at the price tag. Two hundred dollars." The woman tips her head toward him. Her lips roll into a pout and she lets loose a long sigh. "I love it."

"Let's see if they'll go lower." He tugs her arm, leading her into the store where a perky saleswoman waits behind the counter. I step closer to read the artist's name. No one I recognize. But then a thought seizes me.

As the couple exits the store empty handed, I draw close, my mouth shakes but my determination drives me.

"Excuse me, but I noticed your appreciation for that painting."

The woman, who appears to be my mother's age, stops, glancing again at the work in question. "Yes, but they won't come down in their price."

"I don't want to seem nosy or anything, but I know an artist who could paint something better than that for much less."

The man's eyebrows rise. He suspects me of conning them. I give them my most trusting smile. "If you'll give me your email address, I could have her send you sample pictures of her work. I know you'll be pleased."

"She does landscapes? I want one of a river." The woman digs into her purse for a pen. She pulls out a scrap of paper and scribbles.

"That's her specialty." I think of all the river landscapes I've done. I'm sure I can paint from memory. Right now, I need them to agree to at least see my work. If I can sell a painting for 175 dollars, I can pay for a month's worth of groceries.

Her husband nods as she gives me the information. "I'll have her send you pictures tonight.

Will that work? If you like her paintings, she'll work one up and I'll bring it to you here in two weeks."

"That would be great. I can't wait to see what she's done. Tell her thank you from us." They smile and move away from me. I stand with the paper in my hand, convinced I did what I had to do. The clerk in the art store glares my way so I move toward the fountain, sitting on the stone wall. My hands shake as I place the number in my purse. Did I really peddle my work in a mall?

Robert tells me I don't think through what I do. If he had been with me today, he would have stopped my little transaction, telling me I don't have time to paint. Actually, I haven't picked up a brush in months, not since I decided I should be a golfer. But if it brings in money, then my reasons for doing it are good.

On my way home I stop at an art supply store. I carefully select a canvas and brushes and paints. I spend almost what I will make, but I plan to look at this as a start. When I get home, I print out new business cards from my computer. These I will hand out to anyone I meet. But before I go to bed, I pull up pictures I've taken of my best work and email it to the couple—Mr. and Mrs. Shore.

I can hardly fall asleep. Tomorrow I may have my first commissioned work.

~*~

I wake early, the morning light filters through my blinds. Getting out of bed has never been my forte but today I look forward to seeing if I have a new job. I turn on my computer and wait for the screen to appear.

Yes, my answer has arrived.

Dear Bobbi,

Please tell your friend that we would love one of her paintings. Keep us informed as when to meet you at the mall. Her work is amazing.

Amazing. My chest puffs. I sit back in my chair with a smile growing on my face. Soon though, sadness swirls through, replacing my joy. I gave up painting to save my family. What was I thinking? I read the email again. It's only a means to make money—not a career. Not a passion. A way to keep me golfing.

I can live with that.

I have to.

~*~

After class, instead of practicing, I rush home to set up my newly purchased easel. It isn't as nice as my old one, but it will have to do. I face the patio where I can watch my new neighbors move into Mattie's house.

Her necklace is cool between my breasts. I pull it out and study the string of diamonds set along the shaft. Did Mina ever forgive her mother for her accident? I let the pendant drop against my shirt.

I think of my grandfather and swallow the lump that rises in my throat. How long before he's gone? How long before I'm thinking of him in Heaven?

All these thoughts of Heaven and death are doing me no good. I mix together some colors and stare at my readied canvas. In order to paint a scene from memory, I need to transport myself back—back home to where I'm sitting by the river, watching the water rush over the shiny rocks.

My time travel doesn't take long. It never does. Robert says it's my gift—the ability to put myself in a scene and then to paint it for others to see. I shove his reminder away and focus.

I'm there, my toes floating in the cool water, the sun warming the back of my neck. Overhead, crows caw to each other while robins flit through the canopy of oak trees. My hand moves. Soft strokes outline the scene I see so clearly before me. Hours pass. I forget I'm hungry until my stomach reminds me.

I glance at the clock above the TV.

How long have I been gone? This isn't the first time I've left the present when I paint, but it's the first time that it's happened for so long. I set down my brush and blink hard.

I don't believe what I see.

I've painted my best work ever.

23

I don't have long. Q-School is in five days. Since I returned from Thanksgiving, I've managed to sell two paintings, a record for me in such a short period of time. The couple who bought my first painting loved it so much they asked if the artist would paint one for the woman's parents for Christmas.

"I'm sure that can be done." I also fessed up and gave them my business card, admitting I was the artist. They didn't seem to mind.

Actually, they laughed about it and then quizzed me on why I didn't tell them right from the beginning.

"I wanted you to see my work first," I told them. Their check burned in my pocket. I can't believe they gave me three hundred dollars for the painting, declaring it was far better than the original one they fell in love with at the store.

We had met by the fountain, and as I unwrapped my work, my tongue refused to form words. I had never before experienced such pain about selling a particular painting, but this one…well, it felt special to me. Maybe it's because I miss my home so much. I'm not sure. I'd even added a rocky path that led to the tree house. Even though I saw my scenes, I usually added something to them. This time, I added the tree house even though it belonged on the other side of the river in our yard. I wanted this couple to experience what I do whenever I return home—to feel the way the river pulls at my soul and the way the trees beckon me to join them in nature.

"It's beautiful." The woman had stared hard at my work, her gaze not moving from the scene.

It's the reaction I had hoped for.

"It's as though I'm there. I can even imagine how the river might cool my bare toes."

My heart skipped and I let my smile come.

It went too easy.

If only my golf was as good as my paintings.

Drew pulls me aside after class. "You haven't been practicing as much. Have you thought about what I suggested?"

My shoulders hunch around my books. "I'm ready for Daytona. And no, I haven't thought about your offer. I'm going to see this through, and I'd appreciate your support when I do."

"I'll be there. I told you I would." His eyes give him away. He doesn't like that I'm killing myself like I am. I'm glad I don't tell him about my painting. He'd use it to pound in his theory to me that I'm not meant to be a golfer.

"I'm heading to the range. Want to tag along and give me pointers?"

"Can't. I have something to do." He glances down the hallway.

"OK, well, I'll see you tomorrow then."

Drew's attention is focused elsewhere. He nods and heads down the hallway toward the school administrator's office. I watch as he stops before the door, checks his watch, and then enters.

"Hey, want to hit some?" The guy who sits behind me comes up in front of me. It's the first time Jake has asked me to play.

I pull my thoughts from Drew. "Sure. I was headed to the driving range but wouldn't mind going nine rounds."

We walk to the course with our bags and tee off. Jake drives his over 280 yards.

"You're good, Jake. I should have been watching you at the tournaments."

He steps back so I can take my swing. I don't get nervous anymore when I play with my classmates like I once did. I've beaten most of them already, and even though Jake is good, I know I'm better. I position my feet and loosen my shoulders. The day is warm, not at all like Novembers back home. Overhead, a few clouds fill the otherwise blue sky. I focus on a spot two hundred and fifty yards ahead of me. I swing.

"Sorry, Bobbi. Not sure I'd even want to count that one."

I can't believe my shot. I shade my eyes. My ball has gone left about a hundred yards into a bunker. A tremor shoots through my stomach. This can't be. I couldn't have hit the ball so badly.

"Want to take another shot?"

"No. We'll count it." I step back from the tee, my legs shaking from disappointment. Have I lost my edge? Q-School is only days away. A rookie player could hit better than I just did.

I climb into the cart next to Jake, shielding my face from his stare. Everyone in my class knows I'm trying out for the tour. His hand covers mine. "I won't say anything. You had a bad shot. Happens to all the pros."

Sympathy doesn't help. Instead, I want to bawl. What kind of pro lets one shot throw her? Me. I do. I stink as a golfer and I should know it.

Jake takes off in the cart and we find my ball first. I'm usually never in a sand bunker so hitting a ball out of one will be a challenge.

"I've got this one. Give me one shot and I'll be back in the play," I say as I climb out and grab my wedge. Two shots. Two shots it takes to get out and even close to the green. Maybe I shouldn't have stayed up so late last night finishing the painting. Maybe I should have practiced every day instead of trying to make rent money. But what choice do I have? I can't ask my father for money so soon after he's come back home. What a way to look like a failure. I can't even earn enough money to keep myself going? And my student loan doesn't come in until January with the next semester.

I improve as our game progresses but nowhere near the standards I should be.

Jake waves good-bye as I pack my clubs into the trunk of my car.

The school parking lot is nearly empty except for Drew's vehicle. What's he doing here so late?

I lock my car and go into the empty building. My shoes echo in the hallway as I make my way to his office. "Drew? Are you here?" I poke my head around the door frame. His office light is on, but he's nowhere in sight. "Drew?"

"What are you doing here?"

His voice startles me from behind. I spin around and see him holding two empty boxes in his hands.

"I noticed your car. What are *you* doing here?"

He edges around me and sets the boxes on his desk. "What's it look like? Packing."

"Packing?"

"Starting to. By the end of the semester, I'll be

history." One side of his lip rises, and then his full mouth opens into a grin. "Thanks to you."

I drop into the chair in front of the desk. "What do you mean 'Thanks to you'?"

He sits across from me and locks his fingers together. "I don't want to spend the rest of my life doing something I don't love. You were right. I went home that night and thought about what you're doing, and I don't want to do the same thing."

"Is that some sort of compliment? Cause if it is, it doesn't feel like it. So you're quitting teaching?"

"Take it how you want. I know I love to golf and I'm going to try it again."

I want to yelp and throw my arms around him. Instead, I smile. "I'm happy for you. It's what you should do."

"Sometimes making the right decision isn't always easy. I'll have to use my savings to get in shape again and practice non-stop before spring when I try out. And then if I make it, which I plan to, my life begins again."

"I can't believe you're actually quitting and doing this. I'm so happy for you. I mean it. We might even run into each other now and then."

Drew's mouth turns down. Gone is that cute grin. I know what's coming. "So you aren't letting it go?"

"My parents are coming to see me play at Daytona. I plan to make them proud. It's what I have to do."

"You don't have to do anything you don't want to do, Bobbi. Learn from me and my wasted years."

"You weren't at my house on Thanksgiving." My voice falls into a valley. "You didn't see the look of gratitude my mother gave me when she told me how much my golfing means to them. How my golf decision has put our family back together." I look away not wanting to see pity on his face or worse—judgment.

"So that's how it is."

"That's how it is."

He reaches across the desk to touch my hand. Warmth floods my face. I look down and see each individual hair on the back of his hand. It takes everything in me to not flip mine over and grasp his. What is it about Drew? We will never have a future together, especially now that we've made our career choices. But each time I'm near him I think, *what if*?

His fingers move and Drew clasps my hand in his. I bite my lip and look into his face. His eyes tell me what I've wondered all along. He has feelings for me.

"I'd like to stay in touch if we can." His voice is powerful. It reaches inside my heart and stomach and anything else it can get and squeezes tight—so tight I can't breathe.

"Sure."

Sure? It's the only dumb word I can manage. My focus is on my hand and how it feels in his embrace. I wriggle my finger. One finger. He squeezes tighter. I don't know how I will get out of this room without falling apart.

He makes it easier. Drew rises from his chair still holding my hand and tugs me to my feet in front of him.

I'm ready to faint with the rush of emotions I have kept down about him, but right now, they all seem to be rising to the surface at once.

"I'm sorry I wasn't more attentive to you. I'm your teacher and I have this whole set of rules in my head even though we're both adults."

"Yes, we're adults." Thanks for reminding me. I'm acting like a twelve-year-old. You know that feeling you get right before something happens? You know it's going to happen and you can't stop it and don't want to? Well, I get it.

Right before Drew bends over and lays a huge kiss on my lips.

I kiss him back.

I even remember to shut my eyes.

It is that good.

~*~

I decide to take a night off from painting. It isn't that I don't want it, it's because I can't stop thinking about Drew and how he kissed me and how we parted. Sure, I will see him a few more weeks and at Daytona, but our relationship is now forever changed. He kissed me. He told me he cares about me. He walked me to my car with his arm around my shoulder and I let him. I even let him kiss me again before I opened my car door. Right there in public in the parking lot. I let him kiss me knowing that our future together stinks. That probably there will be no future, as he'll be on one tour and I'll be on another.

I don't always act or think with my head. Robert can attest to that. He reminds me all the time of some of the dumb decisions I've made. Funny thing is, he backs this golf decision. Thinking of my brother makes me want to call him. I find my phone buried under my books and dial home.

Mom answers. "Bobbi? I'm so glad you called. I was going to call you." Her voice is faint, high-pitched—not her usual I-miss-you-honey voice. I sit on my couch. Expectation grips my chest.

"What's wrong? Something's wrong."

"I was going to call you after…after I got back from the hospital. I'm headed there now."

"Mom, who's at the hospital? Tell me!"

"It's Grandpa. Honey, he's not good. I need to go. I'll call you soon as I know more." The phone goes dead. I hold it in my hand and start to redial, but end the call. Something major has happened to Grandpa, and I'm sitting here mooning over a kiss.

I pace my living room, circling the stool and watching the clock. How long does it take to get to the hospital? My mother has a cell—she could call me while she's waiting on news. Did Grandpa fall again? When you're alone, you imagine the worst. I do because my mother sounded like it is the worst.

I'm stuck in Florida while my grandfather lies dying in a hospital. Is this how my life will be when I'm on tour? Too far away to be there when my family needs me? I glance at the calendar. Five more days until Daytona. If I drive all night I can be home in seventeen hours. I can check on Grandpa and then catch a flight to Daytona in time.

I pull up my computer to check flights out of Wilkes Barre to Florida. The cheapest flight costs over five hundred dollars. Stupid holiday travelers. I shut my computer off and look outside. The weather up north has been calling for snow. I saw it on the news this morning. I could get caught in a blizzard, and then what. So why drive? Why not fly? Again I open my computer and check the flights forgetting that I can't afford anything.

I'm stuck here while my family is going through a

trial. I kick the couch. My toe twinges, but the pain makes up my mind. Rushing to my bedroom, I pull out my overnight bag. After tossing in a few outfits, I find my keys, shut off the lights and lock my trailer. Seventeen hours is a long time, but I can do it.

24

I'm sick of the radio and the hits from the seventies, but it's the only clear channel I can get as I pass through Virginia. My phone has not rung since I started my trek north. My mother must have forgotten her promise to call, or she has been so busy with Grandpa that she can't get away to call. I hope it's the former.

So far, the roads have been clear, but the weatherman is still forecasting snow. I'm good in snow, always have been, but the thought of driving I-81 in a blizzard after driving fifteen hours does not thrill me.

The bell tone I picked out for my phone intrudes on my worries. I reach for my cell on the seat next to me and breathe a sigh when I see it's Robert. With a quick glance in the rearview mirror, I pull to the side of the road before answering.

"Tell me what's happening," I bark.

My brother will be honest with me, unlike my mother who thinks I'm still twelve and can't handle the truth.

"It isn't good. Grandpa is dying, Bobbi. I wish you could be here."

"I'm going to be there. You tell him—and I mean this Robert—you tell him I'm coming and he is to hold on to see me. He isn't going to die because I am telling him so." My voice is hard.

Robert doesn't have a clue how badly I want to bawl, but I need to keep focused.

"Can you catch a flight this morning? I'm not even sure if he's going to last another hour. He's that bad. I wish you were here. Mom's a wreck and Dad isn't any help at all. He keeps saying things like, 'It's his time. Let him go…' I think he just doesn't want to take care of him anymore."

"He's a jerk. Get him away from Grandpa until I get there. I mean it."

"Are you going to try to come up? I don't know…"

I glance at my mileage. A few more hours. He can hold on a few more hours.

"I'm in Virginia. Give me another six hours and I'll be there."

"Virginia? What are you doing? Driving home? Are you nuts?"

"Maybe. But it was the only thing I could do. Listen, call me if anything changes, but get Dad away from Grandpa. Tell Mom I'll be there soon."

"Drive carefully, you hear me? You must be exhausted."

I yawn and stretch my toes. "I'll be OK. I promise. Give Grandpa a hug for me. And Robert?"

"Yeah?"

"I'm sorry I wasn't there for all of you. I'm so sorry…" My voice breaks. I need to hang up before I do cry and I can't let myself do that. Not yet. Not when I have a possible storm to drive through.

"Don't even go there. Listen, I'm going to be praying for you. Now. And you do the same. I want you here in one piece."

Again, I choke back a sob for the love I have for

my brother and family. We hang up and I turn my radio off. The dark highway hugs my car as I careen back on the road north. Robert said I should pray. When was the last time I did? Does the one with Amanda count? It's been a while. Maybe God won't want to hear from me. Maybe I've been doing my own thing for too long?

"Dear God," I say, thinking it best to address him formally. "Dear God, I really need help right now for my grandfather. Please let him live until I can see him. I need to God. I do." I stop talking out loud. I start praying in my head, telling God all about how tired I am and how long this trip has been and my mother needs someone to take care of her and how Grandpa had this dream for me and now he'll never see me realize it.

I go on and on for over a half hour until the first flakes of snow hit my windshield. Funny thing, I'm not worried. Something about letting God know what's worrying me has taken away the ache that filled my chest since I drove out of Winter Garden.

~*~

By the time I pull into the hospital parking lot, my hands are shaking. I'm starving, as well. The granola bars I'd brought are long gone, as is the bag of popcorn I'd bought at a gas station in Maryland. The ground is covered with fresh snow. Tracks lead the way to the main entrance where Robert told me he'd meet me. He'd checked in with me every few hours to assure me that Grandpa was still alive and that I was, too.

The women's restroom is on the right of the information desk. I hurry inside and catch my reflection in the mirror. I look like a zombie. My eyes are bloodshot, my hair is a mess, and my clothes are wrinkly. Water helps with the hair, but otherwise this is who I am. Grandpa has seen worse.

I remember when I was ten and fell into the mud pit behind the barn. Robert and I had been playing tightrope on the fence when I lost my balance and tumbled into three inches of sloppy mud. Grandpa had come around the side of the barn right when it happened. While Robert laughed, Grandpa reached in his back pocket and brought out his handkerchief and began to wipe my face so I could see.

"You're still the prettiest girl in this whole town, sweetheart," he'd told me as I cried harder.

He picked me up and carried me on his shoulder to the house with a promise of a game of checkers when I was all cleaned up.

Who is Grandpa now?

My mother looks worse than I do. I see her first, slumped in the vinyl chair by the window of the intensive care waiting room. Dad is nowhere in sight. I'm glad. When she raises her head, she discovers me and rushes to her feet, arms outstretched.

"I can't believe you're here!" She touches my face and hugs me again.

Now I cry. Buckets.

My mother eases me to the chair next to her and begins to explain to me in a hushed voice that Grandpa is ill, very ill, and it's nothing short of a miracle that he is alive right now.

"I need to see him," I tell her once my sobs subside.

She nods. "Of course, but I want to warn you—he doesn't look like Grandpa." When she says his name, her voice dissolves into tears. This vigil has sapped her strength, and now I'm angrier at my father that he isn't holding her up.

She takes me to the ICU door. "Do you want me to go in with you?"

"Where's Robert?" I'd rather he was by my side.

"He's with your father in the cafeteria." She waves her hand toward a long hallway. I know where the cafeteria is. I can almost smell the food.

"I'll go in alone. I'll be OK." Again, I lie to my mother. I will never be OK. Not with seeing my Grandpa on his deathbed. But I shrug through the doorway and enter into a room filled with strange beeping noises and lights. She's told me he is in the bed nearest the window. Good. He likes looking outside.

I'm not sure what I expect to see, but not this shrunken form beneath a white sheet. His ashen face is covered with a clear oxygen mask, and his eyes are shut. I locate his hand beneath the sheet and grasp hold of it.

"I'm here Grandpa. It's me, Bobbi. Your Bobbi-girl. Come all the way from Florida to tell you I love you." More words form in my throat but won't pass through my mouth. I've told him I love him and that's what counts. Isn't it? Isn't him knowing he is loved the most important thing to hear as he lies dying? My tears stain the white sheet—making gray spots appear on his chest.

"Please wake up. Please wake up for me Grandpa."

I watch his face for a sign that he hears me. Anything. A blink. A twitch. Nothing.

"He can hear you. That's what the nurses tell us."

Robert. He puts his hand on my shoulder and I turn into his chest, hugging him with more strength than I thought I had left.

"He's dying. I'll never get the chance to make him proud."

"Hey." He pulls me away from him. I love my brother and the tender look he gives me as he cradles my cheeks. "He's been proud of you since the day you were born."

"I'm supposed to golf for him. I'm supposed to win those trophies for him."

"You are enough for him. He doesn't need trophies to be proud of you. Trust me. That's your own head talking—not his."

"How come you think you know so much all the time?" I give him a small smile. My brother is always taking care of me. I want to return the favor. I look into his face and see his exhaustion. "You need to sit down. Go on back out in the waiting room and I'll stay with Grandpa a few more minutes."

"Are you sure?"

"I'm sure." I turn back to the bedside and reach for Grandpa's hand again. He hasn't moved or groaned or made any sign of life since I've come in. I'll wait. I'll wait for him.

The nurse asks me to leave about ten minutes later. "He doesn't know I'm here yet."

"He does. He does." The nurse has a kind voice—the kind every ICU nurse should use with family. I reach over the bed and stroke the only spot not obscured by the oxygen mask on Grandpa's face—his forehead.

His eyes twitch.

I yank my hand back.

The nurse checks the closest machine. "Say something to him," she tells me.

"Grandpa, it's me, Bobbi. I'm here."

Again his eyes twitch until they fully open. He looks up at me—with an expression as if he wonders where he is. He struggles with his mask, until the nurse takes it off his face. My hopes soar—is he going to live? Is he getting better?

A light touch drops onto my arm. "Sometimes patients experience a surge of activity before…"

A surge. Before they die?

I lean over his bed, closer to his face. "I love you, Grandpa."

"You're my girl." His voice is barely a whisper, but I hear him. I turn to the nurse who is hovering beside me. "Will you get my mother?"

She disappears while I hold back my tears. Grandpa is staring at me, and then he winks. He winks like he does when he knows a secret I don't.

"Grandpa?"

My grandfather is a special man. He played golf and won more tournaments than most golfers ever will. He raised a daughter who loves him dearly. So I step aside when my mother reaches the bed.

It's her father, after all. I have my own.

~*~

I find Dad and Robert in the entryway of the hospital. My father gives me a hug when he sees me and begins to lecture me on the dangers of driving all night until Robert steps in and suggests I go home and crash for a few hours. His suggestion sounds good, so he drives my car home as I tell him what Grandpa said.

"The nurse says this happens before people die, but I think it means he's going to live. When I wake up, take me right back, OK. I want to be there." I chatter all the way into the house, forgetting that my brother just drove my car with both legs until I reach the landing.

"You drove!" I grab the banister and hop down the two steps.

"Surprise." His smile lights the room. "Doctor took off all precautions. I'm good to go, well, that is within reason."

"Why didn't you tell me?"

"I like surprises, too."

He's talking about me driving up from Florida. I decide to ask the question. "Can you golf?"

His face pales. "I don't need to. You're the golfer in our family."

I don't know what to say. Robert knows why I'm in school and trying out for the tour. He also knows I don't love it. I haven't told him that I'm painting again and selling my work for more than ever. Right now, I feel as though I'm going to fall off my feet, so I kiss his cheek and tell him I need to crash.

I sleep four hours. It's almost dark when I wake and realize again I haven't eaten anything since the popcorn. I stumble down the stairs and flick on the light in the kitchen. Mom's refrigerator is stocked with the usual supplies. I make a turkey and cheese sandwich before I wander into the TV room where Robert is talking on his cell. He looks up at me when I enter, putting his finger to his mouth.

"We'll be here." He puts his phone on the table and pats the seat next to him. "Grandpa is gone."

I spit the bread out of my mouth and sob.

~*~

The funeral will take place the day I should be playing in Daytona. My father offers to pay for the flight if I plan to go to Florida. He and my mother say they understand if I need to leave. Life is for the living. Grandpa would want me to go. He's gone—there's nothing more I can do. The platitude list grows longer the more I debate.

I brought my clubs with me in case Grandpa improved and I could still play. But play now? How can I?

I hole up in my bedroom. My eyes swell from crying, and I'm sick of all the well-wishers who have converged in our living room. Sure, we have lots of food to sample, but my appetite left the day we got the call.

My father is playing the perfect host, acting as though he and Grandpa were best of pals when, in truth, they weren't. Grandpa wasn't a fool. He saw the way my father treated my mother.

Robert has come in twice, once to pray with me—yeah, I let him. After all, God and I have grown a little closer since my trip—and a second time to tell me he'll back me with whatever decision I make.

I ask my mother if she can postpone the funeral. She looks stricken. Her father must be put to rest as soon as possible. It was his wish. He wanted to be cremated and his ashes scattered into the river.

"The river?" Something about his remains floating in my river repulses me.

Why not the back mountain or where Grandma was buried? She tells me no, the river was where he wanted to be. Maybe if I think of one of my good memories with him it will be easier, she suggests.

So I think about a time I spent with him on the river.

A memory comes to me that evening.

I was eighteen and had gone down to the river to set up my easel. The temperature hovered in the low seventies and not a cloud reared. Caterpillar green leaves cloaked the trees, and butterflies flitted from plant to plant.

If I remember correctly, it was the first time I'd ever travelled back in time to paint. I was not aware of his presence until he touched my shoulder and called my name.

"Where you at, girl? You look like you're in a trance."

My brush fell to my side. I'd been thinking about a time when we were seven and Robert and I had skipped rocks here. I looked up at my grandfather. "I'm sorry. I didn't hear you."

He slid to the bumpy ground next to my easel, wheezing with the effort. "I can see why. It's like you aren't here, but your hand is. Painting like fire." He leaned over to see my work, a low whistle coming from his chest. "You've got talent, Bobbi-girl. That you do, even if you have to leave the earth to find it."

I plucked at the grass. "I don't leave the earth. I just remember things that way."

"Never seen anything like it. Kind of reminds me how I focused when I played golf. If you would ever take golf seriously—you could use that talent."

"I'll never be as good as you were."

"You can be anything you want to be. Just put your head to it. That's what I did. You think someone like me was born into golf?" He laughed in that deep rich tone. "Shoot, my father had to beg the local golf club to let me caddie weekends in trade for lessons. Lucky thing I took to the sport, but it wasn't easy. Nothing comes easy."

"But you played the Masters. That took talent."

He rolled his chin. "Takes perseverance. Takes wanting to pursue your passion."

A knock on my bedroom door spills me back to the present.

Robert sticks his head in. "Dad wants to know if he should book it."

I run my gaze over my clubs that lean in the corner of my room. "Tell him yes."

Grandpa is counting on it.

25

The crowd surprises me. So many spectators out to watch Q-School. I can't help but think that my parents and Grandpa should be here with me. Instead, I flew in alone last night, found a rundown but cheap hotel room, and showed up an hour early so I could get some practice shots in. I honestly don't know what good a few shots will do.

I'm not ready for the biggest day of my life. My dream attempt of going pro happens in minutes. All I can think about is I'm missing the funeral of the man I loved most in this world. I reach for Mattie's necklace at my throat. I'd almost forgotten to put it on this morning.

Not that I'm superstitious or anything like that, but Grandpa told me he carried a coin in his pocket. He said it was one he found during his first tournament. Kept it ever since. I wonder where it is now.

I scan the line of people, searching for someone I know.

Drew texted this morning that he would be here today, even though he's busy with end of semester tests. I look again, willing his face to appear.

No one is familiar and now the people in charge of this whole show are telling me where I need to wait so that I'll be ready for my tee.

~*~

I'm next. The day is one of those classic Florida days—blue sky, cloudless, and low humidity. I could not ask for a better day. What I need, though, is a better attitude.

Drew has told me over and over that most of the game of golf is played between both ears. I believe him today. If I don't stop thinking about the funeral and my family, I'm going to fail, and then where will that leave us?

Dad would give up and move out, and then Mom might lose the farm because she wouldn't be able to afford it.

Even though Grandpa won so many tournaments, he used all his money to travel when he could, and then take care of Grandma before she died. I think Mom once said he was virtually penniless—except for his social security benefits—by the time he paid the burial expenses.

I need to make pro. I tell myself this over and over as I wipe my hands and adjust my cap. I tuck my shirt in for the fifth time and then bend to check my golf shoes. What else can I do?

Robert's final words to me come to mind.

"Before you take your shot, pray that God will guide every stroke and take you where He wants you."

So OK, I will pray. I'm at the end of my wits anyway as to what more I can do. I glance around at the other golfers. Each one looks calm and ready to do this. My hand is shaking.

I don't have a choice. I close my eyes and whisper the words Robert told me to say. I ask God to show me His plans for my future and that hopefully it is as a golf pro.

They announce my name.

~*~

My father greets me at the Wilkes Barre airport two days later. Alone. He doesn't hug me, but grabs my clubs and luggage.

I ask him how Mom is doing, and he shrugs saying something like she'll work it through.

I study his profile. His lips are drawn together. A muscle twitches in his chin. I recognize this expression and dread the forty-five minute ride back to our house. The last time he looked at me this way was the day of the fire, the day I destroyed all his hopes and dreams. Yesterday I did it again. I didn't qualify. The months and months I spent in Florida developing my game mean nothing now. I wasn't good enough.

My whole family can attest to that. I'm not even sure I can spend the night before I get in my car and start my trip back south. As soon as I say hello to Robert and Mom I plan to start driving. What else can I do?

I blew it.

I stretch my feet and let my head fall back against the headrest. My stomach hurts. My head aches. My fingers are tight. Someone, throw me into the river with Grandpa. When I think of him, I realize how empty our place will be now. His chair. Did Mom get rid of it? Or will it always remain as a reminder of him?

"So what are your plans now?" My father's voice is tight and tinged with disappointment.

"I don't know. I need to drive back to Florida to get my stuff."

"Plan on coming back and hanging around here?" He grips the wheel tighter. His knuckles appear white to me.

I'm not sure how to answer. I don't know what my plans are. I've got one more semester of school to graduate, but then what? Work behind the counter of a pro shop? Sure, I can try again.

Robert said that to me when I called him, bawling. "You can try next year. Work on your game all summer and do it again."

Right. Next year. By then Dad will have dumped us, and we'll be forced to live in an apartment over the bank.

Mom got on the phone after Robert and told me it was OK. I had tried, and that's what counts most.

I shut my eyes. Isn't that what mothers are supposed to say? *Try your best. Win or lose, it doesn't matter.* When I took that final shot, my dreams evaporated. I was no one's hero. I couldn't even be one to myself.

We veer into our driveway.

Dad still hasn't said much more than to ask me about my plans. He shuts off the engine and turns to me. "I want you to know I didn't count on you winning. Robert was always the better golfer in this family, anyway. Maybe someday he'll get his shot."

His words explode into my chest. They never expected me to do well? He's been waiting on Robert all along?

I clamp my lips together and yank the car door open, slamming it shut.

My father follows me into the house with my belongings while I race upstairs to my room, throwing myself across my bed.

"Bobbi?" Robert taps on my door. "Can I come in?"

"I want to be alone."

"Let me come in. Please." He's persistent. Always has been.

I roll over on my side and see him standing in the doorway. I should have locked the stupid thing. My eyes are watering and my nose runs like a fountain. He hands me a tissue from my dresser and then scoots next to me on the bed. I snuggle my head against his shoulder, corralling my sobs.

"He never expected me to qualify! He said that. He never expected me to be any good. It's about you, Robert. Always has been for him, and I should have known it."

"That isn't true. It's about him. It isn't even about me. Dad made his choice years ago, and now he can't live with it. He blames everyone around him for his mistakes. He didn't have to get Mom pregnant. He didn't have to quit the tour. But he did. And it isn't your fault."

"But I made them happy. Doesn't that count?"

"You can't fix what you didn't break. You didn't make this mess. Mom and Dad are the only ones who can work this out."

I blow my nose. "And when did you come to this conclusion?"

"Maybe when I told them last night that I don't ever want to golf again. I'm going to college to become a preacher."

I roll away from him and stare into his face. "You're kidding, right? If you think this joke will make me feel better, it doesn't."

Robert shakes his head and that smile appears. "I

start Bible college in January."

"You're serious?"

"As serious as you were about saving the family. It's what I'm supposed to do. My accident was the final piece of the puzzle. I had time to think and study my Bible and pray. And I also saw how you were doing something you didn't want to do. That's how I kept feeling about the thought of golfing again. Sure, I was good, but it was Dad's dream and not mine. One night it came to me that God wanted me to share His plans for us rather than going off on my own merry way. I called the school and sent in an application." He reaches for my hand. "Be happy for me."

"I am happy for you. I'm just in shock. So does Mom agree?"

He tugs me to my feet. "She's on board." He rolls his eyes. "Dad is another story. I love him, but I have to follow God's will for my life, not Dad's dreams. You need to do the same. Figure out what makes you happy and what God's plan is for your life and do it. Dad has to work out his own issues."

"I don't think I can even talk to him now."

"Then don't. But you will someday. We'll figure this one out. So what do you say, want me to beat you at a game of chess?"

The long trip back to Florida beckons me. "Not this time. I'm going to grab my stuff and return to school. Maybe by the time I get there I'll know what I should do."

His smile fades, but he helps me ready my stuff and convince Mom that I don't need two garbage bags of snacks. After a round of hugs and a nod to my father, I put my car in gear and pull out of the driveway. When I see the river, I turn into the access road, shutting my car off. I can't leave without one more good-bye to Grandpa.

Robert told me my mother released his remains at the dock. I force myself to walk down to it and stare into the murky December water. I don't plan on returning for Christmas. The thought of being alone doesn't faze me. Everything has changed at the farm with Grandpa's death. No longer will I greet him in the morning and hear his laugh. I fold my hands in front of me and whisper to him. "I love you, Grandpa. I hope you tell Arnold Palmer hello and shoot your best game yet."

I've got seventeen hours to think. Seventeen hours to wonder why Drew never showed up or called.

26

Only a week of classes remains until winter break. I pull on my jacket and drive to the school, determined to avoid Drew if at all possible. He let me down when I needed him the most. Doesn't he realize how scared and nervous I was? He's been through it before. If his no show is an example of how we're going forward with a relationship, then he's mistaken.

I miss a red light by seconds. My car stinks from trash from my hurried trip home, and I vow to clean it after class. No more long practices for me. I'll finish the week and then decide what to do. On my trip back I thought about how it would be living with a father who has no use for me. I've done that long enough. But where else can I go?

My options are limited, at best. I can finish college and try to get a job here in Florida, pay my loan, and maybe try Q-School again, or I can go back home, get a job, and move out. Robert says to look for God's finger on my life. He says God will open the right doors if I'm looking and not trying to do my own thing.

So far, all the doors have slammed in my face.

I'm late. All the school parking spaces are filled by the front so I drive around back to park. Drew's class is my first one. I grab my pack and enter the hallway.

Another guy waits outside the door, his hand poised to turn the knob. He goes in.

I take a breath and reach for the knob next. It

won't budge. I look through the glass and see Drew's back to the door. I tap on the frame, waiting.

All eyes turn toward me except his.

Drew opens the door. "We missed you."

I step around him. "Save it," I say in a low voice meant only for him. He lets the door close and straightens his shoulders. I don't feel sorry for him. He's the one who let me down.

A few of the guys say hi as I find my seat at the back of the room. Maybe I was wrong to return. I have nothing here now. I can't even bring myself to look at Drew as he teaches. Why did I think we could have anything? He's going on tour and I'll be who knows where?

Life is too uncertain. I think I should be doing one thing, and then it all falls apart. I slump on my desk, scribbling nothings on my paper. My head hurts, this time from lack of sleep. Even though the sun is out, I don't care.

Finally, I look up front when I'm sure Drew is turned around. When I started here I thought he was this big jock. I was so wrong. My lips purse. He's worse than a jock. He's selfish. He could have found a way to be in Daytona, but didn't. If I had an ounce of energy left in me, I would walk right out of here now. Go to lunch. Clean my car. Take a nap.

I don't have an ounce of energy left or guts in me for that matter. I sink in my chair and find a dried up hard candy in my pocket. I stick it in my mouth, sucking on wintergreen.

When class ends, Drew hands out a homework assignment. As he passes my desk, he scribbles something on the paper. "See me afterwards," it says.

Butterflies churn in my gut. I draw out my pen

and cross through his words.

In his dreams.

Later that night, I take inventory of the place I call home. Since coming to Florida months ago, I've purchased two folding chairs. No new clothes. No other furnishings. If I got a job paying more than minimum wage, I might be able to survive—that's it. The newspaper catches my eye. It's a free sample, and so I thumb threw it searching for the want ads. Barmaid. Waitress. Park attendant. Not a whole lot of choices.

The minutes tick by. I heat a bowl of tomato soup and discover my crackers are gone. I'll have to eat it with bread the way Grandpa liked his. Soggy and hot. When I think of him and home, tears well in my eyes and I shove the bowl away.

This is my life. My opened suitcase sits in the corner of the room begging me to unpack it. Last night, I pulled out my pajamas but that was all. For the next twenty minutes, I hang up my clothes and contemplate a trip to the laundry. Instead, I rinse a few items by hand. Wet jeans hang down my bars.

The thought of coming home to this kind of life, day in and day out, depresses me. But surely not qualifying for the tour is an answer, isn't it? Doesn't that mean I'm not good enough and my coming here was all a pipe dream? What was it Mattie said? Superman doesn't exist? I finger my necklace. Mattie was a good friend, and I didn't even recognize it at the time. I saw her as an old lady with too much time on her hands. How wrong I was. If only I had taken more time to talk with her, get to know how she survived her sad life.

My phone rings where I left it in the bathroom. I

race to answer it and see Robert's name. "Hey, how's college boy?"

"Wanted to know how your first day back went. I sure wish you were going to be here for Christmas. It won't be the same. Dad's been mucking around like some old mule, and Mom's been nervous as two hens around a rooster. I don't think their being together again is going to work."

I grip my phone. "Because of me. Right?"

"Not because of you, brat, because of them. I even went as far as to suggest counseling, and Dad looked like he wanted to tear my mouth off. Mom left the room. Guess it isn't cool when your kids act more like the adults."

I curl into my chair. "I'm so sorry you're the one stuck seeing all this. Wish I was there, but the way Dad acted toward me I probably would be mouth-less." A giggle at the picture of both of us without a mouth rises up inside me. The situation is far from funny, but Robert has this way of making everything sound funny or at least not as bad.

"I drove past the art store. The "For Sale" sign is still up."

The store. "Don't even talk about it. I barely have enough money to pay my rent and if I quit school, I'll have nothing."

"So what's the answer? Finish and try to get a job there or what? I wish you had never gone. This place isn't the same without you."

Robert isn't the same because of me. The events from the day of the fire loom in my mind. If I hadn't been so bent to become a famous artist, my family would still be intact.

Not even my father acting like he is now can

convince me otherwise. He loved caddying for Robert.

Robert loved golf even though he says now he doesn't as much as he wants to preach.

"Are you there?" he asks.

"I'm here. I really screwed up my life, didn't I? I'm so glad you know what you want to do." I sound pathetic. So much that I consider hanging up before I go on further.

"Come home. Come home and I'll help you figure out what's next, but hiding away down in Florida isn't going to solve anything. Come home and we'll face whatever your life is to be together."

His words wrap around my heart as I think about our house—our farm and my special place by the river where I said good-bye to Grandpa a few days ago. I can't imagine never living there again.

"I'm not sure I can drive it so soon." Seventeen hours. I could be home by Christmas.

"You can do anything you put your head to. You're my twin." His voice turns husky. I see him sitting on the bottom step by the foyer, his feet stuck out in front of him covered in those corny red socks I got him as a joke for his birthday.

"Even starting over after failing so miserably?"

"I won't let you do it alone."

Tears fall and I lick the salty flavor. They run off my chin and drop into the carpet at my feet. Crying never felt so good. But saying yes to my brother feels better.

27

Amanda is home, sitting in front of her undecorated fireplace. Usually, the entire room is garnished with garland and two heavily ornamented trees by now. Her mourning is still evident in the house void of any Christmas decorations.

I stop here before finishing my trip to the farm, wanting to put off the inevitable meeting with my father as long as I can. My hands cramp from the all-night driving, and I could kill for a huge omelet.

She sits opposite me, a tight smile on her face.

I guess I expected more.

"So you quit college? What are you going to do now, Bobbi? There aren't many options around here. You know that."

I tuck my gloves inside my coat pocket. She hasn't even asked for my jacket. "I don't know yet. I couldn't stay in Florida. I guess I finally figured out that golfing isn't my answer."

Her interest piques and I catch a spark in her eyes. "Answer to what?"

"My family." I hunch closer, placing my elbows on my knees. Maybe if I share, she will, too. I had hoped by now she'd be more like the best friend I knew. Not this hollow imposter.

"Whatever are you talking about? Your family? You mean the thing with Robert wanting to golf? You taking his place? About time you came to your senses on that one." She practically snorts.

I straighten. Maybe talking about me isn't the way to go.

"So how are you feeling now?" I ask.

"Now?" Her eyes grow vacant again. "Not sure what you mean. About Christmas and the baby? Jim wants to try again, but I'm not ready. Not really. Maybe not for a long time." Her voice finally gains emotion. "Why do I want to put myself through such pain again? For what? The doctor said it was a fluke…" She spreads her hands and then wrings them like some scene in a Shakespearean play. The air is thick with her stress, and I smell something burning in the kitchen.

"Are you cooking something in the oven because I smell something…" I wrinkle my nose, and she bolts from her place on the couch, running into the next room of the house like she's on fire.

"My cookies." A wail follows.

"Everything OK?"

Seconds later, Amanda returns with a tray of burnt cookies in her hand. A smile forms on her lips—the first one I've seen since I arrived. "I made them for you after you called. Sugar and cinnamon. Sure don't look like much, do they?"

I meet her in the doorway. "I bet they're good anyway." I reach for one that isn't as dark as the others.

"Don't you even eat that, Bobbi. You'll barf." A giggle erupts from her lips.

I ignore her warning and take a bite, chew, and swallow as gracefully on burnt cookies as I can. "Try one. Really, they're good." I point to the one next to the empty spot.

She looks dubious but sets down the tray and

scoops up a dark golden one.

She takes a nibble, a small nibble, but it's a start. She giggles again. "I remember when you dared me to eat worms behind the garage that one summer. I threw up three times. Never told my mother, even though I wanted to." She pats my arm through my thick coat. "Why on earth haven't you taken that thing off yet?"

Ah. Amanda. "You haven't asked me."

She points to the hall closet. "Hang it up in there. Now…before I have to tell you again and you know how I hate repeating myself."

I laugh.

Repeating herself is Amanda's specialty.

"I can't. I need to get home before everyone is asleep."

"Are you sure? You can spend the night here." She glances upstairs, and I know she's thinking of the baby's room.

"Naw. I want my own bed, but thanks, anyway." I hold my arms out and she comes in for a hug.

"You're the best friend I have. Thanks for putting up with me, and I'm so glad you're home." Her voice breaks.

I can't answer because my own voice takes a leave of absence. I nod and smile as I rush to the front door. The past few weeks have been a barrel full of emotional scenes. I'm too tired tonight to cry anymore. "See you soon." I manage to say as I escape to my car. The icy wind whips my hair as I hurry to start the engine.

Amanda stands in the window waving as I pull away. It's a habit we both fell into when we were little. We would wave good-bye as long as we could see each other's car. One time I had to go to the bathroom so I left my spot at the window, putting Robert there instead. He waved as I would, but Amanda called when she got home.

"That's cheating," she said with a pout in her voice. "I don't have a stand-in like you do."

A stand-in. I think of that phrase now. Robert and I have always stood in for each other whenever we could. Maybe it isn't fair that I have him. Maybe Amanda's mother should have had more children after her. But I do have Robert, and knowing he's here for me means everything.

I don't live far from Amanda, but driving from her place to mine seems like the longest miles I've driven during the entire trip. I round the bend to see the moon lighting up the farmhouse like a spotlight. Shadows fall from the surrounding maples, making me want to pull the car over to take in the scene.

Next, I discover blue Christmas lights blinking in the front windows and red ribbon-wrapped wreaths hanging over the windows. The decorations are the same each year. My mother spends hours transforming our home into a kind of wonderland. She has done the same this year—even with the passing of her father. The Christmas tree is lit in the front room and I can imagine wrapped gifts already piled beneath it.

I slump against the seat. How can I face my father after the way he looked at me at the airport? Part of me thinks it's a mistake returning home. I don't have anything here except memories—good and bad. Maybe I should have started my life over someplace else—Denver, Seattle?

I shut the car off and place my feet in the snow, crunching back to the trunk. Tonight I grab only my suitcase. The rest of my belongings can wait until tomorrow.

The house is dark except for the tree in the front room.

"Mom?" I call out and wait for an answer.

"In here. Bobbi?"

I set my luggage on the kitchen floor and make my way to the front of the house where my mother is standing with her arms spread wide. She pulls me in for a deep hug. "I'm so glad to have you home. Are you OK?"

Of course, she asks how I am. I nod and drop into the chair opposite the couch where I can tell she's been sitting as her folded magazine is plopped against the pillow.

"Tired. Where's Robert?"

"He went to bed early. He said he had a headache." A faraway looks enters her eyes. Is she worried about more than Robert's headache?

I settle across from her and kick off my cold shoes.

The tree twinkles in rhythm to a Christmas melody that the lights play over and over. A leftover decoration from my childhood. And I was right—gifts are piled below the tree. A sense of warmth fills me. Where else would I want to be at Christmas?

"Do you want tea? I can make some. You must be hungry, too. There are sugar cookies."

"The kind with the green frosting?"

She smiles. "Let me get you a plate." My mother leaves me alone to stare at the tree and take in the quiet of the house. Where is my father? Now that I think of it, I didn't see his vehicle in the driveway next to my mother's car. I glance around the room. Nor do I see his slippers or the sweater he usually wears on cold nights.

My mother hands me a plate and a mug of tea. "Here you go. Now tell me about the drive up. I tried to call you a few times, but it went right to voice mail."

"Mom, where's Dad?" Call me blunt, but I need answers.

She plucks at the gaudy afghan I crocheted when I was twelve—pink and white. "I was going to wait to tell you in the morning."

"Tell me now. He's gone again, isn't he? Right at Christmas." The cookie in my hand crumbles. I set the plate on the coffee table before I crush more. How could my father do this to us?

"He left yesterday. Bobbi, this time is for good. I'm not going to fool myself anymore. I know what kind of man he is"—she wipes her eyes—"and I'm not blind, even though I know you think I've been over the years. I wanted everything to work out, but this time…"

"So he's a jerk. Right? He left us because I didn't qualify, and he can't live his life as a golf caddie. Is that it?" My tone sounds harder than I intend it to be, but I'm angry. Not so much at myself—and that surprises me—but at the man I call my father.

"He's your father. Remember that in the coming weeks. We mutually agreed to end our marriage."

"It's over? For good?" Words hurt my throat. They shake and come out sounding high-pitched and that makes me angry too. I rise to my feet and cross to stand in front of the tree. What a joke. "What happens now? He moves out and we stay here?"

She shakes her head and looks down at the carpet. A Berber carpet Dad ordered installed three years ago when he decided the wood floors were too cold. I miss the dings in the wood. "We're going to have to divide our assets."

"Sell the house? Are you serious? This is our farm. It's Grandpa's farm! We can't sell. Where would we live? You love this house." I quickly sit by her and clasp my hands in my lap. "It isn't fair, Mom. Tell him you won't."

She's crying now. I'm so good at making people cry. "It isn't like that. The courts will make me sell unless I can buy him out."

"Buy him out?" So all I can do is echo her like some dumb parrot. "Do you have any money? Did Grandpa leave you anything?"

She's crying harder now and wipes her nose on the sleeve of her sweater. "He went broke from Grandma's illness. You know that. There's nothing. I have nothing but my clothes. Dad bought everything else."

My shoulders fall as I heave out a breath. Nothing. Dad can make us sell the farm so he can have his half. "Maybe he won't. Maybe he'll change his mind. I'll talk to him. Make he'll see we need this place."

She lays her hand on my knee and faces me, her expression taut.

"You will not ask him. This is between your father and me. I know you want to help, but you can't this time. You can't. No one can."

I can't help. But I want to. Maybe Robert and I can come up with something—a way to keep this place so Mom can live here and not in some low-income high-rise. I think of the condos at the edge of town along the river, with blue balconies and clotheslines on each one. My mother can't live there. I won't let it happen.

"What's Robert say? You've told him, haven't you?"

"He knows. Dad told him when he left. I'm

surprised your father doesn't have a black eye with how angry your brother became at him." A smile cracks one side of her mouth. "You would have been proud of Robert. He controlled himself well."

The furnace kicks on. How long before I forget such familiar sounds? I fold the afghan across the cold on my legs. My eyes are heavy, even as upset as I am. "I'll talk with him in the morning. We'll think of something. I promise."

"There's nothing to think about. I'll get a job. Now you go upstairs to bed, and I'll shut the lights off. Tomorrow will be a better day."

I take my mother's advice and slip up the stairs to my room. I don't turn the lights on because if I do, I will cry. I love my room. I don't know how I can say good-bye.

~*~

My favorite time of day is when the sunlight first streaks through my window. This morning is no exception. My curtains are still open as I didn't mess with them last night, so I have a clear view of the mountains in back of our home. The barn's cupola glistens from melting ice and the bare branches that held my tree house twinkle in companionship.

My toes find the end of my bed and I stretch. First my arms, then my legs. Part of me wants to close my eyes into the nothingness of stupid dreams. The other part, the responsible part, knows I need to be here for my mother today and the coming days.

Tomorrow is Christmas, too. We need to come up with a plan before then, or we might as well take the tree down now.

Robert and my mother already sit at the kitchen table when I enter, scuffling in my dirty clothes.

He rises and gives me a big hug. His shirt hangs on him, making him look as though he's ten years old again and dressing up in Dad's work clothes. "Welcome home. I missed you." His smile is in place but I know it's for Mom's sake.

She gets up and fills a cup with hot water and sets in before me with a tin of teabags.

"How did everyone sleep?" My voice rasps. I clear it and ask again.

"So you know." Robert doesn't have to say anything else. His gaze crosses to my mother who busies herself with her scrambled egg. It looks cold and dry, but she persists in picking at it.

"Mom told me last night. What are we going to do?"

"You're both not going to do anything. It'll work out." Finally, my mother pushes her plate away and leaves the room.

Robert sighs and his shoulders slump.

"Afraid there isn't much we can do. Dad's made his mind up. He's done. He's planning to sell his business and move south. He needs the money from the sale of this farm to do it."

"We need to find a way to save this place. It was Grandpa's and he wanted Mom to have it, not Dad." I cross my arms the way I do when I want my way. It used to work. Not anymore, though. I study Robert's outfit again. He's wearing a tie, too. "Where are you going?"

"I told Dad I'd meet him later at the office to discuss options." His lips turn down.

"What options? What are you talking about? And

since when do you dress all up to talk with Dad?"

Robert turns his head toward the backyard. He isn't a good liar, nor can he avoid the truth well. "I'm not only meeting Dad. He has this friend who wants to meet me. This guy wants to talk with me about going to Florida, too, to play golf."

My mouth drops open. "You're kidding, right? You're going to college next semester to become a preacher. Why would you even remotely consider moving south with him after what he's done to Mom?" I don't believe we're having this conversation.

My brother has lost his mind sometime in the past week. I watch for signs that he's joking—a curve of his lip, a twinkle in his eye. Nothing. I think I'm going to be sick. "You can't save Dad. You told me that yourself. And what about your promise to help me find God's plans for my life? Was that a lie, too?"

He stands and empties his cup into the sink. "Maybe I was wrong about going to school. Maybe I want to play golf instead."

My glance goes to his leg. He notices and shifts his stance straighter. "You're crazy, Robert. Do you know that? He's made you crazy, and I won't allow that." My voice rises with each syllable. "Dad has destroyed our family, but he won't get you."

"Listen to you. You're the one who's nuts. I'm doing what I want—unlike someone who thinks she's a golfer and isn't."

Ouch. I brace myself against my chair. How can he say that? Someone once told me that love and hate are close emotions. I get that. I get that in a huge way now as I glare at Robert.

He holds my stare for only seconds and looks away.

"I'm out of here. Tell Mom I'll be back later." I shove away from the table and grab my coat from the hook in the back doorway. My keys are still in the pocket, and although I haven't brushed my teeth or changed my clothes in three days, I don't care. I need to get space to think, and that won't happen at home where Mom is bawling upstairs and my brother has turned into the biggest traitor on this earth.

28

Not many places of business are open early the morning of Christmas Eve. I find that out as I scan town, driving up and down the streets. I notice that Dad is at his office already. I should have figured he'd camp out there. I'm not in the mood to talk to him yet—especially after Robert's announcement. I might give him that black eye that Robert didn't.

I grip the wheel as I spin on some ice. I still can't believe what Robert said about going south. He knows he'll never be able to play golf as well as he did before. Doesn't Dad know that? Are they both delusional?

Or is there another reason Robert is promising Dad he'll go with him? I pull in front of Dee's Ice Cream Hut and even though it's a freaking thirty degrees out, it's still open. Maybe a chocolate shake will clear my brain. I take a quick glance at my hair and no makeup, wipe sleep from my eyes, and tuck my coat around me. The place is empty except for someone mopping the floors. I place my order, grab a straw, and steer toward the back of the establishment where my family sat after my softball games in high school.

I look like a loser. Feel like one, too, but who wouldn't? A puddle forms around my feet where I walked through a bank of snow near my car. Great. Now I'll catch pneumonia, and my mother will have to care for me when all she needs right now is more to worry about. The milkshake goes down fast. I didn't realize how starving I was. I go back to the counter to order fries.

The clerk gives me another look—so she's all dolled up—but who cares? This is Dee's Ice Cream Hut.

The fries help. One by one I dip them in catsup and suck on the ends. I'm so absorbed in my ritual that I don't notice the parka standing in front of me. I look up. The fry never makes it to my mouth.

"Hungry?" Drew pulls out the metal chair across from me and lowers himself into it.

I swallow the piece, gagging.

He's dressed like an Eskimo, complete with a knit cap and gloves dangling from his hands.

"What are you doing here?" It seems that's all I ask him.

"You were pretty hard to find, but your car sticking halfway out on Main Street was my best clue." His blue eyes shine—bluer than any time before.

My hands have catsup on them. Probably my lips, too, but I'm too stunned to wipe them.

"You're supposed to be in Florida." Witty comeback. Right. I unzip my coat and then think better. My clothing is wrinkled.

"I've been looking for you. And besides, it is Christmas."

"So your mother demanded an encore performance?" At least my memory is still intact.

He sets his gloves to the side and unzips his parka. Where did he get that thing? It must weigh more than me.

"You remember everything. Maybe you can remember how I kissed you not so long ago."

My toes curl. They do and I'm not joking. How

could I ever forget that kiss? "I remember. I also remember a promise to support me in Daytona."

His face relaxes. "Oh, that. Is that what you're mad about?"

"Oh, that?" Again I echo. I need to think before I speak. "It was Q-School. My big shot and you weren't there for me."

He starts to roll his eyes and thinks better—my guess because he stops mid roll and puts on this serious face. "My brother ended up in the ER. I couldn't leave him. I tried to call you, but it went to voice mail. Figured you were concentrating."

"The ER?" I like his brother. I grab a napkin, waiting for something good.

"Fire ants. Seems he's allergic and swelled up badly."

"Fire ants. You couldn't come to Daytona because of an allergic reaction to fire ants? Really?"

He props his elbows on the table. "I don't want to fight, Bobbi-with-an-*I*. I've missed you so much already."

Oh, yes, I've missed him as well. He's who I think about when I think about my future and the mess in my family. He's my safe place, but then I remember how Drew let me down. Does going to the ER count as a good enough reason? I meet his look and feel my milkshake gurgling in my stomach. He smells like mint. Fresh mint. I smell like a dog that needs a bath.

"My family is falling apart."

His hand stretches to cover mine. "How can I help?"

I pull my hand into my lap. "Please meet my brother."

~*~

Christmas morning wakes me at six AM. I'm still tired—worn out from avoiding Robert, who looks at me with loads of guilt. I haven't discussed what he told me with my mother yet. Why worry her? She's got enough on her mind.

My room is chilly. I snuggle under my covers. Yesterday after Drew left the restaurant, I drove around town until I could find items that would pass as gifts for my mother and brother. Since I'm broke it wasn't easy, but I managed to find a pretty bracelet for Mom and a calendar planner for Robert. I borrowed some wrapping paper and put them under the tree before falling into bed early.

~*~

Ho Ho Ho. I think today rates as my worst Christmas in my life. Worse than the time Dad left us before, because this time it's forever. My teeth chatter so I reach for my robe and slippers and go downstairs to the thermostat. No wonder. It's set on sixty. I tick it up a few notches, grateful to hear the furnace kick on.

Next I plug in the Christmas lights so when they come downstairs we have some form of festivities. The coffee maker is ready to go—my mother set it last night. I press the on button. Soon the aroma of freshly brewed coffee reaches my nose.

The cinnamon rolls are in the fridge so I take them out, pop the can and stick them into the oven. A tradition even though nothing else seems to be anymore. I think about calling Amanda to say "Merry Christmas" but change my mind. Instead I curl up on the living room couch and watch the tree lights twinkle.

Drew agreed to come over tonight to meet everyone. He said by seven his family is done celebrating and he'd be happy to come over. My plan is for him to talk with Robert about how hard the golf pro life is. Since my brother won't listen to me, he might pay attention to Drew—someone who has been on tour.

I shake my head. I still can't believe Robert can be that stupid. What about all his talk about God showing him His plans for his life? Was it all nothing? I glance to the coffee table and see his Bible sitting there. I pick it up, the leather flaps falling back in my hands, opening to Jeremiah. Robert has marked one passage all in red. It's been a while since I've read anything in mine. A long while. I can barely make out the verses. One he has underlined. Twice." *For I know the plans I have for you…*" That verse again.

A preacher once said you'll know when God is talking to you if you listen with your heart. I trace the verse with my finger and squeeze my eyes shut. "Are you telling me something, God? Do you care that much about me?"

But has it done Robert any good? One day he wants to be a preacher and the next day he's going off to Florida with Dad to try golfing again. How dumb is that? How dumb is it to think you can be a pro when you'd not even played in almost a year?

I close the Bible, setting it back on the table. How dumb is it, indeed? How dumb was it for me to think I could take my brother's place in Florida and golf like a pro? I like to think I'm pretty smart, but as I think about what I've done this past year, my eyes and heart open up. Was I insane? Did I really believe I could go as far as someone as good as Drew?

My stomach rolls. Is this how someone feels when they've been found out? Tears form in my eyes, soon spreading to my cheeks.

"Bobbi, are you all right?" My mother stands in front of me, dressed in her fifteen-year-old paisley robe, her hair pulled back with a sweatband.

"I just realized how stupid I was going off to Florida like I did. Why didn't you stop me?"

She sits next to me and throws a blanket over both of us. "I tried. You were adamant."

I cross my arms. "I can't believe I was thinking I was good enough to turn pro and that Dad could caddie for me someday. It amazes me how he went along with it."

She touches my cheek. "You were pretty good. You worked hard at doing what you thought was the right thing to do. I love you for trying."

"Well, it didn't work, did it?" I snuggle against her. I'm sure I look pretty pathetic with my puffy eyes and sleep head hair. Good thing she doesn't mind.

"We're going to make it. You watch and see."

I think about Robert and his options. Should I tell her his plans? She'll be crushed if she knows. But then, maybe she can talk sense into him if Drew can't.

"What about Robert? Do you think he's going to make it?" My tone is cautious.

"The doctors say he's healed and will only get better."

"No. I mean about giving up golf forever and going off to college."

She thinks a few minutes before speaking. "He gave up golf a long time ago. He's signed up for school, but with your father leaving us…"

"Mom, what if Dad moves away from Pennsylvania? What if he makes us sell this place and sells his business and leaves us forever? What would that do to Robert?"

She knits her fingers together, her forehead does the same. "I think I'll worry if that happens. His father is everything to him."

Bingo. Robert is acting as crazy as I did.

"Let's wait and see, OK? I have other things on my mind, like today being Christmas, and someone needs to wake that sleepyhead up." She smiles and pats my leg. Soon she's calling up to Robert and the three of us are sitting around the tree with our gifts, pretending that everything is all right again.

~*~

I avoid Robert most of the day with inane chatter.

In another hour, Drew will arrive and knock sense into my brother's head. Then maybe, maybe, I will think about speaking to Dad about the farm. I couldn't fix the family with golfing, but I might be able to with a little diplomacy. We can't move and Mom will never find a job. Those are the facts. Dad is going to have to accept them.

The front doorbell rings. I glance at my reflection in the hall mirror. I'm wearing a red sweater and little makeup. I don't want him to get any ideas or even guess my feelings toward him. My family comes first.

"Hey, you look great," he says when I open the door, letting a rush of frigid air in with him. He's dressed in his parka again minus the gloves and cap. He looks great, too.

Keeping my distance from him is going to be hard. It's all I can do to not throw myself into his arms and kiss him.

"Merry Christmas. Was Santa good to you?"

"He is right now."

Drew hands me his coat and his touch lingers on my arm. Heat rushes to my face. Since fanning it is out of the question, I move toward the living room where Robert and my mother are waiting to be introduced.

My mother raises her eyebrows, giving me that knowing look.

"Mom and Robert, meet Drew. He was one of my teachers in Orlando. We found out we live near each other and he's up for the holidays, so I thought he could come over and see our place." I'm rambling. I know it but can't stop.

Thankfully Robert steps forward and shakes Drew's hand.

Mom welcomes him and invites him to sit by the tree on the couch next to me.

I'm not one for awkward situations. Today is no exception, but if Drew can talk any sense into my twin then bring it on.

"So you taught my sister how to golf?" Robert shoots me a look as well. He knows Drew spent many hours on the course with me because I've told him.

I didn't tell him that I was attracted to my teacher and on more than one occasion those feelings got in the way of my goal.

"Not really. She knew how to golf pretty well before I got her. Just some fine tuning." His gaze catches mine.

Really, God? Did you have to make his blue eyes so attractive?

"I taught Golf Psychology. Most of golf takes place right here." He points between his ears. Robert has heard this before, I'm sure, but his expression shows interest. "I hear you're a golfer, too."

My brother tips his head. Is he going to tell Drew about his accident? "I enjoy a good game. Too bad the weather isn't better. We could go a few holes."

I want to smack Robert. He has hardly been on the course since he started walking. He knows that, too. "My brother is planning to attend Bible college and study to be a pastor."

Drew settles into the cushion next to me. His warmth slides onto my side of the sofa, caressing my side. "Is that so? Sounds like a good plan to me. When do you start?"

Robert works hard at not glaring at me. "This January, that is, if my options don't change."

At his words, my mother perks up. "What options, Robert? You're all paid up for this next semester. What are you talking about?"

Here it comes. I give Robert what I hope is a triumphant look. He bites his bottom lip, obviously not intending to include Mom in his decision about Dad. Maybe now he'll wise up and we can get back to what's important—saving our farm.

"Dad," he gives Drew an apologetic look. "My father might be moving south and has asked me to come with him. I'm sorry, Mom. I was going to tell you as soon as I decided." His face is the color of fresh peaches.

My mother's mouth hangs open so wide I can see the gap from a missing tooth. Maybe bringing this topic up was a mistake.

Drew looks at me now with an expression I've

seen him give students in the classroom.

"You're moving?" my mother squeaks.

"Dad said if we lived where it was warm year round, I might be able to get my game back. He said he'd hire the best trainers, and when I made the tour, he'd caddie for me. Just like he always wanted, Mom. You know how miserable he is here. He hates his job."

"You wanted to be a pastor. You said God called you." I can hear her better now.

So can all of us.

Robert shuffles his feet. His embarrassment is almost unbearable.

"I played on tour. It isn't what you think." Drew's comment surprises me. I didn't even have to prompt him. I relax my grip on the couch arm. Maybe this conversation will go better than I thought.

"You played? How come you got out?" Robert turns his attention to Drew, leaving my mother to wring her hands on her lap.

"Long story, but I was thinking about going back and trying this spring. I thought teaching wasn't my thing. I was wrong."

"You were wrong?" My voice sounds like my mother's. We could be twins.

"I was wrong. Sometimes you think you should be doing something else and forget to look into all the details. After I quit my job, I had plenty of time to remember. The long days, long flights, and times without ever seeing those you love. I don't want that again." He gives me a look—one I can't read.

"*If* you even make it on tour, which I doubt you will, you're going to be away from everyone you love the rest of your life. Travelling is exotic at first, but then there's the practicing and more practicing all to make a dollar. Is it really worth it?"

My knees knock together. I shove my hands between my legs. Where did all this come from? Drew quit teaching because he wanted to play. He was good. He *is* good. What's happened?

I search my mother's face, trying to evaluate how she's holding up. First, she loses her marriage and now her son. She's staring at the tree, her eyes half-closed.

I've gone too far.

"Robert, maybe you and Drew could talk another time. I just realized how tired I am, and Drew must be tired out, too."

"Sure. It's been great to meet you, Drew."

"I'm sorry, Bobbi. Didn't realize how late it is, and it is Christmas." He turns to me. "Maybe we can get together tomorrow. Lunch?"

"Sure. Tomorrow."

He rises, shakes Robert's hand, and then gives my mother a small hug. She smiles and thanks him for coming. "Would you like a Christmas cookie before you leave?"

Drew rubs his stomach. "My mom filled me up good. Thank you, anyway."

I hurry him to the door, ashamed again how this evening played out, but curious about his plans. If he isn't going to try out, what's he going to do?

Drew leans close to my ear. His hot breath sends chills across my neck. "I'll call you in the morning. Merry Christmas."

~*~

Robert meets me in the TV room the next morning. He's dressed in sweats and looks like he didn't sleep all night. He plops next to me and reaches for the remote, turning the TV off. "I'm sorry. I've been a jerk." He reaches for my hand and squeezes. "Forgive me?"

"Are we talking about you going off with Dad or giving me that dumb piano tape for Christmas?" I squeeze back.

"Both. I prayed all last night. I guess I got off track, thinking I could help Dad if I went with him and make his dream come true. Guess playing the hero runs in this family."

I laugh. Hard. It lifts my heart. "You are a goof. You'd think you'd learn from my stupidity, wouldn't you. At least you didn't go to college for something you don't like to do. I get an extra bonus. A student loan that comes due in three months and I'm unemployed."

"I promised I'd help you, didn't I? I meant it at the time and I mean it now. From here in PA, not Florida." His mouth turns down, and I feel sorry for my brother. In some ways we are so much alike. We love our parents and want to help.

"Maybe we can still do something for Mom. I haven't talked with Dad yet since coming home. I'm not even sure that he'll talk to me, but I hope to convince him that Mom needs this place."

"Sure about that? It's a big place to take care of alone."

"Of course I'm sure. She loves it here." My arms find their comfort zone in a crossed position. Today I plan to track my father down and make him see what he's doing to us. I might not be his dream golfer, but I'm his daughter and he needs to listen to me.

"Are you ever going to get it? We can't fix our

family."

"Save that for a sermon. Right now, I need your help. You need to tell Dad your plans and then let me at him."

"When are we going to talk about you and your life? You haven't even mentioned painting again."

I never told him about the paintings I did in Florida. When I moved home, I stuffed my supplies in my closet and haven't even thought about them. As always, a longing wells up inside of me at the thought of painting again as a career. Is it even a possibility? I have not driven past the art store out of fear that it's been sold. Not as though I can afford it or anything. I reach for Mattie's necklace that I sleep in. The jeweler who appraised it said it was worth more than five thousand dollars. I dismiss the idea of selling it.

What can I do with that amount, anyway?

We hear sounds of our mother waking and puttering around in the kitchen.

Robert pats my head and goes in to talk with her.

I turn on the TV not wanting to hear that conversation.

Robert has come to his senses.

Now if only my father will.

~*~

When I was in the third grade, I wet my pants because the teacher would not call on me so I could use the restroom. Water trickled into a puddle beneath me, and George, who sat nearby, called out to the teacher about what I'd done.

She hurried me to her restroom and cleaned me up. Next she called my house.

My father answered. My mother chose that day to get her hair permed. I remember waiting in the office in wet pants for him to pick me up, my legs crossed and my chest throbbing with fear. I knew he would yell at me for disturbing his day off. He always did. That day was no exception.

As I near his office late this afternoon, that same fear rises in my throat. Fear that he'll yell at me for disturbing his life again. I didn't tell my mother where I was going, but Robert knows. He was the one who told me where to find him. I guess Dad wasn't any too happy with Robert's choice. He'd called him a sissy and told him to get out.

Hearing what he'd said to Robert inflamed me further. Robert had been willing to sacrifice his life for his father. If we hadn't talked, I know he would be packing now.

Maybe there is a little Superman in me after all.

I think these thoughts to buoy myself as I park. Dad's car is here. Alone. I wonder how he spent Christmas. And with whom? I glance at my watch. I had to cancel my lunch date with Drew, but he said it was OK. He'd be around until after New Year's. We agreed to meet in a few days.

The weather fits my mood. Dark, overcast. Wind whips my cheeks as I leave the car. I'm still not used to the bone chilling cold here. A dusting of snow covers the walk, but footprints mar the sidewalk to his office.

My brother's big feet make me grin. It wasn't easy for him to come here—to tell Dad good-bye. He and my father have always had this bond. A bond I couldn't be part of and never will be after today.

The door needs a paint job. My father was never much on maintenance and especially with his office.

Every spring my mother would come in and do a thorough cleaning of it so that he wouldn't be embarrassed, she told me.

I don't think he cared. He never did stop thinking about his past life—the one before twins.

I rap on the door. Nothing. I turn the knob and go in, relief flooding my insides that the door is unlocked. "Dad? Are you here?" I find myself praying, asking God to help me through the next few minutes. Funny thing, praying calms me. Maybe Robert is on to something. Maybe I have been missing something.

"Bobbi? Come on back."

He's in his office, which means I'll have to sit across from his monster desk. The desk we were never allowed to play around or on. The sacred desk. I hate that desk.

"Merry Christmas, Dad," I say as I enter the room. The place is torn apart. Boxes lie everywhere, half-filled. "Looks like you're packing."

He grimaces and points to the only chair not filled with books and files. "I'm selling the business. I'm sure your mother told you already. Sorry this had to happen."

"Are you? Sorry? I don't think you are."

He wipes his hand across his face. "I don't want to discuss my marriage and personal decisions with you today. Seems like you have your own life to clean up."

I swallow back the mean words I want to throw at him.

Robert warned me he would be nasty. He also gave me a mini sermon on turning the other cheek.

I won't go that far today but I won't take his bait either. "Mom's pretty upset. You're making her sell the farm. It's Grandpa's farm. Not yours."

"Too bad you never saw who paid the mortgage and replaced the roof or painted the place, or you wouldn't say that." He sighs. "Listen, girl, we have to sell it. It's what happens in divorce settlements. No one wins."

"Seems like you are. Throwing Mom out and making her work in some dumpy store to make a living."

"There are plenty of other places for her to work and it won't kill her."

I rest my hands flat on the desk. "Isn't there anything I can say to make you give her the farm? Dad, I love that place. So does Robert. I always expected I'd bring my family there someday for holidays. You can't sell. You can't!" I lose it and start to cry. The absolute last thing in the world I want to do in front of my father.

He tosses me a box of tissues.

I shove it aside and fumble to my feet.

This scene with him reminds me of past scenes. My father always wins. Always.

"You won't get that place." I grit the words between my teeth. "I promise you. I'll find a way to buy you out." Then I stumble from the room, my anger blinding my way.

But I will never forget his laugh as it follows me out the door.

29

My mother comes into my bedroom dressed in black polyester dress slacks and a mauve sweater with two fake pearls at the neckline. She sticks out one foot to show me her loafers, circa 1972. It is two days before New Year's Eve and she's going out to apply for jobs. I told her this morning that no one is hiring until after the holidays, but she's determined.

"You look nice." I'm packed under my blankets even though it is after 9 AM. My energy level is at zero. Maybe I'm coming down with something. Depression, probably.

"Robert typed a resume for me, although I don't know how raising two kids and keeping house counts for much."

"Here." I slip out of bed and move her over to my dresser. Digging through my jewelry box, I come up with a pair of long silver earrings. "Wear these." I hold them in my palm. She takes them and puts them into her ears.

"Thanks sweetie. They look nice." Her confidence is waning.

I give her a big hug. "You'll do awesome! Do you know where you're going first?" I pray it isn't the mall. The shops rot there.

"The mall. There's a cute card shop I like."

I hold back a groan. "How about downtown where they built some new businesses? Isn't there a dress store there or something? Mom, you can't work at the mall. On Friday nights it's filled with teenager make-outs."

Her smile fades. I know today is hard for her. At two, she and Dad are seeing a lawyer.

I offered to go with her but she refused. She wants to be independent, she told Robert and me. Does independent mean not taking help? I don't think so.

Her car pulls out of the driveway a few minutes later. I jump into the shower and plan my day. Drew asked to meet him for lunch at the pizza place on Main. Curiosity about his plans makes me go. I wear my best fleece and jeans, and by the time I'm ready I'm late.

The delicious odor of garlic greets me when I push through the entrance doors of the pizzeria.

Drew waits at a side table, a soda in his hand. He rises when I draw close, reaching down to kiss my cheek. I almost reel into the next table.

"What can I get you?" He nods toward the counter.

"Root beer, please. Did you order yet?"

"Pepperoni, large. Will that work?"

He remembers my passion for pizza. I wait while he brings my drink and then shuffles back into his chair beside me. His nearness ruffles my composure.

I sip and then cough from the bubbles. I'm acting like a high school girl with a crush. Again. When will I grow up?

Drew is watching me with the grin. "You never said you forgave me. Do you?" He looks at me intently, wearing his teaching face. Serious.

I think about my answer. He let me down but so did my father, and how many times did I forgive him? I lost count years ago. "Sure. You're forgiven. Now, are you going to tell me why you aren't trying to go on tour again?"

"Right after you tell me what happened with your brother."

"You never go first." I enjoy his teasing. It reminds me of my relationship with Robert—but more.

"Beauty before age."

"Now you're making it hard for me not to go first." The toe of my boot meets his. I nudge him. "You have this way about you."

"A way you like?" He moves his chair closer. Will he hear my heartbeat?

"Maybe." I never was coy, but today I'm learning. I clear my throat. "My brother decided to go to college. Here. Not in Florida. So thank you. You helped me."

"And your mother? How's she doing with all that's happening?"

"She's actually on a job hunt today. Where I should be, too." I frown, remembering my state of unemployment. "I tried to get her to wait until after the holidays, but she's determined. I also met with my father. He won't let the farm go. He wants his share. That's the part that's killing me. I know my mother wants it, but she can't afford to buy him out, and I don't have that kind of money. So in a few months I'll be homeless. Unemployed and homeless. Good life, huh? And my brother says he'll help me. Help me what? Put back a life I destroyed a year ago?" When Drew doesn't laugh, I stop.

There it is. My life laid out on a pizza table.

"I don't have room for romance, Drew."

He takes my hand. "There's always room for romance. My turn now. I'm moving back here. When I figured out that I didn't want to go through all that touring again, I had to make a decision. I wasn't happy in Florida. I wasn't happy at that school teaching Golf Psychology. I was happiest teaching others how to golf. So why not do it here?"

"What do you mean here?"

"I'm buying Keystone Hills Golf Course. It needs some upkeep, but by spring it should be ready to go. My brother plans to come up and help me run it."

His features light with excitement as he tells me about his venture and plans to make Keystone one of the most sought after places to golf in the area. Fifteen minutes pass before he stops, realizing he has been doing all the talking. "I'm sorry. I am so ready to do this I can't think of anything else."

I rest my chin on my palm. "I love your energy. Your passion is amazing. I'm so happy for you." He's made the right choice about his life. I can't help but compare his plans to mine and wish I can feel that same surge he has now. "If I can do anything to help, please let me."

"Thanks for listening to me go on and on. I sign the paperwork once the lawyer gets through—and the surveyor and everyone else involved. I can't wait to walk on that course and know it's mine. It's taken all my savings, but I have this feeling about it. I can't describe it, but when you know something is right, you know."

"It sounds right to me. I'm so happy for you." I mean what I say. I'm so pleased and could listen to him all day, but I want to get home to see how my mother made out on her search and her meeting with my father. So much is happening in my life right now, I find it hard to focus on what I should be doing. I've never been one to flounder, but it seems I am now.

"What are you doing on New Year's Eve?" Drew gathers up our plates as he asks.

"Same thing I do every year. We sit around the tree and make stupid resolutions. Last year I resolved to become a famous artist. Look where that got me."

"It got you to me." He wriggles his eyebrows. Just a little.

"It got me a student loan payment. A twisted ankle. And no career."

"Greet the new year with me."

The only other date I ever had on New Year's ended in disaster. I had turned eighteen and Amanda set me up with her cousin. A popular band was playing at a new restaurant in town, and she and her fiancé wanted to go.

Dick, her cousin, said he'd be my date. I went so far as having my hair done at a salon and I bought a fancy red shirt to wear. When they picked me up, Dick said hello and that was about it for the night until twelve o'clock struck and he grabbed me in a bear hug and locked his lips on mine—plus his hands—and wouldn't let go until I pushed him away. No, it wasn't fun. It put a sour taste to what most people believe should be a fun experience. I'd rather sit home and watch the ball go down.

"What are you thinking about? I lost you." Drew is waiting for an answer.

I know in my heart if I go out with him on the supposedly most romantic night of the year—*if* you are with the right person—I might not be able to turn back. Especially since he will be in close proximity. And am I ready for a relationship when I can't even get my life under control? "I'm going to pass, but thank you. I think I'll spend it with my family again this year."

His smile falters, but he revives himself and scoops up my coat when I stand. Drew is a gentleman for sure when he isn't on the course. I recall his brash treatment of me when I messed up a shot. He didn't mince words then.

We part at our cars, promising to catch up after the holidays. I hurry back across town and over the bridge to the farm, hoping my mother hasn't left for her appointment at the lawyer's yet. She might change her mind to let me go with her. When I pull in, I discover her car is gone, as well as Robert's truck. The flag is down on the mailbox. It's early for the mail but I check it anyway.

I pull out a stack of bills and flip through them until my hand stops on a formal looking letter addressed to me—from Florida.

~*~

The letter about Mattie comes on the same day my mother files for a divorce, gets her first job, and I reject Drew.

When my mother returns from her appointments, she is whistling. I think it's a Christmas jingle. She tosses her bag on the counter and joins me at the kitchen table where the letter lies open in front of me.

"I'm employed," she says. "I actually have a job where someone is going to pay me for my work." A smile wreathes her face—the biggest one I've seen in ages. The smile takes years off her appearance. She doesn't even play with her fingers as she tells me, like she normally would when she's talking. My mother is confident, and I admit this change surprises me. "Are you going to ask me where?"

"Yes! Where? I'm so proud of you."

"The Brighter Boutique. They opened before Christmas and did well with the crowd of ladies my age. The owner told me I would be perfect because I am friendly and can wear the styles. I even get a 20 percent discount. Can you believe that? I start next Monday at nine o'clock and work until five. What a perfect shift. I'll be home to make supper, but then you could get something going for us since Robert might still be in classes." She stands and retrieves her purse, rummaging through it. She pulls out a sheaf of papers. "I have to fill these out for my first day. They actually will pay part of my health benefits. Can you believe that?"

"Wow. You lucked out, Mom. I'm so happy for you. How much will they pay you?"

My question stills her. "We didn't even discuss that. I guess I should have asked, but with benefits it must be more than minimum wage. You would think so, wouldn't you?"

She's more naïve than I thought. "You should probably call and find out. I would if I were you."

"Yes, I guess that's a good idea." Her eyes drift toward the window. "I thought I asked everything."

"How did it go at the lawyer's? Did Dad show up?"

She sits back down and puts her purse to the side. A look of firm determination appears. "We agreed to everything. I should have known we would. It's been coming for years. We were ready."

"What about this place, Mom? Is he making you sell?" I hate to press for details but I must know.

She turns her head slowly back to me. "There isn't any choice. It's half his. I stopped by a real estate office on my way home." She seems to realize I'm here and reaches across the table to grab my hand. "It'll be OK. We can find something cute. We'll sell stuff we don't need, like some of my good dishes and Grandpa's chair and my sewing machine…" She stops, a sob cutting off her words. "I'm sorry," she says and rushes out of the room leaving me with my letter.

I want to tell her about the letter. I fold it in half and tuck it in my fist, instead. I'll show it to Robert when he gets home. He'll know what to do about Mattie and her decision.

~*~

The real estate agent comes to our house the next morning after breakfast. I haven't had the chance yet to talk with Robert because last night he was out with friends. The agent is nice, although she looks like she should be working in a fashion design studio instead of in northeast Pennsylvania. Her boots come to her knees, and her coat is made of brown wool. Around her neck, she's draped an argyle scarf.

"Let's take a tour of the place so I can give you comps later and we'll know how to price it." She carries her clipboard as my mother leads her upstairs through our bedrooms and back downstairs to the cellar.

I debate following them outside and instead watch from the window as they stumble around the barn and garage, my mother's arms waving from her side as she talks about each place. I wonder if she's telling the story of when I fell out of the tree by the back of the garage. I skinned my leg up pretty badly—so bad it demanded a trip to the ER. Or is she telling her about the pond up back and how we spent so many winters ice skating there? I squeeze my hands together.

I remember the letter from the lawyer who asked me to call him. I still don't understand why—part of me is afraid it's because I was the one who found Mattie. Maybe I'm being sued by her daughter? She seemed so nice and grateful to find the journal. I wait in the living room, propping my feet on the coffee table. Shortly, my mother and Greta—what a name!—return and start filling out listing papers.

"I don't need comps, but I'll send you some. I think you could ask two hundred and fifty thousand for this place and get it." She beams like she did my mother this great service.

My mother sits next to me with the pen in her hand.

"Your husband will have to sign these, too, since you mentioned he owns half of this property. Would you get him to sign or do you want me to stop by his office?"

"Please if you don't mind. Stop by the office."

I nod. The less my mother has to see him the better.

When they finish, Greta shakes our hands and leaves by the back door as though she's a close friend already. I don't care for her, but say nothing since Mom chose her.

"Want a cup of tea?" I pick up the tea kettle.

"I think I'm going to take a nap, if you don't mind. I'm worn out."

My mother never takes naps, but she does today for over two hours. During that time, I work up my courage to contact the legal office on the letterhead. Harvey Brandshaw, Esq. Orlando.

"May I speak to Attorney Brandshaw, please? He sent me a letter recently concerning Mattie Montrose."

Elevator music comes through the phone as I wait. I tap my fingers to the tune, almost forgetting why I called.

"May I help you?" A man's voice booms at me. I pull the phone away from my ear. I explain who I am and why I'm calling.

"Ahh, dear Mattie. She was one special lady, wasn't she? When she came to me not long ago to change her will, I was in shock, but then she told me about you and how you had touched her heart. She wanted to help you in some small way and now she has."

"What do you mean? Are you talking about the necklace because if you want it back I can mail it to you." I finger the club, praying he doesn't want it.

He chuckles in an entirely different tone than he talked.

I like him better now. I've chosen to call from the TV room and monitor the doorway for my mother. She's gotten up, but said she was running to the grocery store. I don't want her walking in on me as I speak.

"Not at all. Mattie had other plans for you. She was a sweet one, wasn't she?"

"I liked her." I wish he'd get to the point and explain if I was going to jail or not. I cross my ankles, then my fingers. I change my mind and shoot up a fast prayer. By now, my stomach is doing flips and I wish I'd drunk tea, anyway. Not the soda I'd opted for.

"Well, Miss Bobbi. Do you mind if I call you that? Today is a life-changing day for you. Miss Mattie asked that after her passing, I get in touch with you to let you know she left you money from her estate."

"Her estate? I thought her estate was the contents of the trailer." I picture the packed boxes of photos and trinkets that went to charity.

"Oh, no. Quite the opposite. She amassed a large estate. From that, she's left you the sum of one hundred and fifty thousand dollars. Shall we mail the check to your home address or would you rather direct deposit?"

The phone slips from my fingers. I pick it back up. "Direct deposit, please."

30

The real estate agent said she won't list the house until after New Year's Day so we won't have any strangers trooping through now.

My mother asks if we should take the tree down early.

Robert says no, since it's our last holiday in this house we have the right to enjoy all of it.

I don't tell them about Mattie's gift yet. When I hang up from the lawyer, I grab my purse, get in my car, and drive out to the park where I'd hiked that fall. The trees are bare and muddy piles of snow cover the rocks. I push up the trail until I get to the highest peak, my breath coming out in bursts of cold.

"I don't believe it!" I say over and over. All that money and she lived like she did. Why would she leave it to me? She hardly knew me more than a few months. I sit for over an hour asking God what's going on. I haven't trusted Him with my entire life, and still He allows this windfall. I don't deserve this money. My chest tightens as the memory of the moment I trusted God to save me once again surfaces. I remember wanting to tell Robert how I felt, but didn't. Instead, I let myself be embarrassed of what I'd done. Why did I turn away from Him? Why do I always follow my own course?

A cold wind slaps my cheek. Maybe it's time to listen and stop running. I close my eyes and pray.

~*~

New Year's Eve I wake up with the urge to talk with Drew. Even though I turned him down for a date tonight, I miss him. I also want to tell him about the windfall and my plans.

He answers on the first ring.

"Hey. Are we on again for tonight?" His voice tickles through my body.

"Can you meet me for a few minutes at the coffee shop in town? I have something to discuss with you."

"Sounds serious. Sure. How about in an hour?"

I run for my shower and tell Robert I'll be back soon. Guilt that I haven't shared everything with my twin makes me almost turn back, but I don't. Robert will tell me to pray about it. I did pray about it when I sat on the mountain, but God didn't give me any clear direction yet.

Drew beats me to the shop and a steaming coffee waits for me. I drop into the chair opposite him, my heart taking an extra beat as I admire the way he looks this morning in a blue sweater and jeans. His minty breath sweeps me into another place. Even his nails appeal to me—clean and broad as he grips his cup.

"What's going on? I didn't expect the call, but I'm glad you thought of me."

"Did I ever tell you about this woman named Mattie who lived next to me in Florida?"

He squints. "I don't think so. What about her?"

I pull out the necklace. "She gave me this when she died. It's worth some money, but not enough to do anything with. The other day, I get this letter in the mail saying to call this lawyer. Seems she was rich and left me something more."

"Something more? More jewelry?" He takes a deep sip of his coffee.

I shake my head. "No, like in money. A lot of money. Money enough to buy my father out and save our house."

His cup scrapes the table. "Wow. Enough money for you to start a new career, too?"

Again I shake my head. "No. It isn't meant for me. I think I was given this to save our farm. So my mother has a place to live." It's exactly enough to buy the half of the house. Maybe this is how God is revealing his plans for me.

"Can your mother afford the upkeep on the place? It isn't cheap to maintain a farm, let alone a house."

"You think too much. You're buying a golf course. You're going to have the same problem. Besides, she'll have me and Robert. We'll pay our share." I toss my empty cup into a nearby receptacle. "Of course, she'll manage. She's like that."

At least she always was. My mother is a survivor. She'll be happy to stay there when I give her the money.

"Have you thought about your life at all, Bobbi?"

"This is my life."

"You spend most your time thinking about everyone else and you don't have a clue how you're going to live the next few years. Going to work at a department store selling sports equipment?"

I pull back my shoulders.

Here's the Drew I met on the courses.

"I haven't gotten that far."

"You can't spend your life bailing everyone else out. It doesn't work. You have to figure out what you want first so you're in a position to help others."

"From the mouth of a Golf Psychology teacher?"

His jaw tightens. Maybe I've gone too far. I'm tired of people not getting how much I want my family safe. My family is my life.

"Isn't your brother going to college? I don't hear you saying he's going to take a job to keep the place."

"Robert knows what he wants in life. I'm happy for him. Besides, he's gone through so much and deserves this."

"And you haven't?" He bends over the table. "Who spent almost a year in Florida at a school doing something she didn't like to convince her father he can stay with the family and relive his dream?" He shoves his cup aside. "Listen, call me when you figure it out. Right now I'm sick of seeing you throw your life away." He actually stands up and strides out of the coffee shop without a backward glance.

I want to shout at him that I'm not throwing my life away and that I'm not playing everyone's hero as he insinuates. Instead, I grab my purse, wait a decent amount of time, and then stalk to my car. Driving around town until my gas is almost gone, I pass the art shop and cool down. The "For Sale" sign no longer hangs in the window. I don't know why, but my heart sinks a little when I see this.

I pull into the parking place by the door. I will visit with Arthur. Tell him I'm back in town for good. The doorbell jingles as I open it. Right away, I know something is different. It doesn't smell the same. The interior has been filled with paintings from artists I don't recognize. A woman with long black hair pulled back into a ponytail greets me with a nod. She resumes her paperwork at the desk behind the front entry. The place is silent except for the tick tock of a large clock over the fireplace.

Maybe I'm in the wrong town.

I edge up to the counter. It's made of Formica—not the pretty granite Arthur brought from Italy. "Excuse me. Is Arthur around?"

She looks up like I've interrupted her universe. "I don't know where he is. He sold me this place and moved out of town."

Sold the shop already? "Do you mind if I look around?"

"Help yourself. Sale items are up front."

I work my way around the sale items and find similar items lining the walls in the back. The artists represented here have no sense of design or color or balance. A toddler can paint better than these artists. My chest aches as I go from painting to painting. Inferior quality. Junk you would buy at a hotel selling starving artists' work. Maybe it's good Arthur left town. He'd be spitting ice cubes if he saw what's become of his place.

Why did he sell to her?

The answer comes to me. It's because I didn't try to find a way to buy it. And now Arthur's Art Shop is a hole in the wall. A blight on the street. A place I'll never enter again as long as I live here. Fury wells inside me that this new owner doesn't know good art. She will sell these paintings to people as though they are something to be admired. She'll be stealing from them and future generations who look at this work.

I leave without another word.

On the street, I almost bump into the mailman who is rustling through his bag of mail. I know George well enough to not chase the disgust from my face.

"Saw the new place, huh? Nothing like Art's." He drops three letters into the slot by the door.

"I can't believe they call that art."

"Nothing like that painting you did for the wife and me. We still have it hanging over the fireplace. Get lots of compliments." George has a baby face. He looks sixteen even though he's pushing sixty.

"Thank you. I'm glad you enjoy it." I wave good-bye and rush to my car, eager to get home. I need to talk to Robert and my mother about the house. I cross the bridge, round the curve, and pull into the driveway behind an ambulance with its lights flaring. As I jump out of my car, two EMTs carry a stretcher down the back steps. My mother is lying under a sheet that is pulled up to her neck. An oxygen mask covers her face.

Robert is immediately at my side. "She's going to be OK. Come on, we'll follow in my truck."

She doesn't look fine. I touch her cold hand. "Mom, are you OK? I'm coming to the hospital with you." She looks at me, but the EMT pushes me away as he slides her into the back of the ambulance.

Robert tugs my shoulder so I follow him and climb into the passenger seat. He presses the gas to catch up as the ambulance circles out of our driveway with my mother on board.

"What happened?" I'm breathless with the memories of the last time an ambulance arrived on our property. Robert's face is the color of snow. He grips the wheel and his knuckles rise from his hands.

"She complained her chest ached. Next thing I know, she's on the floor passed out. The medics think she might have had a heart attack." He glances my way then forces his gaze onto the road. "Pray for her now, OK. Pray while I drive."

My throat closes. I push it open. "I'm praying right now."

"Out loud. So I can hear, too."

"OK." I press my hands together, shut my eyes tightly. "Dear God. Please be with Mom right now. Help the doctors make her better. Please. We need her so much." I can't help it. Tears run from my eyes and I cry. Big sobs.

Robert touches my arm. "He heard. That's what counts. She's going to be OK. She has to be OK."

I want to believe him, but I think of Grandpa. Death happens. Bad things happen. I've learned that lesson too much this past year. Now Mom. "She's been under stress with the house, Dad, and her new job. I should have helped more."

"You did everything you could. Let's not go there." His tires squeal as he veers into the ER parking lot. Within minutes, they put my mother in a closed cubicle.

Robert and I are told to stay in the waiting room with half a dozen other people in various states of illness. An hour goes by before the front nurse calls us. I rush to the counter before Robert, who is getting a drink of water.

"We're going to need some insurance information. Will one of you come back and meet with us?" It's not a nurse, it's a clerk, and I don't know what kind of insurance Mom has. I go anyway, hoping it will get me closer to the back.

"She has insurance through my father," I tell her. I don't want to call him, but they suggest I do. I pull out my cell and punch in his name.

"Dad? It's me. I need your insurance information. Mom's in the hospital."

His voice explodes in my ear. I finally get the information, but only after I tell him what I know. He says he's on his way. I want to tell him don't bother, that you are the reason she's here. But I let it go when the nurse comes along with Robert to tell me we can go back to see her now.

The hospital smells antiseptic—like the one where Mattie died. I was born in this hospital but feel no real connection to it. We follow the nurse to cubicle three. She pulls the curtain back for us to stand next to Mom's bed.

I shut my eyes fast. She looks like she's dying.

Robert puts his arm around me. "It's OK," he whispers. His comfort helps as I open my eyes and stare down at this lifeless person on the bed.

The nurse adjusts the blanket. "She's going to be transferred to CCU. The doctor will speak with you soon. She's had a heart attack and needs surgery."

I cover my mouth, biting my lip until I taste blood. "She isn't that old," I say as though my reasoning will change everything.

"Heart attacks can strike anyone, especially if they have been under severe stress or it runs in their family. There are many reasons this happens. I'm so sorry. Why don't you go back out in the waiting area until we get her transferred, and then you can visit again?"

The evening drags. I drink two sodas and eat a pack of vending machine cookies.

Dad shows up an hour after I call him.

Robert gives him the update and he sits on the opposite side of the room from us, drinking cold coffee. His hair is disheveled and he's wearing an old pair of jeans with a sweatshirt and jacket. Not his usual attire. I can't help but wonder what he was doing when

I called. I don't ask though. I don't want anything to do with him.

At six o'clock, we are told we can go upstairs to meet with the doctor.

Dad follows us into the elevator.

None of us speak.

I inch toward Robert to place as much distance between my father and myself.

The elevator plays music, soft piano notes.

I think of Mom and the radio channel she plays every morning. Something classic. She'd enjoy this song.

The door slides open and we wait for Dad to go first, following him down the hall to the nurse's station. A woman dressed in paisley pink greets us and motions us to where the doctor waits in a cubicle.

"I'm Doctor Stevens. I know this is happening fast but her cardiac cath shows a 95 percent blockage of one of her coronary arteries. We're prepping her now for bypass surgery and she'll be going to the operating room in a few minutes. I'll come out to talk with you when the surgery is over. When they get her settled in the CCU, you'll be able to see her briefly. Do you have any questions?"

I sink to the chair against the wall as my father and Robert pepper the doctor with endless questions—getting the same results. My mother is very ill and needs surgery.

We shuffle out to the next waiting area to begin the long wait.

"Bobbi, can I talk with you in private, please?" My father's voice startles me from the magazine I'm trying to focus on. He's standing by my chair, his hands thrust deep into his pockets. He has this habit of rocking back on his heels, and today I swear I will push him over if he starts to do it.

"What about?"

He motions toward the hallway.

I follow, my feet hugging the carpet as I do. He's the last person on this earth I want to talk with today. My teeth ache as I grit them.

He leads me to a soda machine where no one else is standing.

"I want to know what happened. What's your mother been doing?"

"What?" My mouth falls open. "You know what she's been doing. She's been divorcing you. She's been selling the only home she ever knew, and she's been pounding the pavements getting a stupid minimum wage job so she can live in some one bedroom apartment by the tracks. What do you think she's been doing?" I gasp for air at the end of my speech.

"I knew she was upset, but not to this extent."

His reaction floors me.

"Upset. You knew she was upset. Dad, what planet are you living on?"

He shakes his head to the side. Confusion settles into his eyes. It hits me. My father is clueless as to how he affects others.

"She suggested the divorce. She said I wasn't happy and she couldn't make me happy anymore. Doesn't she understand she's my whole reason for living?" His eyes close. Is my father going to cry?

"What are you talking about? You're the one who keeps leaving her. You're the one who has all the affairs, Dad."

His head shoots up.

Yeah, I hit a nerve and I don't care. "I saw you."

And it's out.

He turns away from me, his back bent. "You never told me." I can barely hear him.

"Well it isn't something a daughter wants to tell her father, you know. You cheated on Mom and she stuck by you. All these years and you haven't cared. Look what you did before Thanksgiving. You came back only because you thought you could live your golf career again through me after what I did to Robert. You hated me, Dad. You still do." My chest is on fire. Words I thought I'd never say to my father spill from my mouth. Ugly words. I don't stop until I break him and when he finally sinks into the chair against the wall, I turn and leave him. I leave him like he has left us more than once.

The hospital exit is down the next hall. I push through the door into the parking lot where a gust of cold air strikes my face. My coat is inside in the waiting room and I stand freezing in the cold December air, my hand shaking against my arms.

The relief I expect to come doesn't. Instead, sadness raises its head and almost chokes me. If there was ever a chance to repair my family, I've blown it by my recent actions.

A hospital employee dressed in a parka comes out the door. She looks my way. "Honey, don't you think you should put a coat on? It's probably close to twenty degrees out here. You'll catch a cold and be in there as a patient soon enough."

"I'm fine. Thank you." I rub my arms and move closer to the brick wall. Finally, I feel Robert's keys in my jeans pocket from when I'd picked them up after he left them lying in the ER. I search the parking area and discover I'm in the lot where we left the truck earlier.

Maybe I'll leave for a while. The doctor said her surgery might take a few hours or longer.

Fifteen minutes later, I pull into our driveway. The car heater is on full blast and I'm reluctant to get out and make a dash for the door. When I finally do, I enter the back way and note the mess the EMTs have made in the kitchen where they found my mother. The chairs are pushed back and her sweater lies in a heap. I pick it up and caress the soft fabric while folding it in half.

The teapot beckons me. With my mother's favorite cup in hand, I wander upstairs to her bedroom, searching for what, I don't know. Her bed is made with her favorite quilt—birds and lavender flowers. I sit on the edge and let my gaze wander. It drops to the nightstand at my right. She's written some notes in her familiar penmanship. I pick up the paper and smell her perfume on it.

The letter is to my father.

It's a love letter. I read until the end and put it down, flushing and angry at the same time.

My mother loves him and wrote the letter to ask him to try again. She blames herself for everything that has happened in their life including getting pregnant. She even offers to sell the farm and move anywhere he wants to move to be with him. Even Florida.

I fall backward on the bed, my head slamming into the pillow shams. They give with my weight. Plush. Groaning. I look up. The ceiling is painted beige with little ridges feathered around the far edges. She once told me she wanted to put a picture of mine up there so it would be the first and last thing she saw when she fell asleep and woke.

I called her silly and offered to paint something

but never got around to it. I glance at the bedside clock. In another four hours, it will be a new year. A new year with new dreams and hopes and disappointments. I want my mother to be here to experience all of them with me. My hip aches as I roll to my side. The letter stares at me—reminding me that my father and mother are a couple. No matter what the situation. No matter if they are apart or together, I can't change how they feel about each other.

Tears trickle from my eyes. I wanted to keep them together, and then I wanted to keep them apart. Do I know what's right anymore? Is their business any of my business? This whole last year of college was for my father so that he would be happy again. But did I ever ask him what he needed?

The answer rises in my throat and makes me run to the bathroom in the hallway. My insides land in the toilet. I slide to the cold linoleum and wipe my mouth with the back of my hand. "I never asked."

My voice echoes off the pale green bathroom walls. I assumed what my family needed without asking or caring that they might want otherwise. I rise to my feet as my cell phone starts to vibrate. One glance shows me it's Robert.

"Hey. How's Mom?" I catch sight of my reflection in the mirror. Bloodshot eyes greet me.

"Where are you? The doctor came out and said they're moving her to recovery. It went well, Bobbi. She's going to be OK. Now get your butt back here with my truck."

"It's good news? Praise God."

"Praise God, indeed. He hears our prayers. He heard yours."

I shove my phone into my pocket.

God heard my prayer. He really heard me.

I swallow hard and drop back to my knees. "Please forgive my doubt, Lord. Please forgive me for running ahead of You and making my own plans. Thank You for healing my mother and thank You for opening my eyes to Your love." When I finally rise, I add one more prayer and hope He's still listening.

31

The clock on the waiting room wall reads 11:45. In fifteen minutes, it will be the New Year. My father is asleep on the sofa, and Robert has gone to the cafeteria to see if they are still serving anything.

I saw my mother when I came back but she's been sleeping. We should go home, but I won't be the first to suggest it.

Dad nodded when he saw me, but that's it.

Robert grabbed me in a bear hug, his smile spilling off his face.

On the drive back, I made a decision. I'm done playing Superman. I'm turning in my cape for good and going to focus on putting my own life together and let everyone do the same for themselves.

By the looks of it, Dad isn't going anywhere. His love for Mom has been pretty evident since his arrival at the hospital. Maybe if I stay out of the way, they will work out their own problems. If they don't, it isn't on me.

Most of the hospital staff has gone home.

I was told they work on a skeletal crew on the holiday although tonight is a big one for fatalities. A few cleaning ladies nod to me when I use the bathroom. Thanking them would sound dumb, but part of me wants to. Instead, I return to the waiting room and pull my jacket around my shoulders.

The temperature has never been warm in here and

right now I'd give anything for my bed.

"Hey, they're closed. Not even coffee." Robert comes up to me. He holds salted peanuts in his fist and offers me some from the half-eaten bag.

"No thanks. How about we all go home until morning? They say she'll sleep a long time yet and everything went well."

He shakes his head. His eyes are bloodshot and his clothing looks like something he's taken from the trash. "Not me. Here. Take the keys and go get some sleep. I'll stay with Dad."

Having permission to return home appeals to me more than camping out in a cold waiting room. Besides, I want to call Drew and wish him a Happy New Year if I can. I take the keys and head out to the parking lot. It's well lit, so I'm not worried about anyone bothering me.

Fireworks sound off to my right.

I look up and see flashes of colorful lights rising over the rooftops. A smile works its way to my lips. I do have something to celebrate this year.

My phone rings as I reach the truck. Drew's name shows on caller ID.

"I was going to call you. Happy New Year."

"Where are you? I drove past your house and the lights are all out. Is everything OK, or are you partying somewhere and forgot to invite me?"

"I'm in the parking lot of Memorial Hospital." I unlock the truck and get in. The engine soon warms the cab.

"What's the matter?"

I hear the fear in his voice. My lips curl upward. "It's OK, now. My mother had a heart attack and they did a bypass. She's going to be fine."

"Wow. I'm sorry, Bobbi. How are you doing with it?" Now his concern comes through.

I smile again. "I'm tired, but OK. I was going to call you. You know, to wish you a Happy New Year."

"How about telling me in person?"

I glance around the parking lot expecting to see him walk toward me. The only person I see is a tired security guard taking a cigarette break. "Where are you?"

"Meet me at the golf course. You're fifteen minutes away."

The golf course. The one he's buying, of course. "At this time of night?"

"It's OK. I know the owner."

I imagine his blue eyes twinkling with his joke. "Warm it up. I'll be right over."

The drive takes me less than fifteen minutes, a curvy road out past town and across the South Bridge. When I come over the crest of the hill, I brake in delight. White lights spotlight the driving range. Only Drew's car sits in the parking lot. I climb down and look around until a whistle catches my attention. From about fifty yards away, Drew sits in a golf cart. He zooms over to my side.

"Hop in." On my seat lies a warm plaid blanket. He's wearing his parka again.

I do as ordered, pulling the blanket around me. "Are we taking the grand tour tonight?"

He presses the pedal and we take off across the course arriving at the top of the hill at the first tee. Drew shuts off the cart. The silence hugs us.

"Look over there," he says, and points to our right.

Fireworks light up the sky dazzling us with brilliant colors.

"Pretty amazing view, don't you think?"

"You bought this course for New Year's Eve, didn't you?" I snuggle deeper into my blanket, enjoying the show and my company.

Drew snakes his arm around my shoulders. It's warm and comforting.

I rest my head back.

"I'm sorry about your mother. But I'm happy to hear she'll be OK. What do you think caused it?"

"A number of things." I pause. How much do I share? "The most important thing is my father showed up. I know he still loves her without me doing anything."

He whistles again. "You didn't do anything, huh? Hard to believe. Did you lose your superpower?"

I twist in my seat to study his face. He's kidding, but it's funny how well he knows me. "I gave away my cape. No more meddling or fixing. They're on their own."

"I'm happy to hear that Miss Bobbi-with-an-*I*." Drew's hand comes up and he caresses my cheek. "Maybe you can focus on you now."

I remember our kiss. How can't I when his face is so close to mine? "I plan on it. Once I figure out what to do next."

His hand returns to the steering wheel and he starts the cart up again, zooming across the fairways. "Where are we going?" I raise my voice to be heard. Drew doesn't answer, but instead heads toward the driving range.

"The driving range? You really do own this place." I like the idea of having the place all to ourselves. When he pulls up, he shuts off the cart and jumps out. I put aside my blanket to follow him to the tee. A set of shiny new clubs waits for us.

Drew pulls out the driver and hands it to me. "Merry Christmas."

"It's New Year's."

"I'll get to that. For now, Merry Christmas. Come on."

"Really? I didn't get you anything." I take the club in my hand and follow him to the tee, amazed at his generosity, but curious to his plan.

He places a ball from his pocket onto the ground. "Hit it."

His eyes are smiling when I look into his face, then he nods to the club I'm holding. "Hit it like you've never hit it before."

The shaft is cut to my height. The grip fits my hand better than a pair of fancy racing gloves. I give it a practice swing. It's been weeks since I've hit a ball. Can I make a decent shot? I look out at the course and admire the lay of the land. This is a beautiful course. I played it a few times with Robert when we could afford to. My jacket slips to the ground.

"Go ahead." Drew stands back away from me, but his voice is a whisper in my ear. Hit it. How many times have I heard that in my life time? How many times did Robert tell me to try to hit the ball the best I could? "You aren't a quitter, Bobbi. I know you can get this game," he'd say.

"You just want someone to chase your lost balls." I'd tell him in return, but then I hit the ball and each time it flew a little further.

Tonight my memories collide with reality. Grandpa's face appears before me. He's holding his coin. I glance down at my neck where Mattie's pendant hangs, reminding me to focus. My first hit of the New

Year should be memorable. I hang my shoulders forward, loosen my grip, and waggle my middle.

I swing.

Blood rushes through my veins as I track the course of my ball. When it lands at two hundred and eighty-five yards, I let out a whoop and twist around. "Did you see that? Did you see how far it went?"

Drew is next to me in a flash, locking his arms around me, swinging me into the air. "I saw it. I saw it." He finally slips me to the ground but doesn't let go. "And now I want to wish you a Happy New Year. If you'll let me."

I look up into his face again. The tenderness in it brings an ocean of waves to my chest. "You're sweet, Drew. Really sweet."

"Think you might have time in your new life for someone so sweet?"

My legs almost collapse beneath me. Oh, yes. Oh, yes. Aloud I say, "What are you suggesting?"

He tugs me closer against his him. "A proposition."

I wriggle my eye brows. "A proposition?"

He takes the club from my hand and puts it back into the bag. When he returns, seriousness has replaced his playfulness. "I need someone to help me here at the course. I think you're the right person. Your shot just proved it. I'll pay you well and let you have all the free golf you want."

"You want to hire me? To teach golf?"

He closes the gap between us, wrapping his arms around me again. "Admit it, Bobbi. Golf is in you. I knew it even more when I watched you hold that club tonight and swing. The distance was the icing on the cake. You're a natural. I want that at my course. I want you at my course."

I think of the prayer I'd said tonight on the way back to the hospital after finding my mother's letter to my father. My heart swells with the memory of my words spoken in earnest. I wish my brother were here to see how God answered it.

"Is that the only reason you want me here? To teach your customers how to golf?" No, I'm not a flirt but, hey, it's New Year's Eve with fireworks and the whole deal.

A grin forms on his lips. "I knew the minute you stumbled through my classroom door I'd be saying your name correctly the rest of my life. I just had to convince you."

"Have you?" I touch his day's growth of beard. The stubble electrifies my fingers. When he bends to kiss me, I close my eyes and exhale.

Mattie was wrong about one thing.

Superman is real.

Epilogue

Eighteen months later.

It's one of those perfect Pennsylvania days. Crystal blue sky, temperatures in the mid-seventies, and the smell of lilacs rushes around me in a dance to usher in summer. I'm waiting for Drew and Mark who are inspecting the final tent for the tournament. Already the parking lot is filling with locals who signed up to help support our first event.

I wander into the pro shop where the staff has already hung the sign. I can't help but stop and admire the banner: First Annual Art Charity Golf Tournament.

Next to a table laden with donated prizes, the grand prize is displayed on a large easel. I run my hand over the oak frame. This painting is still my favorite.

Amanda said she wanted to hang her new family portrait over her fireplace now, anyway. "Besides," she told me, "it's time someone else enjoyed one of your creations."

I hadn't wanted to take her painting, but she'd insisted. Who can argue with a new mother?

I linger over the work a minute longer and then move to the next table, where I've placed some of my latest art.

After our honeymoon, Drew built a studio for me over our garage. If I lean just right, I can see the river.

"Bobbi! The place looks wonderful!" I turn to see my mother, who is leading my father into the clubhouse by the hand. It seems she runs more than their new sporting goods store now. I hide a smile.

Dad doesn't look too upset though. In fact, ever since Mom left the hospital, he hasn't stopped smiling.

She pulls me into a hug. "Where's that son-in-law of mine?" Her necklace and earrings compliment her peach blouse and linen pants.

"He's finishing with the set-up. Should be here soon. You look great, Mom. Do you sell that shirt in your store?" I finger the dainty collar.

"Not yet, but give her time." My father steps next to us and chuckles. He told me last week at dinner that buying the store was the best decision he ever made, short of marrying my mother. I swear it's like the two of them can't get enough of each other.

He reaches for my hand. The first time he did that at my wedding, I didn't know what to do. I looked at my mother who was fixing my veil and she nodded, a tiny smile appearing on her lips.

Today I grasp it and hang on a full minute. "You look great, too, Dad. Are you ready to win?"

He shrugs. "Let's leave that to your brother. I heard he's been practicing between his Bible classes."

"Maybe I shouldn't have given him those lessons all spring." I watch the double entry doors and see my twin coming toward me.

No one would know that once upon a time he couldn't walk. He strides toward us, but reaches me first.

"Congratulations on your tournament. By the looks of the parking lot, your favorite art charity is going to be very happy." His smile reminds me it's time for something I need to do.

I leave my family standing together while I hurry behind the counter, searching for my purse. When I look up, Drew has already arrived and is making small talk with them.

"For I know the plans…" Again, that still small voice whispers in my heart.

I'm glad I listened.

My hand finally finds the folder and I glance at Drew. He nods and motions for me to come over.

Perhaps I could have found a better moment, but today seems right. I work my way back to the people who mean more to me than golf or art ever could.

Drew pulls me close.

My mother's eyes widen, waiting for the news I'd hinted at earlier.

I take a deep breath and pass around the ultrasound picture. "The doctor says it's a boy."

I smile at Robert. "And a girl."

Thank you for purchasing this Harbourlight title. For other inspirational stories, please visit our on-line bookstore at www.pelicanbookgroup.com.

For questions or more information, contact us at customer@pelicanbookgroup.com.

Harbourlight Books
The Beacon in Christian Fiction™
an imprint of Pelican Ventures Book Group
www.pelicanbookgroup.com

Connect with Us
www.facebook.com/Pelicanbookgroup
www.twitter.com/pelicanbookgrp

To receive news and specials, subscribe to our bulletin
http://pelink.us/bulletin

May God's glory shine through
this inspirational work of fiction.

AMDG

www.ingramcontent.com/pod-product-compliance
Lightning Source LLC
Chambersburg PA
CBHW020417260626
47156CB00007B/2431